HURTS LIKE BRAND NEW SHOES

Cyntrenna Palmer

DEDICATION

This novel is dedicated to James and Versie Mae Palmer who taught me to keep the course, in spite of the shoes worn.

DEDICATION

This novel is dedicated to James and Versie Mae Palmer who taught me to keep the course, in spite of the shoes worn.

ACKNOWLEDGMENTS

Romann Edwin Williams, thank you for providing me the support, tolerance, prayers, and environment to fulfill this dream. You will always have my eternal love and gratitude! #IOWY

My three reasons for being, Robert, Roceana, and Randell, I am who I am because of you. Your belief in me allowed me to become the woman I was destined to become. We are one! We did it!

My Grand loves, Kenzi, Maecyn, and Reign, thank you for coming into my life to show me unfiltered love.

Kelvin R. Moss, my brother from another classy mother, thank you for pushing me to completion. Your belief/encouragement is one of the many reasons I love you like five and five!

Stacy Addison-Gregory, you are the pearl in life's oyster. Thank you for seeing my vision and giving me the shoehorn needed to breakthrough.

Farah Williams, I know you are our angel looking down from above. Thank you for exemplifying the strength needed to live bravely and courageously. Rest well, our angel, rest well.

CHAPTER 1

BE IN STEP

It was a lazy Saturday morning and I needed to find a way to get out of the bed to stop sulking and pining over love lost. Or as I knew love to be, at such a young age, and thinking it would never to be found again. Plus, if I didn't leave the house my grandmother would find chores for me to do. She believed that an idle *anything*, except your "pocketbook"—vagina, would be the devil's playground. I could smell breakfast cooking of salmon patties, grits, and bacon. My grandmother was a "country from scratch" cook. I quickly got ready and while she was distracted talking on the phone, I told her I was going to my friend's house. She shooed me off not listening to me and I decided I would visit my cousin across town in Parkway. My high school sweetheart, Drew, and I had broken up. She lived in his neighborhood and went to school with him. I lived across town from them and attended a different school. Everyone had been discussing the fight that took place on the track at South Plantation High. I went to see what was being said from my cousin.

Drew was a popular senior at South Plantation, who wore glasses upon his boyish face but his body was that of a blessed muscular god—thanks to being a member of the football team, track team, and wrestler. Everyone knew we were an item at my school, Fort Lauderdale High, and many at his school. We'd been together for a couple years. I'd met him at my best friend's cookout, Angie. Angie invited him to the cookout because they had been talking until they found out they were related—distant cousins. He had a *very* nice athletic body and I couldn't keep my eyes off him.

He was obviously smitten with me because he kept initiating conversations with me. He had me at "hello." I felt confident that I caught his attention physically. I played tennis and was very tone. My hair was thick and long, which was usually kept in a ponytail. I am of a darker skin tone, thanks to burning rays of the Florida heat. Without hesitation, I will admit that I wasn't a typical "girly-girl." I would be in step with more of the tomboy who was slowly blossoming into a young lady. I wore no make-up, didn't shave my hairy legs but never had a shortage of suitors due to my coke-bottle shape.

Drew and I flirted and talked the entire time. He even gave me a ride home. Drew was not your typical "Broward County Boy." He came from a very religious home and had both of his parents in the home. Drew's parents had a nice home and made a good living. He drove an Audi and he had the rims with the booming system. He was unlike the "city boys" who drove the Monte Carlos, Broncos and Chevy Impalas with the bass-driven speakers and spinning rims. We banged Lisa Lisa and The Cult Jam to my house. Arriving at my house, he left without my phone number. To my excitement and surprise, several days later he drove by my house. I was buying ice cream from the ice cream truck. We talked about the cookout and he stated he had been thinking of me since that day. He decided to take a chance and drive by, in hopes of seeing me outside.

Drew was my first relationship and first love. I wouldn't be honest if I said that being with him was a bed of roses. There was always outside interferences due to Drew's roaming eye. I was determined to make it work, by standing toe-to-toe with him, and with having no hard evidence other than hearsay—I stuck it out! Drew was everything I wanted in a boyfriend. No matter what my close friends told me about him getting quite close to a new girl at his school from Indiana. She played basketball and it was said that they were kissing in the hallway and he walks her to every class. I chose to believe him because I wasn't emotionally prepared to be without him.

You can choose to be "Ray Charles" to the truth for only so long and life has a way of forcing you to deal with reality. Life will snatch the rose-colored glasses off and stick your nose in the shit you are avoiding. This day came for me when Angie had gotten her license and was allowed to have limited use of her mother's car. Off we go to South Plantation to surprise my boyfriend, who was practicing for the state in hurdles. We arrive there and as we are getting out of the car, I see a white girl wearing Drew's letterman jacket. She was walking to the track and I saw his last name proudly displayed across her back. Ain't this 'bout a bitch (in my Bernie Mac's voice). So all along what everyone has been telling me was true. Now I have no choice but to get a toehold on the situation.

As I stood there as a ball of unfiltered emotions, it was at that moment that I became filled with rage. How can he be so cruel? What a liar! I asked him about the rumors and he callously denied them. Only for me to find out that it was all the truth and I had been played for a fool the whole entire time. I looked over at Angie and said, "I am going to fuck him up and her up!" Before Angie could respond, I took off like Usain Bolt in full stride sprinting towards her. I was like a lion or tiger about to pounce on the prey as shown on the "Animal Channel."

Before I could reach her, Angie's yelling caught Drew's attention. He ran off the track towards us in state record time to come between us. "Get out of my way! I am going to fuck her up! Then I am going to beat your ass!" Drew attempts to diffuse the situation,

"Stop, Rona! Do not touch her! What are you doing here?" I am not listening to him but trying to get past him to pounce on her. "I came out here to surprise you. Why is she wearing your jacket? So this is the bitch you have been kissing in the hallway? I am such a fool for believing your no good ass! I hate you! It's over!" I turn my attention to the girl and begin yelling at her, "Did you know about me? Who are you to him, bitch?" "I'm his girlfriend! I don't know you!" she said. Angie jumps in the middle of us in an attempt to quell things, "Rona, stop it! It's not worth it. Stop! Let's go! You've seen it for yourself. Now you know." Drew agrees, "Rona, calm down! I'm sorry! Stop it! You can hit me all you want just don't touch her! You will go to jail."

The anger, which was misplaced and misdirected to her, was now solely laser-focused on Drew. I hit him with all my might. I knocked off his glasses and broke his gold rope necklace with the gold medallion. I tried to Mike Tyson him. I was going to make him feel all the pain I was feeling. In complete tears, Angie peeled me off of him and we went home. I was heartbroken. Drew and I had previous spats and would often break up to make up, but this time was different. It would take Jesus Christ himself to make me take Drew back this time.

My heart was broken in half. I got home and went straight into my room to cry some more. I couldn't talk to my family about it because I was forbidden to date in the first place. As I lay in my bed paralyzed with emotional disbelief, my phone rings. I try to pull myself together and answer my phone. "Hello, Rona speaking." It is Drew's raspy voice, "Hello. Let's talk about what happened. I feel that all that was uncalled for. Why did you try to fight her? You broke my glasses and scratched me all up." I am thinking this must be a complete joke. He calls me with no apology and making me out to be the culprit. "Are you serious right now? You broke my heart, Drew! How could you do that when you know how much I loved you?" I begin to sob uncontrollably. He responds, "I met her and we started talking. I love you and care for her too. I didn't tell you about her because I knew you wouldn't go for it. With her, she didn't care. She knows I talk to other people. I want both of y'all but I know you would have a problem with it. Please don't make me choose because I care about both of y'all." I decide to step on his toes, "Drew, since you can't make a decision then I will make it for you! We're done! I'm not going to be with you and only you while you deal with others. You never loved me! You don't hurt anything you love." I found my strength and gathered my composure while hanging up the phone.

I needed to keep my mind off Drew. After hanging out at my cousin's house in Parkway all that day, I left to catch the city bus home. As I walked down the street to the bus stop, I see a nice sports car pass by jamming Madonna's "La Isla Bonita." This car was flying down a residential main thoroughfare doing at least sixty miles per hour. I think to myself, "What an idiot driving like a bat out of hell!" Just then, the car slows down and turns down the street I am walking on. The car is literally on two wheels. Then the car stops right next to me. Could he have heard me? No way! I'm tripping! Then the driver steps out and walks in my direction. The driver is a light-skinned, slender guy with light brown eyes and freckles. Not so bad on the eyes and standing about five foot ten inches. So far so good, as I think to myself. Then he opens his mouth and, to my horror and dismay, he has gold teeth! Gross! As he's talking to me, I can only see his four top teeth in gold with rubies and diamonds spelling out the letters of his name—EARL. Are you serious right now? I'd never been a fan of the gold teeth. For me, it held a negative connotation: drug dealer, thug, hoodlum, d-boy and no one I could ever take home to mama. Gold teeth are very popular in South Florida. It is often a sign of wealth. I was asked if I wanted an open-faced crown for my sixteenth birthday. I declined the offer.

"What's your name?" I was put on the spot and out of all the names in the world and I replied with my name, "Rona." "What's your telephone number?" Once again, out of all the numbers in the world and I respond with my correct phone number. "I'm going to call you later. My name is Robert Earl, girl." He then walks back to his car blaring music from Power 96.

As I watch him drive off, my heart is still beating out of my shirt! I thought he was going to rob me the way he approached me. Now I'm kicking myself because I gave him my actual name and phone number. I begin to find comfort in the fact he did not write my info down. This was before cell phones were a staple. In the mid 80's, if you had a cellphone then you were "balling." Few people had cellphones with the attached battery pack, which was bulky and quite heavy. Besides, what kind of guy would approach a girl walking and not even offer a ride? I would've declined had he offered anyway. I catch the city bus back home with Drew still heavily on my mind. Heartbroken, alone, and hoping to awaken from this nightmare to find it was all a bad dream. No chance of that, this was reality.

I finally arrive home safe and sound. Since I'd been gone most of the day without checking in with my grandmother, she made it clear that I wouldn't be leaving the house anymore today. My grandmother was "old school." She didn't believe a young girl should be "ripping and running the streets." If you weren't at home or in viewing distance, then you were accused of being "fast" and "smelling yourself." In other words, being grown before your time. This would be her perception of me. She would give me the name of "Reckless Rona" because she believed I was always wreaking havoc. In some ways, I purposely lived up to the name. This is why you have to be careful of the seeds planted with your children. I don't believe that my grandmother was intentionally trying to break me down or set me up for failure. She was just making an observation based on my actions. I was never the conformist. I was the first grandchild and set the bar for all after me to reach. Having had no blueprint or older sibling to emulate, I had to learn by trial and error for experience. Often times, trial by fire and I had no idea how hot it could and would get.

CHAPTER 2

BE IN STEP

My grandmother yells for me after hearing the phone ring. "Rona, telephone! Rona, telephone! Girl, pick up the phone right damn now!" I finally reach the phone, "Rona speaking." "This is Robert Earl, girl. I met you yesterday and you gave me your number." "Oh yeah." I am freaking out on the inside due to receiving the call I had no intentions of taking. "I remember," and my response is without any excitement. "Where do you live? I was going to come hang out with you." "Sunland. The house right next to the park, near the tennis courts." "Ok, straight. I'm on my way," were his last words before he hung up.

After a restless night and still in disbelief over the break-up with Drew, I decided I needed a welcomed distraction. Heck, it's not as if he's home crying his heart out over me. He has a girlfriend. Truth be told, he had a girlfriend when I was his girlfriend. If that ain't a complete hot mess dot COM! Even though Earl is not my usual jock-type that I go for, he can take up some time while I heal. As promised, he arrives a couple hours later by the city bus. He sat in my yard, that's all I was allowed to do in regards to dating. By the time the sun went down, he better not be around—as stated constantly by my grandmother and father. We spent hours just talking about everything and nothing. He seemed like a nice guy. From initial appearances, he seemed like a good guy—just not my type.

Talking for hours we built up an appetite and he wanted to know if I wanted to go to Burger King for a bite. It was in walking distance since neither of us had access to a car. I asked for permission to walk to Burger King and after giving him a long speech regarding not taking me off to have sex and having me back well before dark, she allowed me to go. To say that I was pleasantly shocked that the lecture only lasted about ten minutes, is putting it lightly.

Grandma interrogated him every time he needed to use the bathroom or request a drink of water to cool off from the humid weather of South Florida. Surprisingly, she didn't know his people. Grandma damn near knew all of Lauderdale. Miss Frazier was a staple in the northwest section, also known as "the city." It was simply named as such because the city police served the area and not the county. Grandma came to Florida when she was sixteen years old and was born in 1918. She'd seen the city change in many ways and knew the goings-on of the mean streets from the sanctuary of her home, thanks to her secret weapon. Like any other superhero, Grandma had super human powers thanks to the invention by Alexander Graham Bell—the telephone. With her deep network, there was nothing that occurred in Lauderdale that Miss Frazier didn't know about, including and never limited to me.

As we walk and talk to Burger King, he starts to open up and tells me what he wants from me. He begins to place his claim, "Check this out! When I saw you walking down the street, I wanted a closer look because you are fine as hell. I came to kick it with you because I wanted to see what you were about. You just broke up with that 'clown' and now you've got me. I'm no longer in a relationship and I choose you to be my lady. I want you! You're smart and a good girl. I'm going to take care of you and you won't have to ask your family for no money because you're mine. There are so many chicks out here that only want me because I have money. I had to make sure you weren't playing me for my money. So we're going to eat then catch a cab to pick up my car, and then we're going to the mall."

I am now trying to process all of the info that he has just given me. You chose me? I got you? Are we now in a relationship? I'm thinking to myself. Go and get his car? But he caught the city bus to my house. Take care of me? Giving me money? Now that's a major no-no! I was always taught not to ask, nor take money from a male. For the simple fact that I had no job and no means of repayment, except with sexual favors, which would mean I was a prostituting whore. I don't want to be a prostituting whore. I still loved Drew. I'm now in a relationship with someone I don't really know well but saying all the things I wish that Drew would say.

I threw caution to the wind and I played along. After leaving Burger King, we hop into a cab and head to the beach to get his car from Ed Morse Chevrolet Dealership. We head to the service center and he picks up the nicest car I've ever seen outside of the imported exotic cars. The car was a 1986 Chevy IROC Z28, with gold rims and a T-top sunroof with a half-rag top. Wow! He tosses me the keys and says, "Let's go," as he hops into the passenger seat. Houston, we have a problem! As beautiful and nice as the car is, it also has a very serious flaw—it's a stick shift. I can't drive a stick! I stand outside of the car and say, "I don't know how to drive a stick shift. I can't drive a stick." He responds as he gets out to drive, "I will teach you how to drive *your* car." The beauty of the car held my attention and I didn't catch the hint he was dropping. Off we went to the Galleria Mall as my hair blew in the summer breeze. This just may be a good summer after all. Could it be I've met my rainbow after being ravaged by the storm called Drew? Could it be?

We walked hand-in-hand at the mall and peered at all of the merchandise that I've seen in my favorite magazines: "Seventeen,

Teen, Cosmopolitan and Vogue." I'd never been the flea market type chic, no "shade," but it just wasn't my style. I wasn't into the urban wear. My style was more so preppy. Provocative clothing, such as the "daisy dukes" and spray-painted shirts, weren't my thing. I liked the designer bags, Swatch watches and Saks Fifth Avenue clothing but that's not what I wore. I said I liked them *but* my grandmother loved Sears and Roebuck more. My grandmother basically clothed me only from Sears. Nice clothing but not very fashion forward, at the time.

I was simply a girl from the hood who went to school with the white kids from wealthy families. There are some definite advantages of integration and the still long-lasting effects of Brown v. Board of Education. The rich white kids taught me about the finer things in life, proper speech, reckless abandonment and disregard for rules and laws—maybe that's not a positive. They savored the urban culture. It was an even exchange because I assimilated into their culture and they embraced and satisfied their curiosity of being urban. I was often made fun of because I spoke proper English or that I talked like a "white girl." It didn't help any that I played on the tennis team too. I was called "white girl" like it was a plague or something.

Earl asks, "Are you going to just walk around the mall or are you going to buy something?" I replied, "I don't know what I want yet." What I really meant was that this is a super expensive mall and I don't have any money except the quarter to call home for emergency. I hadn't seen any of his money and I don't steal. He then takes the lead and we head into Saks Fifth Avenue and look at purses. He states, "A woman should always carry a purse. Where's your purse?" I say, "I thought we were just walking to Burger King." He then told me, "Pick out a purse, wallet, and keychain. Do you like this one?" He picks up a blue signature Gucci bag. "Do I like it? No, I love it," I exclaimed. He then pulled out the biggest wad of cash I've ever seen and pays for the items. He carries the bags and we head to buy me a blue Swatch watch to match my purse. "Since we're next to the beach, buy a bathing suit. We might go swimming," he commands.

To say that I'm caught up in the matrix is an understatement. Here I have this random dude showering me with gifts. How can you refuse or not get caught up? Everything I had been told was morally wrong and sinful, I found to be beyond exciting and highly addictive. I would soon learn that everything that feels good to you might not be good for you. But at this very moment in time, I threw caution to the wind and decided to see where this would lead. Worse case scenario, we stop dealing and I am still left with a $3,000 shopping spree. I am blown away by the one hundred dollar bathing suit and damn near a whole new wardrobe with accessories. After buying out the mall, we headed to my house because he had to go to "work."

Now the reality is setting in. My grandmother is going to kill me if I stroll in with two arms filled with bags and no job or source of income. She will be convinced that I did something "strange for change." I talk to myself, "What to do? Think! How do I get my stuff in the house without getting killed?" She will already be suspicious because we left on feet and now coming back in a new sports car. It would take Jesus Christ himself to convince her otherwise. I need to think of something quick because we are almost to my house. As he is talking to me about something, I'm completely in thought praying about this dilemma. "Dear God, It's me, Rona. Please don't let my grandmother be sitting outside in the yard, on the porch peering out of the front picture window or sitting in the living room talking on the telephone. Lord help me get all these bags in the house without my grandmother killing him *and* me! Please, Lord, please! Amen."

Then I pretend to have to "pee" *really* bad! I interrupt him and tell him that I'm going to get out of the car really quick because I had to use the bathroom. He offered to stop at a gas station but I declined due to my having a serious dislike of public bathrooms. I'd rather hold it until I get home. He began to drive even faster to get me home. Oh no! My heart was beating out of my chest but I had to play it cool. I really didn't need to go that bad but my nerves had me about to wet myself. Turning off Sunrise Blvd. to 16th Ave, I could see my house from across the park. I lived right next to the large city park that was previously known as Sunland Park. It has since been renamed to Joseph Carter Sports Complex, but it will always be Sunland Park to most, including myself.

Pulling up in front of my house and the coast appears clear. Earl was blaring music and I told him sternly to turn it down. That type of noise would draw her out. She was the neighborhood watch and very little did she ever miss. Since I was six days old, I was in the care of my paternal grandparents and father. My grandfather had passed when I was in the 9th grade and my father was in and out of jail due to his drug addictions. My grandmother had been the only constant in my life. She was unable to finish school due to having to raise her siblings. She was the oldest and her mother's untimely death during childbirth left her as the "mother figure." Having had to be the woman of the house well before she even had a chance to know herself as a child. Due to her caring for the smaller children and helping her father tend to the farm, she never finished grade school. This would not be the case with me. She ensured that I had a good education and that I would become learned. It was if she would live vicariously through me. This was the reasoning behind her stern demeanor. She simply wanted more for myself than she had.

I jumped out of the car and told Earl to wait a minute. Leaving the bags in the car, I went into the house to find out where my beloved "gatekeeper" was. "Ma, I'm home! Ma, where are you?" No answer. I roam through the house and the coast is clear. I run back out to the car to hurriedly retrieve the bags while I could with no friction with Grandma. "Thank you for everything! I had fun with you." Earl said, "This is just the beginning. I'm going to treat you like a queen because you are my queen. You are mine! I'm coming by tomorrow to teach you how to drive a stick." "Ok. It will have to be after church." "Bet that up!" and he leans in to give me a kiss. Turning my head just in time to avoid his lips, he plants a kiss on my cheek. "Good night!" "We are going to have to work on your kissing skills too." He turns around and closes the trunk. He gets into the car, blaring the music while burning rubber down the road.

I'm praying that Miss Nezzie, the nosey neighbor, wasn't watching me to report back to Grandma. If so, I'm done! It's over. If she tells grandma that I was kissing then I would be a definite goner. I wasn't allowed to date and was told that books were my boyfriends. "Get your education, gal! Dam a man! They only want one thing and your education can get you *everything*!" Grandma always had strong feelings on putting your life on a shelf while chasing a man. "Keep your nose in your books. You hear me?" I had these words permanently imprinted in my head.

Unpacking the bags and hiding the evidence of my shopping spree, I called Laverne—who was the big sister I never really had. I was laying across my bed really giddy about the day's turn of events. "Guess what, Laverne?" "What?" "I met a guy who took me shopping at the Galleria Mall and bought me everything I wanted." "Who is this guy?" I answer, "His name is Robert Earl. He lives in Lauderdale Lakes. He went to Boyd Anderson." "What about Drew?" "It's over! I'm not going to be with him anymore. He's a cheater and liar. I am tired of boys carrying a man's name. He can go be with her. She can have his cheating ass," I state. "Sis, you need to be careful. He just met you and buying you all that expensive shit. What does he want in return? Does Grandma know?" Laverne now starts to giggle, "She is going to beat your ass." "Ha, ha, ha! What's so funny? I got everything under control. I got this." Why did I have a feeling that these were my famous last words?

After getting off the phone with Laverne, I begin to think about what she said. Her reaction wasn't what I expected. I didn't know at the time how cryptic her words would become.

CHAPTER 3

BE IN STEP

Sundays were usually spent in church all day and with the family. As usual, Sunday school and 11:00 am service was mandatory unless you were damn near dead. I'd been attending Piney Grove Baptist Church since birth and had no say, nor opinion, when it came to church. Grandma made sure that I got "the word" in me every Sunday. After church would be Sunday's dinner and Grandma's favored dessert dishes. Grandma, being from the backwoods of Georgia, was very familiar with her way around the kitchen. How could she not? She'd been cooking since she was about 8 years old; she made everything from scratch and one could usually smell her cooking from the driveway.

We would eat Sunday dinner and sit around in the yard and talk. My Aunt Pearl and Uncle Herschel usually came over and spent the day. Aunt Robbie would also come by after church and visit. There always would be history lessons told of Jim Crow, segregation, the assassination of Martin Luther King, Jr., and the hanging of Sam—who was accused of staring a little too long at a white woman. They would reminisce on days of old and the youngins', like myself, would take it all in. Little did I know that I was being taught life lessons well before I had even started out in life.

The house phone rings and I am told that the phone was for me. I leave the history lesson and go to answer the phone. "Rona speaking." "Hey! I'm coming to scoop you so I can teach you how to drive a stick. Get ready, " and Earl hangs up the phone. Here we go again! Is he trying to get me killed? Grandma has an audience at the house and she is sure to put on a good show if he comes to pick me up from the house. Man, how do I end up in these situations constantly? I know. I will get my tennis racket and balls to head to the tennis court.

The tennis court was my safe haven. Grandma never complained about me playing tennis. Honestly speaking, it was because of her I was so good. Whenever I would become angry at her "old school" rearing and discipline, I would take my racquet and head to the tennis court. Talking back was never a wise recourse, so I would spend hours on the racquetball courts and tennis courts. I had drawn a circle on the racquetball wall, which represented my grandmother's head. I would attempt to hit the ball in the hole from any place on the court and with only one bounce. It was these drills that prepared me for tennis and was the sole reason I played so well. Tennis brought me much popularity because I was the only black girl who played tennis in my county. I wasn't just a black girl who played tennis; I was also a "beast" on the court. Many of my opponents had been playing tennis since they were able to hold a racquet. Not to mention, they also had personal coaches. However, I dominated the court and had been undefeated through high school. I was the Serena and Venus Williams before there was a Venus and Serena Williams.

I hadn't been on the court long when I heard Earl turning the corner onto my street blaring Jam Pony Express DJ's music. The music escaped through the T-tops. I ran toward the end of the street to catch him before he came to my house. I hop in and we head off. "We're going to Winn Dixie parking lot off Broward Blvd. so you can learn how to drive *your* car." "My car? What car?" I was completely confused. "I'm giving you this car so you won't have to catch the bus or catch rides to school." "Are you serious? You're giving me your car? What will you drive?" I ask. "I bought a new corvette convertible and it's in the shop getting 'souped' up. I was going to sell this car until I met you. Didn't I tell you I was going to take care of you because you're mine? I'm also going to take you shopping for school clothes since school will be starting back soon." I think to myself that Grandma is going to kill me! "Ok, but you just bought me some clothes," I answer. "Those are just for now. I can't have my ol' lady not on point. Come on, I'm Robert Earl and you're Robert Earl's girl. We stay fresh! I will take you and buy you the clothes I want to see you in."

We arrive at our location and he proceeds to show me the clutch and its purpose. Listen to the engine and it will tell you when it's time to shift gears. When the engine strains it is time to shift. Wow! The symbolism of it all is mind-blowing. He gets out of the car and tells me to get behind the wheel. Feeling nervous, he assured me that it is not difficult. He kept repeating that I can and will get the hang of it. His continued support and willingness to teach me was soothing for my nerves—somewhat. I turned the key to start the car and I hear nothing. He tells me I have to press the clutch in to get the car started. Ok, let's try it again.

I pressed the clutch and turn the ignition—vroom—and the car chokes out. He angrily tells me that I am messing up and making it more difficult than it is. "What did I do wrong?" "Everything! Once you start the car, take your foot off the clutch and give it some gas. Dam!" "How am I going to learn anything if you're going to get mad when I do something wrong? Don't worry about it." I start getting out of the car. "What are you doing? Where are you going?" Earl asks. "I will walk home. Forget it!" I said. "Get back in, honey. I will teach you. I'm sorry." I would have this opportunity to view his "other" side--his mean, short-tempered and quick to "pop off" side. I didn't like this! I wasn't used to this type of behavior. I dismissed it, but I would come to be quite familiar with this "Dr. Jekyll, Mr. Hyde."

Within a couple hours, I was off driving in traffic and choking out in the road less and less. I was getting the hang of it. He tells me to take him to Cambridge Square because he needs to check on something. Off we go to Lauderdale Lakes. Cambridge Square was a large apartment complex with one way in and out. Most people who lived there were on section 8 or had low-income based rent. I would later learn that he lived here and this completely confused me. He has so much disposable income and a nice car but lives with his mother in government housing. This wasn't what I had expected. I figured he came from a nice neighborhood with a nice home like Drew.

Though, this by no means was atypical in the hood. People often would buy a new car and "trick it up" while living in government housing. Cambridge Square wasn't a terribly bad place and it did look nice. However, with the onslaught of the crack epidemic in the 80's, this housing complex started to spiral downward. Residents began to chase the high rather than having pride in where they reside.

By no means was I an authority on drugs but I had seen firsthand what it did to both of my biological parents. My father had been drafted, due to the Vietnam War, right out of high school. As a result of his experiences abroad, he came back as an IV drug user, who later transitioned to crack cocaine. He had run through the plethora of drugs: marijuana joints, heroin, speedballs, freebasing, snorting and smoking base—also known as "crack." He had been a functional addict up until he encountered that "white girl"— cocaine. She took him to unimaginable lows and looking for his next "hit" became his full-time job. Having no legal source of income, he supported his drug habits by stealing. His usual charges were strong-arm robbery, breaking and entering, and shoplifting.

My biological mother had left me at six days old and befriended the "white girl" too. I don't know much about her usage first hand, unlike my father, because she wasn't around. I'd only seen her a couple times, once or twice, in almost eighteen years. Due to both of my biological parents using drugs, I ended up in the care of my paternal grandparents who legally adopted me. My Grandfather died when I was barely a teenager and all I had in this world was my grandmother. She was my rock and the only constant in my life. Using any type of drugs or fraternizing with drug dealers on any level was never an option.

I pull into the complex and park the car as Earl instructs me. He tells me to sit tight until he handles some business. I obey. He gets out and approaches the young guys loitering on the playground. They seem to get right when he approaches. They all dap him up and begin to hand over their money to him. Every single one of them gives him money and I found this to be very interesting. I wondered why he was collecting money? Did he win a bet? Did all of them owe him money? If so, for what was the money owed? I hit the button to wind the windows down and turn off the car so I can hear what's being discussed. Earl asks, "How much do you have left?" The guy replied, "Not that many. I will get them off by this evening." "I got my ol' lady with me. Give me a li'l bit and I will re-up. Make sure you help 'Knock-Knock' sell his rocks."

Get what off, I wonder to myself. Rocks? Is he referring to rocks like stones? Something is fishy and I am going to find out exactly what is going on. Based on Earl's interaction with the five to seven guys, he was the head honcho—their captain and leader—and they were his soldiers. I'd never seen anything like this. How did such a small guy in stature command so much respect? Grandma always said, "Follow your first mind!" Something was telling me what I had witnessed was not right. It may be even illegal. As to exactly what was going on, wasn't clear to me just yet. Suddenly I see Earl take a swing at one of the guys and knock him to the ground. All of the guys simply watched as Earl began to mercilessly stomp him out with no intervention. Earl tells him, "If you don't have my money by this evening I'm going to kill you!" Someone in the crowd yelled, "Nine, nine, nine!" The crowd dispersed and Earl jumped into the car and said, "Let's go eat." I complied but my mind was racing at the speed of light. I really didn't have an appetite. I wanted no food but answers to the gazillion questions I had unanswered. I was completely perplexed as to how to broach the topic. What was he doing? Whatever it was, it had "no good" written all over it.

Cambridge Square was a one-way entrance and I was always told to avoid these places. High-crime and drug areas often have the entrances and exits sealed to only one way so law enforcement can secure the perimeter easier. They would watch like hawks, hovering over the outgoing and incoming traffic. If they suspected drug activity, the car would be pulled over upon leaving the complex. And this was exactly what happened to us this day. As we were leaving out of Cambridge Square, a police car came from nowhere with the sirens blaring and blue lights wildly flashing. My stomach is now in knots. I've never had a reason for the police to pursue me. Little did I know this would be the beginning of many more to come. "Be calm. Pull over where you can," Earl says and he starts to pull out the car registration and insurance card.

"Why are they pulling us over? Do you think someone reported the fight?" I ask. "What fight? We just left my house sleeping! That's our story," Earl demanded. The police officers approach the vehicle on each side with their holsters unsnapped and hand on their service revolver. The two white officers had an obvious familiarity with Earl and also a blatant dislike of him. "Robert Earl Jackson, you already know the drill. Present me your license." "I'm not driving. You pull me every single day. You know whom the fuck I am! Shit, you probably got my license memorized," Earl rudely stated. "Do you consent to a search of the vehicle or do I have to call in the drug dog?" the officer asked. "You can call Sheriff Nick Navarro and I still I don't give a fuck! Hell no, you can't search my shit. I just say no to drugs and you should start saying no to those doughnuts and stick to the coffee. That uniform is looking mighty tight," Earl's verbal tirade continued. I am witnessing this and in complete shock. Who is this renegade? I'd never seen this side of him, either. Drugs? Is he crazy? You can't talk to a cop like that.

I am left to simply wonder what had I gotten myself into. "We are going to get your ass and send you straight to Rayford. We got our eyes on you. It's just a matter of time," the officer warns. "Shut that shit up and tell it to deez nuts! I keep a lawyer on retainer for y'all pussy ass 'crackas.' I am a law-abiding citizen. You won't ever catch me with my hands in the cookie jar. Now let's cut this shit short, my ol' lady is hungry." "Just remember what I said. It's just a matter of time, Robert Earl." The cop leans down and meets me at eye level. "You seem like a good girl. What are you doing with somebody like *him*? Does your parents know their daughter is riding around with someone like *him*?" I am left to wonder again what does all this mean? Why won't anyone just spill out what exactly he is guilty of? "Don't talk to her. And how the fuck you sound 'someone like *him*?' This is racial profiling and harassment. Please believe I will be informing my attorney," Earl fires back. "We look forward to it. The answer will be, as in the past, suspicious activity that gives us probable cause. Don't choke on your meal, Robert Earl."

Earl cranks up the music and motions for me to start driving. He appears to be completely unaffected, nonchalant, and definitely not afraid to speak to the officers in a disrespectful manner. He seemed more annoyed than anything else. He is the complete antithesis of me; I am a literal ball of nerves. I've never experienced anything like this. I didn't think anyone was above the law and to speak to an officer in that manner could land you in handcuffs heading straight to jail. You cannot pass "go" and there is no collecting $200 in Monopoly money.

I am quiet and reserved because my thoughts are running wild. In my limited experience with the police, they are there to help and catch the criminals. I was never one to get into any legal trouble and I viewed them as my ally. I am left questioning myself: Do I know this guy? Why does he hate cops so much? What did the officer mean "someone like *him?*" We arrive at Wendy's on 19ᵗʰ and 441 and go in to order. "Why did you talk to those cops like that? They are going to take you to jail if you continue," I say. "Fuck those 'crackas!' They harass me daily. They are simply mad that I make their yearly salary within a month. That's why I keep an attorney on retainer. He costs a lot but he keeps me out of jail," Earl boasts. "But why would you need a lawyer if you weren't so cocky with them? It doesn't matter how much money you have because the lawyer will have it all if you keep it up." Earl begins to laugh, "That's what I like most about you. You have all the book sense in the world and know nothing about the streets. Don't worry; the attorney won't take all my money. That's why I pay him $5k per month. If those 'crackas' plant something on me, I have an attorney and bondsman on payroll. Let me get you fed so I can drop you off home. I have to 'straighten a package' and I will come and get you later." That is just fine with me and sounds like music to my ears. I am ready to go home because this has been more than enough excitement for me. Also, I hadn't talked to Drew and I missed him. Even though I am trying to move forward, I just can't stop thinking about him. I can't go back out with him but I can't turn off my emotions, either. Sigh! Teenage love can be a bitch!

CHAPTER 4

BE IN STEP

My senior year is about to begin in approximately a month. Earl and I had been dating for a few months. He asked me to speak to my grandmother about allowing me to go to Disney World with him. And how am I going to broach this topic? Going out of town with a boy? I can just hear Grandma saying, "Oh, hell to the naw and you can go when pigs fly." She had loosened up the reigns where he was concerned, mainly due to his charming ways and expensive gifts. Time was winding down because he wanted to take me for the 4th of July and that was less than a week away.

I had settled in to being with Earl. He was getting my hair done weekly, giving me a weekly allowance of several hundred dollars, and taking care of the monies associated with my senior year: senior pictures, class ring, cap and gown, and the senior ads. Grandma always said I was the most expensive out of her grandkids and I was pretty sure that she wasn't mad about Earl being my sponsor. As long as I kept my legs closed. I never was the "gold-digging" type. I just had champagne and caviar taste on a Kool-Aid and ramen noodle budget. I wasn't allowed to work while being a student. I don't know where I would fit in a job considering I was quite involved in many extracurricular activities. My primary focus was being a student and that was my only job.

I reached out to my Aunt Barb to assist me in convincing Grandma to let me go to Disney World. My aunt was like the big sister I never had coupled with being a "cool mom" and aunt. She was quite the looker, too. Barb stood a statuesque 6'2" with the most beautiful caramel-colored skin and a sophisticated chic style. She loved her heels high, in spite of her above averaged height. Some times we would put on heels and dance around just taking in this life and moment. She had a good job, and unlike my father, making her self-sufficient and totally financially independent. "Auntie, I need a favor." "What do you need, Rona?" "I want to go with Earl to Disney World for the 4th of July. Will you talk to Grandma so I can go?" "Are you having sex?" "No!" "You know I've told you a thousand times, when you are ready I will take you and put you on the pill." "I know." "I will talk with Mama. Just stay out of trouble and do no back talking to her. If you can do that, I'll take care of the rest." "Thank you so much, Auntie. I will!" I hated lying to Aunt Barb. I had been having sex. I just didn't feel comfortable enough to tell her. I was never that overly sexual girl. While most of my friend's were talking about having their "cherries popped," I had no such stories to truthfully share. My parents were strict and kept me on a short leash. In order to fit in with the crowd, I lied about my sexual trysts.

I had lost my virginity at thirteen years of age to a senior at Dillard High School named Ernest Bradwell. He took me on my first date to the Swap Shop Drive-In movies and in the backseat of his car was where my virginity was lost. I did not find it enjoyable but very painful. I am sure this was the reason I did not engage in sex again until I was sixteen years old with Drew. Drew and I would have sex with regularity and it was because he wanted to. My immaturity and inexperience caused me to feel like sex was an act you did for your boyfriend. No self-satisfaction but for his pleasure only. I never had sexual urges or sexual desires by my own voli-tion. Whenever Drew and I had the chance to be alone, we usually engaged in sex. Drew was more sexually experienced and sexually open. That was probably what added to his value, and him being a hot commodity, because he could get a girl sprung sexually.

Earl was different, however. He hadn't tried to have sex with me. The most we had done was kiss and hold hands. I appreci-ated him taking his time and not rushing into sex. Unbeknownst to me, it was all a part of the plan to disarm me and it worked! Unbelievably, Grandma granted me permission to go but come back the same day. I informed Earl and he replied, "Pack some-thing sexy." Sexy? I don't have *anything* "sexy." Here we go again! He keeps me so confused.

The morning of the 4th arrives and Earl, Kenny the god broth-er, and Tameka, Kenny's girlfriend, come by fore day in the morn-ing to pick me up. I throw my bag in the trunk and jump in. I was super excited to be spending the day at Disney World. Earl then informs me that we are going to get a room and relax before going to Disney World. "Ok," I reply. Even though I'm wondering why we can't go straight to the "happiest place on Earth." Since I had to be back home before midnight and it's nearly a three-hour drive each way. All I know is I better be home before midnight or I'm not go-ing to be able to leave the yard until I am grown. Earl assures me that we are going to have fun and make it back in time.

I befriended Tameka, who I found out was really good friends with Pam—Earl's ex, and got to know her. She was a cute, red-boned but clearly very young. Tameka appeared to be 13 or 14 years of age and Kenny was maybe 15. He was short and small-framed which made him appear even younger. Tameka readily filled in the blanks I had in my mind unvoiced. She was young but street savvy. She told me all about Pam and Earl's six year relation-ship. She also shared that Pam was obsessed with Earl and wasn't handling the break up well. I try to keep my cool to continue to get information. Notably, I couldn't imagine having a boyfriend of six years and I'm only sixteen years old. How do you date anyone at 10 years old? I didn't even like boys at that age. When I was 10 years old I was in the fifth grade and wasn't even attracted to boys yet.

Tameka and Ken had been together for years too. I would later learn that both of their mothers were drug-addicted and they were basically raising themselves. They clung to each other and had to be far more mature than their immature years because of real life adult situations. They were openly affectionate and obviously sexually active. She would lie in his lap and on him constantly. They were always holding hands or some type of touching. It was if all they had was the other and they hung on for dear life.

Meeting Tameka helped me understand Earl better. Although we'd been dating for several months, there was still much about him I didn't know. She had told me as much as she felt I needed to know without betraying Earl. It was clear that she looked up to him as a big brother-in-law. She had known about me before meeting me. He had told her that he had a new girl and it's finally over with Pam. She told me that they broke up often and would get right back together, but this time was different. She told me he must really like me to choose me over Pam. Earl provided for her and took very good care of her. I didn't ask what she looked like because I didn't care. She offered up that I looked better than Pam. I was never the one to feel the need to compete with *any* chic. I was the oldest out of my three blood sisters and four half-sisters, and was viewed as an alpha female. I didn't check for any chic. End of discussion!

We arrive in Kissimmee, Disney World is actually located in Kissimmee but Orlando is listed as the location, and find a hotel. We check in and get separate rooms for each couple. Earl had driven there and wanted to rest up before we spent the entire day at Disney World. We go into our respective rooms and Earl takes off all of his clothes and gets into bed. He instructs me to do the same.

I was completely uncomfortable and caught off guard. To stall for time, I told him I had to call my Grandma and let her know that I made it safely. He relented and I called home. "Hey Grandma!" "Rona? Where are you? Is everything okay?" "Yes ma'am. We just got here. What are you doing?" "I was on the other line talking to my friend Verdell. Well, go on and enjoy yourself and make sure you are home by midnight. You hear me? Tell Earl he better have you back home no later than midnight. And I don't mean 12:01, ok?" "Yes ma'am."

I hang up the phone wishing she hadn't been on the other line talking. Otherwise, the phone call would've been a marathon phone conversation. Any other time Grandma would've talked my head off about the local gossip, church talk and drama. I was kind of hoping for the Miss Frazier interrogation. This could have possibly prevented or delayed the forthcomings. I guess Earl was ready to make good on his investment. My sexual ignorance did not allow me to have a voice or choice. It was simply the usual feeling that this was a necessary evil in having a boyfriend.

My parents did not provide any sex education. We were only told, "not to do it!" Conversely, my Aunt Barb did say that I could come to her when I was ready. Yes, I'd been sexually active but not because I was ready. It was often forced, coerced, and often times, I was simply an unwilling participant. Honestly, I hadn't come to her because I wasn't ready because I wasn't the overly sexual chic. I didn't desire the sexual contact because I felt I was too young and too focused on other things. I also didn't have many opportunities to be left to my own devices, other than school and church.

I hung up the phone and the lion began to eye his prey. Earl is lying under the covers naked and stroking himself. "Take off your clothes and come here." "I don't want to lie down yet. I'm going to mess up my hair before we get to Disney World." This was a meager attempt to stall again. Earl is tickled by my stalling and asks, "Don't I keep your hair done? You get it done for me. So I will be the one who messes it up. And I will pay for you to get it done again." I breathe deeply and think to myself that I am in love with Drew but I guess I have to move on like he did. "Ok."

Miss Cleo could have even seen this coming. And so the consummation occurred...

CHAPTER 5

GET TOE TO TOE

Spending the day at Disney World and in the blazing heat and humidity had worn me out. On the drive back I slept soundly. I didn't feel bad about the sex either. I didn't feel good either. It just was. I doze off and dreamed of a rewritten future. The original plan was to attend college and Drew and I would be together—and maybe even marry. We would live happily ever after. Marriage was optional, though. I never dreamed of being a bride. I dreamed of being a doctor or lawyer. I would have a good job, nice car, and Drew. This, however, would no longer be the case.

Where does Earl fit in my future? Is he interested in college? What are his plans for the future? We've spent a lot of time together, yet I didn't know his future—or even present plans. Our time mainly consists of him basically "straightening packages" privately and I am simply along for the ride. In my mind, I am trying to picture us together in the future. I keep drawing a blank because I truly don't have enough to paint a clear picture.

We arrive home by the curfew and I slept the whole entire ride home and was now wide-awake. I gather my belongings and go into the house while waving goodbye. Ken and Tameka had no curfew, house rules, or a Miss Frazier so they were free to come and go as they pleased. They were living the life, or so I foolishly thought. I could only dream of that type of freedom. Grandma wasn't having it!

Grandma and I had some small talk and I showed her all of the souvenirs. I even bought her a keychain back. She said she had prayed for our safe return and could sleep restfully now that I was home. What is going on? Whenever I don't want my ears talked off, she is in full throttle mode—which was daily. Now she has grown less talkative and something just isn't right. "Grandma, what is wrong with you?" "A hard head makes a soft ass, Rona!" "What's that supposed to mean?" "I'm going to give you enough rope to hang yourself. You are going against the way I raised you." "I don't do anything. I go to school and get good grades while playing tennis, in clubs, cheerleading and I never get into any trouble. Why shouldn't I be able to go off with my friend?" "I'm hearing stuff about your friend and I don't like it. I got some people on it. I'm going to get to the bottom of it. Until then, he's no longer welcome here," Grandma states. "What? Why? That's why I can't wait to graduate and go to college. You liked him a minute ago." "I was tolerating him until I found out who his people are. I don't like what I am hearing. I don't want him around here and you need to stay away from him too. If you keep ripping and running behind him you aren't going to nobody's college. And I am done with it."

As heated as I was, I am not dumb or crazy. She was obviously mad as hell with me. The only time she barely talks is when she is trying not to kill somebody. I am that somebody. She went to her bedroom and slammed the door. I retreated to my room in an attempt to figure out what Grandma was so mad about. What had she found out? I am sure I will find out in due time and this I know for sure as soon as she is fully armed/ informed for war/battle.

I might as well call Laverne and fill her in on my trip. Maybe she will take my mind off Grandma constantly tripping. "Hey Laverne. What are you doing?" "I just got back from my boyfriend

Smokie's house." "Oh, so y'all are an item h'uh? So y'all are going out now?" I ask. "Yeah and I hear I'm not the only one who got a man. Word on the street is that your dude is a shot caller," Laverne teases. "What's that supposed to mean?" "A baller with twenty-inch rims on the Impala." "Girl, you are crazy. He doesn't have an Impala," I answer. Laverne begins to laugh at me, "Girl, and you are as 'green as grass.' You're smart as hell and dumb at the same damn time! I'm trying to be down. Does he have a brother? Shit, I'll even fuck with his daddy if he got "bread.' Shit, real talk!" "Laverne, you're a hot mess. He has a little brother but he's in middle school. I've never met his daddy. I only know about him having a mom," I said.

"Don't be stupid! You better get that money. Drew was broke and you loved his nerdy ass. Earl got major 'cheddar,' you better love and fuck the shit out him. You know a lot of 'chicken heads' are checking for him. I wonder why he's fucking with your 'white' ass?" Laverne begins to laugh hysterically. What I have grown to love Laverne for is her no nonsense, brutally honest opinion. As kids, she beat me up daily. I was afraid of her partly because she looked like a cross between a monkey and Chia pet—a "monchia" as I referred to her. She only had hair at the top of her head and the sides were broken off and fuzzy from rubber bands too tight.

Laverne was a brawler. She lived right down the street from me. Her house faced mine. She disliked me as a young kid and fought me daily up until was in the 5th grade. Becky, the neighborhood hair braider, was braiding my hair on the bleachers next to my house. Laverne rolls up on her bicycle like a "female Debo." I told Becky that I had to use the bathroom, in an attempt to prevent the impending beat down and embarrassment. Becky sternly told me that I was not going to run from Laverne anymore. She believed that's the reason Laverne kept beating me up. She told me that I was going to fight her today. What? Is this chic crazy? Laverne isn't human but a "monchia"—part beast. No mere mortal, adult, or child could beat a "monchia." King Kong has nothing on her. Or so I thought.

"I don't know why you're getting your hair done. You still ugly!" Laverne starts. "At least I have hair!" I reply. OMG! What did I just say? This newfound bravado because of Becky is going to get me killed. Laverne gets off her bike and walks to the bleacher and tells me to fight her. I sit still in complete shock because I don't want to get pummeled by a "monchia." As I am attempting to process this thought pattern, Becky pushes me in to her. I honestly don't recall fighting her but I did remember biting her from head-to-toe. I was not in the mood or had the time to be beaten by a "monchia" this day. I think it was intense fear that caused me to react in a fight or flight situation. When I finally snapped out of it, Becky had pulled me off of her and Laverne was crying. My how the tables can and will turn. Laverne proceeded to tell me she was going to take her bike home and come back to beat me up again. Again? I don't know which fight she was talking about because I didn't get beat up by the "monchia" from that day forth.

The dynamics of our relationship changed from foe to family. She was like a big sister, protector, and street educator from that day to this present day. I learned a lot from her. She has my back. I take heed to most of her advice but when it came to men—not so much. Laverne is a man-eater, a female gladiator and I was simply a spectator in the coliseum. "What do you mean, 'Why would he want me?' And you have such a potty mouth," I seek clarification from Laverne. "Have y'all had sex, yet? And don't lie!" "Only once when we went to Disney World. I just got back from Orlando and it was fun!" I answer. "The sex was fun? So you liked it?" Laverne is laughing again, "I knew he was going to 'pop that cherry.' All that money he's spending on you. I hope you gave him his money's worth." I'm completely embarrassed, "You're so nasty! No, Disney World was fun. I'm not like that. I'm definitely not like you! That was the first time." "That's his 'coochie' now. He's paid for it."

Laverne is completely tickled by all this. "I'm getting ready to go because you're tripping. I'll call you later. School is starting soon and I have to go get my schedule from school in the morning."

The final weeks of my summer continued with Earl and I spending time daily. Our days consisted of eating out, going swimming, and making endless visits to "da stroll to straighten out packages." I was like his chauffeur. He had given me the IROC Z-28 and my days were consumed with his unknown dealings.

Grandma wasn't kosher at all with the idea of him giving me a car that expensive. She clearly stated that he was not welcome at her house. So I had to park the car at the park at night.

Little did I know that life as I had known it to be would drastically change. I'd grown to accept the relationship with Earl and had fallen in love with him. I'd finally gotten over Drew and under Earl's spell. Entering my senior year with a new guy, new car, new wardrobe and accessories and exiting in this new way of life! Stay tuned...

CHAPTER 6

GET TOE TO TOE

I was a senior in high school but a freshman in the game of life. I would soon be promoted whether or not I was ready. Almost as soon as my senior year began it was over. As the bell rings to change classes, I suddenly became supremely nauseated. I sprint for the girl's bathroom and proceed to puke up my guts. What is wrong with me? I'm usually the picture of health. I've never thrown up before. What could I've eaten at lunch that didn't agree with me? I finally finish dry heaving and I must now pull myself together before I'm late to gym class.

I dress out for class and run to the gym in record time to prevent from being late and having to do late laps—running around the gym for fifteen minutes. The P.E. coach calls out for me to go see my guidance counselor. I do as instructed and go to see my guidance counselor completely confused as to why I am being summoned. I've always been an above average student and stayed out of the dean's office. Without requirement, I'd gone to summer school every year in high school. I couldn't take classes this past summer if I wanted to graduate with my class. If I had taken English over the summer, I would have graduated in December rather than in May.

I'm called into the guidance counselor's office to be informed that I've received several more scholarship offers. My grade point average was above a 3.0 and I'd been named to the All-State Tennis Team the past two years. I had the choice of an athletic or an academic scholarship. The guidance counselor gave me the three letters of intent to take home and discuss with my parents. The guidance counselor praised me for being an outstanding student. I needed to come to a decision regarding my college choice and it wasn't a very difficult decision to make. The game plan would be to go as far away from Grandma without actually leaving the state. I wasn't ready to leave the state but I was putting distance between her and I. That was the only thing I was sure of.

School was a breeze! I only went to school a half-day and could graduate in December, if I chose to. Earl enjoyed being able to see me half the day without the watchful eye of Grandma. For all she knew, I was in school all day. As long as I didn't skip school, which I never did, the school would have no reason to call her about me. I may have been hardheaded but I was no complete fool. School had never been open for discussion.

Word spread fast around school that I was not just the driver of the nice car in the student parking lot but the owner. My car was nicer than most of the cars in the faculty parking lot. I was popular in school but girls and I seemed to have issues. The girls didn't care for me much but the guys liked me. The odd thing is that I hadn't dated a guy at Fort Lauderdale since my sophomore year. There was usually jealousy because of the jock you were dating but I didn't even date a guy at my school. Drew and I had been dating for years and he went to another school.

As I head to the parking lot to leave campus until tennis practice after school, I notice that cake was smeared over the windshield and the half rag was cut. I couldn't believe my eyes. School has only been in a minute and the "chicken heads" has started. I sat in the car unable to see out the windshield. I crank up the car and turn on the wipers to clean off this mess. I am so hurt and angry that I begin to cry. Now I have to go show Earl what the jealous "chicken heads" had done.

I just don't know why some females are like "crabs in a bucket." Pretend to be your friend while green with envy; they spectate in the shade of your shine. I naturally gravitate to boys. Girls made me feel less than I was. "Why you play with boys all the time? I heard you let those boys 'hunch' you. Why does your hair look like that? Why you talk 'white?' You think you are 'white!'" was constantly the taunting and demeaning questions hurled at me by the mean girls. Can I dare to be different? I was raised from a different grade! Why do I have to lose my sense of identity to fit in with the cliques? No, thank you, I'll pass. Thankfully, Grandma had raised me to not care what I am called or asked about but what I chose to answer to.

Unlike the girls around school who went for "bad" because they had a group behind them, I stood alone. I was taught if I can't be a leader, I damn sure better not be a follower. And to never start a fight but to always finish it! This thinking made me a target. I lived in Sunland Park, where it was safe to roam and play during the day but at night it was a completely new cast of dark characters. It wasn't uncommon for a young girl, like myself, to be in the park at night and get raped, or even murdered. For this reason, Grandma kept me on a short leash.

I was bussed out of my all-black neighborhood to schools that were in mainly all-white neighborhoods. I immersed, or better yet—assimilated, into their culture. How could I not? I spent more time with the white kids than I did with my friends in my neighborhood. I was interested in everything: The Chess Club, cheerleading, tennis, Spanish Club, and the Key Club. I was never one hung up on color, it's only upon looking back that I notice the disparity in multiculturalism. However, many of the neighborhood kids never let a moment pass to remind me that I think and/or act like a "white girl." The inference is like it's a plague, something disgustingly bad. "You think you're 'white'" was almost the obligatory salutation.

Sunland Park was kind of cliquish. We lived in the houses that were southwest of the park. There were only a few homes surrounding the park, mainly apartments. I would later learn that the apartments were low-income and mainly located on the southeast side of the park. On 15th Terrace and 16th Ave, I named "Senior Citizens Row," there weren't many kids. Retirees, who had adult children with their own families, owned most of the homes. Once you go east and pass the tennis courts, there are younger families with many kids left to their own devices.

Fighting was the city's pastime and this is how you got your street credibility. Absurd isn't it? It is what it is. I wasn't one to start a fight but often had no choice but to finish it. I was often a target because I didn't mess with many of the girls from Sunland. Sunland taught me how to be strong and we all know that only the strong will survive. As for the weak, the weak is devoured. There aren't any punks claiming Sunland Park. You proudly claim that you hail from Sunland because you've earned your stripes or ranking. I found it comical that everyone seemed to have an opinion on whom I was and I hadn't quite figured that out, yet. The typical girl from Sunland was all about "dat life" and I was still trying to see what this life was all about.

There were only a few girls that I truly believed were my friends. I could count them on one hand and have several fingers left. I grew up around mainly boys. On "Senior Citizen's Row," there were seven boys my age and I was the only girl. Our days consisted of such great childhood memories playing games: football, kickball, dodge ball, flipping on mattresses, climbing trees, and racing bikes. Wow, what a grand childhood. I grew up as one of the boys, so the transition into puberty was awkward. My "homeboys" grew into young men who were more interested in getting into girls rather than hanging out with their "home girl." We all started dating and spent most of our free time with our significant others. We grew up and stayed close but our day-to-day dealings had become far and few.

I arrive at Earl's house and the tears had dried up but my eyes were still red from crying. Not sure if I will get "Mr. Jekyll or Dr. Hyde." I knock on the door and pray that all goes well. "Who is it?" "Rona." Earl opens the door and says, "Hey honey!" He smiles until he notices my disposition and asks, "What's wrong?" "Somebody cut the rag on the car and placed cake all over the windshield at school."

"So why are you crying?" "Because they've messed it up." "I'll get it fixed and washed. What are you crying for? It's nothing. I've got some stuff to do. Follow me to take it to get fixed and while they are fixing it I'm going to show you something." "Ok," I replied.

We dropped off the car and headed to the beach. We park and head into one of the beach stores to buy an overpriced bathing suit. I try on several and model them for him. He decides on one and we head across the street to go swimming. We swim and talk while enjoying the beautiful Florida sun and salty Atlantic Ocean. We grabbed lunch and then head across to get a hotel room to nap. We have sex and fall asleep.

I wake up in excruciating pain. I'd never felt anything like this type of pain. It literally feels like Freddy Krueger is inside me trying to cut out. Falling to the floor on my knees while holding my stomach, Earl tries to comfort me. In desperation, he asks what he can do to help me. He keeps asking me, "Do I need anything? Can I help you with anything?" How am I supposed to know why I feel like I am being ripped apart from the inside out? He gets me off the floor and places me on the bed. I decide to lay down a bit until the pain subsides.

As the pain lessens, it suddenly ends as quickly as it began. Lying in Earl's arms with my head on his chest, I feel secure and loved. Feeling his bony chest on my cheek, I listen to his heartbeat and breathing. Unconsciously, my breathing pattern and heart beat takes his cadence. As I'm lost in the music of our life's beat, then Earl breaks the silence. "You are going to be my wife and the mother of my children." "You think so?" Earl confidently responds, "I know so. I chose you. I'm Robert Earl, girl!" I find him and the topic amusing, "You're so cocky. Chose me?" "Remember that first day I came to your house and we talked all day? I knew then. You're smart. You look good, too. You're a good girl. You're 'green.' That's why I chose you." "What made you stop and talk to me that day?" "What do you mean, 'why did I stop?' You were wearing your little shorts like the white girls with this body. I got up on you and saw your face with that long hair. So I grabbed you."

"I should've said I had a boyfriend," I tease him. "It wouldn't have mattered. If I want you then you're mine. If you still would've been with that clown with glasses, I still would've got you." "No, you wouldn't have. If I had a boyfriend then I wouldn't have talked to you." "You're mine now and forever. I bet not catch a nigga in your face! All that 'he's a friend' shit don't fly with me," Earl commands. "So I can't talk to my friends?" "Not if they are dudes." "You can't tell me who to talk to! I don't cheat and I don't really mess with girls like that. You have to trust me. If you don't trust me then we don't need to be together." "I can and will. See that's why I know you're 'green.' Niggas don't want to be your friend. They want to get in between your legs. I don't trust anyone but God and my mama. It's not about trusting you. I don't trust them niggas! I can see I'm going to have to break you in because you're so stubborn and hardheaded. Let's go and get your car. You need to get home before your Grandma calls in the F.B.I."

CHAPTER 7

GET TOE TO TOE

Grandma usually cooked great breakfast on the weekends. Since we weren't rushed for school, she usually went all out for breakfast on the weekends. A typical breakfast would be truly southern: salmon patties, bacon, eggs, grits and flapjacks (pancakes). After devouring breakfast, we knock out the required chores before we are allowed to leave the house. I then head to the tennis courts to get a couple hours of practice in before Earl and I get together. Since he and I had started dating, I haven't been as focused with tennis. I need to get focused before my last season. I plan on going out with a bang. My goal is to go undefeated this upcoming and final year. I would always make it to the districts, without a loss, only to get handed my defeat by Claire Evert—who is Chris Evert Lloyd's little sister. Well, she graduated last year and I was pegged to take districts this year.

Laverne comes to the courts to keep me company while I practice. I welcomed her distraction, although my mind should be on tennis. She always makes the time pass by sharing her constant adventures. "So when are you going to hook me up with one of Earl's friends with money?" Laverne begins. "I don't really be talking with his friends and I don't really know them. I don't be

41

around them," I responded. "Why? They don't like you?" Laverne questioned. "No, it's not like that. I don't be around them. Like, I'm in the car when he's talking to his friends or he goes outside of the house to talk with them and I'm on the inside. I never really thought about it though," I said. Laverne begins to laugh, "Hell naw! He got yo' ass on lock! You on lockdown!" I begin to feel some type of way, "No, I'm not! You know what? I'm going to see him in a little bit and I will talk to one of his friends for you." "All right. That's what's up. We'll see. Don't mess around and get beat up!" Laverne states as she is laughing hysterically. Just then I hear Grandma yelling out of the front door to me at one hundred yards away, "Rona! Rona, telephone! Ronaaaaaaa!" I yell to her that I am coming and I bid Laverne adieu. I run across the park to go answer the phone. "Hello!" "What are you doing? Who were you talking to? What took you so long to get to the phone?" Earl begins to interrogate me. "I was…" and before I could complete my sentence I am interrupted. "Bring your ass here now! I've been waiting on you. You got fifteen minutes!" Earl then hangs up the phone after his demands.

I throw my racquet and balls in the car and head to him as summoned. Being all sweaty and in gym shorts, I was in no condition to be in his presence. I just knew he wouldn't be happy when he saw me in my P.E. attire. As I turn into Cambridge Square, I see two police officers posted at the entrance watching all traffic like a hawk. I pulled into the parking lot and I see "Knock-Knock". He nods an unspoken "what's up?" and I get out of the car and approach him. "Hey 'Knock Knock.'" Before he responds to me, he looks from side-to-side nervously, "What's up?" "I have a friend who wants to meet you." "Knock-Knock" is interested and asks, "How she looks? What school she go to?" "She's not ugly. She goes to Dillard." "I went to Dillard and I might know her. What's her name?"

Suddenly Earl appears from nowhere and smacks me dead in the face! We began fighting and I was just reacting naturally to being struck. As we lock up and fall to the ground, I just pounce on him like a poorly hit ball in tennis. It wasn't uncommon for me to fight boys growing up, but to have one strike me as damn near an adult was very foreign. I was sincerely fighting him like there was no tomorrow and I noticed that there wasn't any retaliation. He was pinned under me while I punched his lights out. I got off of him and stopped throwing blows as my thoughts came back to me. I am trying to figure out what just happened? What am I doing? Before I could fully process everything, Earl starts in by saying, "Don't ever disrespect me again!" "Don't you ever touch me again," I demand. "Then stay out niggas faces! Have you lost your mind?" "Have you lost yours? I talk to whomever I want and every time you touch me I will fight back," I promised him.

I stood there toe-to-toe in his face. I meant each and every word spoken. I wasn't going to have him putting his hands on me. This was completely uncommon and unfamiliar to me. My parents barely had verbal fights, no less than punching the other. Earl looked at me and realized I meant business and apologized. We hopped into his car to make his usual "straightening of the packages" and he pulls up and gets out to talk to some guys. We usually didn't stay any longer than a few minutes but this was different. The conversation was much longer and a bag is given to Earl as heads back to the car. He places the brown bag in the glove compartment. He appeared to be seemingly agitated and anxious as he drove to the next stop. He parks down the street and walks a half block up the street to some guys standing outside some apartments. Another long conversation and I decided to touch myself up in the mirror and looked for a hairbrush to freshen up my ponytail. There was nothing in the console and I then checked the glove compartment where the mysterious brown bag lies.

Curiosity gets the best of me and I take the bag out and open it. Inside is a Ziploc bag filled to capacity with Chiclet-looking squares—all evenly beige-colored and square-shaped. I proceed to start breaking them in half through the bag. What was I thinking? I didn't even know what it was. To me, it was like bubble plastic waiting to be popped because you just can't resist it.

After some time Earl arrives at the car and asks for the brown bag. I placed the one Ziploc into the bag with the others and handed it to him. "What were you doing?" Earl asks as he inspects the bag. "Just playing with them. I didn't take any. What are they anyway?" I ask. Earl pulls out bag to discover crackled remnants of the once perfect squares and demands to know, "Why did you crush my *rocks*? Damn, that's what I get for fucking with a 'square.' Don't be going through my shit! I was just doing a friend a favor by dropping that off. His car broke down and he needed me to drop that off before the police came. From now on, don't involve yourself in things you have no part in. In other words, don't be snooping and we will be ok. I'll be right back!"

Oh my goodness! *Rocks!* He has *rocks*? Heck, I touched and played with the rocks. He sells rocks. What in the world? Is this how he gets his money? I don't mess with dope boys, at least not knowingly. Everything that I had seen associated with drugs had been negative. Nothing positive ever came from it. Noted, I was raised by my grandparents, as a result of my biological parent's drug addictions—namely crack cocaine also known as the rock.

One thing I noticed about Earl was that he was a smooth talker. He had a way of justifying his greasy acts with squeaky-clean responses. Either I was just too naïve to believe the truth or he made me think otherwise; regardless, I turned a blind eye to the alleged dealings. Believing that he wasn't slanging rocks because he was not on the corner all the time like the dope boys. He spent too much time with me. It wasn't uncommon to know a lot of dope dealers. Once the crack epidemic hit in the 80's, many people jumped on the bandwagon to make extra money. A small invest-ment yielded a much larger return. My homeboys would slang a little dope to buy school clothes, cars, etc. I knew of the existence of crack first hand because my father was addicted to the drug for many years.

I started to feel nauseated and wanted to lie down. We went back to his house and I lied down in his bed. He said he had some business to tend to and for me to nap and he would be back be-fore I awakened. I drifted off to sleep thinking about the rocks I'd seen. I started putting it all together and realized why the police constantly questioned him—due to being an alleged drug dealer.

I wake up four hours later and Earl hasn't come back yet. All of a sudden I feel like I am going to erupt and make a mad dash for the bathroom. I'm literally vomiting up my guts. As my body thrusts violently in and out, bringing up anything recently ingest-ed, my ears pick up a voice calling my name and I answer, "I'm in the bathroom." Earl comes in and sees me facing the commode and asks, "You've been throwing up?" "Yes." A big smile erupts on his face and he says, "Honey, you may be pregnant. That's why your stomach has been hurting." "I'm not pregnant! I can't be preg-nant." Earl seems bewildered and asks, "Why not?" "I have to go to college. I can't get pregnant. Plus, Grandma and Barb would kill me." "I'll take care of you. I got you!" "Don't tell anybody! I don't know what I'm going to do," I demand. As much as I wanted to con-vince him that I wasn't pregnant, I also tried to convince myself of the same. I'd never been sick a day in my life. Now I am throwing up my guts often. I'm just going to continue on and hope it goes away. Dear God, please make it go away!

Maintaining the façade in school became more and more diffi-cult. I was literally throwing up every morning and throughout the day. I'd lost quite a bit of weight very quickly. I'd exhausted every excuse known to man to tell my teachers as to why I was late to my classes. Anything was better than the truth, which was that I had "morning sickness" all day long. I had become so weak and anemic from the constant nauseating feeling. A half a day in school became too much. I wait until my senior year to start skipping school and classes. With no time to spare in my senior year, my bad habits kick in the final seconds of the match/game. I'm not even sure if "bad habits" is the right verbiage or simply fate, destiny, or the consequences of choices made.

My sickness did not subside, if anything, it got worst. I'd attempted to go to school here and there, my attendance was based on the severity of my "morning sickness." The rumor mill was abuzz due to my weight loss and poor attendance. A classic case of a good girl gone bad. School wasn't the only place abuzz with my newfound condition. Earl was around telling anyone with an ear that I was pregnant. I'd asked him not to tell anyone until I knew for sure. I had no plans, none that included a child. I was never the type of girl who fantasized about having a husband and kids. No, that wasn't my fairy tale. My aspirations were to be a doctor or lawyer. I viewed children as a hindrance to those dreams. And this was primarily the reason I had such a hard time taking the "rose-colored glasses" off and accepting and dealing with reality of the matter.

CHAPTER 8

GET TOE TO TOE

Since Earl and I had the talk about me possibly being pregnant, I had been staying with him. I hadn't been home in nearly a week. There was no way I could go around Grandma sick without her finding out. People in Cambridge Square had been telling me that my Aunt Barb had been asking about me. Beyond a shadow of a doubt, I knew this had Grandma written all over it. After I stayed out for the day, the mere thought of enduring her wrath paralyzed me with complete and utter fear. School wasn't even a topic open for discussion. I had pulled the ultimate act of "smelling myself." My anecdote was to keep running until I knew what to do. Little did I know that I was already on running on empty.

Barb was often in Cambridge Square because that was her territory as a meter reader with Florida Power and Light. I knew I had to proceed with caution while out and about driving during her work hours. I basically stayed in all day until I felt the coast was clear to venture out in the evening. There is a commanding knock at the front door as I am sitting in the living room. Earl goes to the door and looks out the peephole. He opens the door while informing me that it is my Aunt Barb. The day of reckoning has arrived. Barb was an intimidating figure when she wanted to be, with her amazon-like build. Pushing past Earl she demands to see me. I was glued to the couch as she walked in and came toward me with aggression. She grabbed me by my shirt and jacked me off the floor forcefully. "You are taking your ass home. Who do you think you are? Do you call yourself running away?" I dared not say anything. Anything would set her off even more. "Let's go and you stay away from her, Earl. You don't mean her any good keeping her out of school."

The ride home consisted of Barb telling me how I am ruining my life. She didn't want me to make the same mistakes she'd made. Barb had a good job, nice car, and stayed fashionable. However, she had become pregnant when she was fifteen years of age with my cousin, Sterling. In spite of being a teen mom, Barb graduated high school, attended college and landed a good job with the utility company. She was able to graduate high school because Grandma raised Sterling right along with me. What hurt the most is that Barb had always been available to talk in hopes of preventing exactly this situation.

We arrive at Grandma's house and it feels like I'd been gone forever. I can see Miss Nezzie and Mr. Prince on their porch eying me. They speak to Barb and she respectfully speaks back. "Barbara Ann, I see you found her." "Yes ma'am. I did. I told mama not to worry that I would." "I knew she would get herself in trouble when I would watch her go down the street and hop in the car with him. Then she started parking the car down the street for her to come and go," Miss Nezzie informs. I mean, really, just discuss me like I am not present, why don't you? There isn't a need in the world to even try and explain or say anything. All I can do is buckle up and hope I survive this ride. Barb snatches me by the arm with her nails piercing my skin and takes me into the house while calling out for Grandma. She brought me home like a hunter proudly displaying their captured game. Grandma informs her that she was in the backyard and Barb proceeds to drag me to the backyard to finally face Grandma.

Grandma was hanging up clothes on the clothesline while talking to Miss Ethel. She turns around and looks at me in pure disgust. She snarls while looking me up and down for inspection. There is no way to deny the obvious disappointment on her face. I was never one to blatantly disrespect Grandma. I've always tried to measure up to her requirements and make her proud.

As I stand before her, there are no words to explain my actions and complete disregard for her feelings. "Where have you been, Rona?" "With Earl," I mumble. "So now you think you are grown? Smelling yourself? Have you been going to school? I just knew that boy meant you no good. You ain't seeing him no more. You hear me?" Grandma seeks acknowledgment. Again, I didn't dare say anything. "He better not call, come by here and if I find out you have been driving his car you will have hell to pay. You hear me, gal?" "Yes ma'am."

Then all of a sudden I feel myself about to barf again. Before I could brace myself, I begin to throw up. On my knees, I violent begin to vomit. I had not thrown up like this before. This was by far the worst it had ever been. The timing could not have been worse, either. I was so overtaken by the nauseating feeling that I had no idea what Barb and Grandma was doing. I am convinced they were watching and would know immediately something wasn't right. "What in the world? Lord, give me the strength to not kill this damn gal. She has gone off and gotten herself pregnant. Barb, is this girl pregnant?" Grandma asks. "If she is, Mama, her and that child is about to die." Barb begins to take off her shoes and her facial expression reminds me of a bull seeing red. She begins to walk toward me in a highly aggressive manner. She grabs me by my shirt and jacks me up lifting me off the ground while eye-to-eye with her over six-foot frame. "Rona, are you pregnant?" Barb demands to know. "I don't know." "Why are you throwing up? Have you had sex with him? Did you have sex with him *after* I've been telling you for years to come to me and I will put you on the pill?" Barb rages.

I begin to cry. I was far too afraid to confirm what they both have assumed. "Yes, only twice." "What do you mean only twice? It only takes once. I can't believe that you didn't come to me."

I find myself on the grass looking up at Barb. Since I obviously lost time and events, I can only surmise that Barb decked me. She must've knocked the lights out of me and did it so well that I didn't even see it coming. If they are this angry now, if I am positively pregnant it will only get worse. Barb snatches me up and begins to shake me violently and uncontrollably. Maybe this was her way of attempting to shake some sense in me. Grandma chimes in, "I knew her hot ass was going to get herself in trouble. She's pregnant! That's why she's throwing up. She done gone and got pregnant. How are you going to play tennis and go to college 'knocked up?' I tried so hard to make you out of something. Everything I've tried to do and now you've gone and made a mockery of it. Get out of my face! I'm so disgusted with you and you've brought shame on this family and me. No matter what you do for y'all hardheaded kids you just don't get it." Grandma sadly states. "I'm going to take her to my doctor tomorrow and find out for sure and how far along. If she isn't, I'm going to make sure she is on birth control pills. If she is, Earl and I need to have a talk. After we leave the doctor's office will determine the topic of discussion. Don't even think about leaving this house and I will be here in the morning to pick you up. Now get out of my face and space," Barb angrily says.

I retreated into my bedroom, which seemed a little unfamiliar. I hadn't been home in over a week but had been in contact with Sterling and my half-sisters to keep Grandma aware that I was still among the living. The feelings of total amazement, shock and confusion take over my body. In the back of my mind, I'd thought that I could be pregnant. But I didn't want to be pregnant! In actuality, I didn't necessarily want *any* kids. There was a great divide between a senior in high school and a teenage mother. I was adjusting to my senior year and looking forward to college life and beyond. I'd envisioned the future many times but none with a child.

I called Earl to make him abreast of the declaration of war from Grandma and the to-be-announced conversation he would have with Barb. He has no idea of the trouble we are in right now. If I'm pregnant, then the conversation won't be good. If I'm not, it still won't be any better because it is a known fact that I've been sexually active. "Hey honey!" Earl answers. "Hi. Well, they know that I may be pregnant." "What did they say?" "It was World War Three. Barb jumped on me." "Do you want me to come get you?" "No, please don't come over here! Grandma said that you can't call, come or see me anymore. Plus, I am sure the whole neighborhood will be reporting if you came anywhere near Sunland." "Your Grandma must be crazy or senile if she thinks that we are not going to be together. I've already started looking at some spots. You've got my baby and we are going to be a family. That's just how it's going to be," Earl assures me. I don't understand how he can be sure amidst the chaos.

I have gotten myself into a world of trouble. "I'm scared and I don't know. I don't want to be pregnant! I don't want any kids. If I am pregnant, I want an abortion. I think, but I'm scared of that too. I don't want to die from an abortion and I don't want to die at the hands of my family, either. I'm still a young girl and I've been forced to make adult decisions before becoming an adult," I unload to him. "Why are you stressing? Everything will be okay. You're having my baby and you're my lady. We're family. That's all there is to it," Earl kindly states. "Barb is taking me to see her doctor in the morning. I'll know then." "Time you find out, give me a call. I love you!" "Okay." I was unable to say "I love you" back. It's not as if I don't care for him because I do. I just can't even focus on that right now. My doctor's visit will determine the rest of my life. To be a mother or to not be a mother is the resounding question.

As expected and promised, Barb came by in the morning and took me to see her physician, Dr. Matos. The short ride to the doctor's seemed more like a cross-country drive. Barb was silent. There was no need for her to verbalize her feelings. Her face told the complete tale. She, too, was completely disappointed and disgusted with me. The painful silence was worse than the physical beating she gave me yesterday. This was completely unknown territory to me. I'd always been the good girl with good grades and a bright future. I strived to keep their approval and stay in their good graces. Could all that work over the years have been in vain?

CHAPTER 9

GET A TOE HOLD

My name is called and the nurse advises me to provide them with a urine sample. After this is done to disrobe and place the gown on with the split in the back. I obey. Today is the day of reckoning. I don't want to be a parent, no less, a teen parent. How am I to be responsible for another life when I am trying to figure out life for myself? I follow all the directions the nurse provides me. Now I wait for Dr. Matos to come in. The door opens and Dr. Matos appears. "Hello, young lady! I'm Dr. Matos. You're pregnant," she informs me. "So I am pregnant?" I ask looking for confirmation. "Yes, I will examine you and tell you how many weeks along you are." Dr. Matos replied. She then places her gloves on and proceeds to check me vaginally. As I lay back on the examining table I begin to cry. "I don't want to be pregnant!" I stated out loud. Dr. Matos completes the examination and removes her latex gloves and faces me. "You're about three months minimum and I wouldn't advise a termination after three months. It looks like you're having a baby," she said.

The tears begin to flow uncontrollably. Barb enters the room without any sympathy, empathy, or consolation. She walks right up to me and slaps the hell out of me. The slap rendered me bewildered and I came to with her shaking me to death while yelling, screaming, and crying out to me. "What have you gotten yourself in to?" she asks, "What have you done? You are going to have this baby and I'm going to take it. When you show me your degree, I'll give the baby back." "But I don't want a baby!" I replied. "Well, you are! Deal with it!" Barb fires back sternly, "That's the consequences of bad decisions. This is going to kill Mama."

We drive home and I go into my room and cry my heart out. I got on my knees and cried out to God. There was nothing else left for me to do. I begin to talk to God in prayer, "Dear God, I'm so sorry about everything that I've done. Please help me, God. Make this a dream please. I don't want to be pregnant *or* have a baby! Please make me not pregnant and I promise I will live right. I don't want to be pregnant! Amen."

I decide that I need to try and lose this baby. As soon as I get home I begin to use the end of the bed to apply pressure to my stomach. I do this for several minutes to no avail. I'd cried myself into a tizzy and now I have a headache. I go into the bathroom medicine cabinet and take out a bottle of aspirins. I am still crying and very upset and I decide to take the entire bottle of aspirin. In my twisted thinking, I believed that one of two things would occur—or both: I'd lose the baby and/or wouldn't have to wake up to this nightmare. I take about twelve to fifteen aspirins and go lay down. I want to wake up from this nightmare.

Unsure as to how long I had been sleep when Grandma burst into the room with her hand on her hip. She was yelling my name in a pitch that could wake the dead. She tells me to call "that boy" to come over so we discuss what he is going to do now that I'm pregnant. Just then it dawned on me that the aspirin overdose attempt did not work. I guess I am going to be a mother.

I called Earl as Grandma requested. He said he was on his way and he sounded completely overjoyed that I was pregnant. He didn't appear to have any hesitation about talking with Grandma.

The joy in his voice was not mutual. This was not what I wanted and this was not a part of the plan. Earl tells me he will be right over and assures me that everything will be okay because he was going to take care of us—the baby and I. Earl emphatically states, "We're a family now, babe." We end the conversation and I try to get my thoughts together for this meeting with Grandma. This will be, no more and no less than, a massacre. I'm petrified! And then the doorbell rings.

"Come in and who is it?" yells out Grandma. "It's me, Grandma, Robert Earl," he states. "Come in boy! I'm not your Grandma. I'm Miss Frazier to you, boy!" and then she yells for me to come. "Go have a seat in my living room" and she goes into the kitchen to turn down her dinner and takes her apron off as she heads back to the living room. "You know Rona is pregnant because you helped make her that way. So what are you going to do about it? Are you going to keep selling drugs?" as she delivers her hits without warning. I simply sit in shock and stuck on the word "drugs." Earl begins to laugh, "Drugs? I don't sell drugs." Grandma goes in for the jugular again, "You ain't nothing but a damn drug dealer. Selling them rocks! I 'den heard about you. And now you've ruined her life too. She'll end up raising that child by herself and you'll be dead or in jail." Earl replies, "I don't sell no drugs. I'm a businessman. I don't stand on nobody's corner. I'm above that. I got Rona! I'm having a house built for us and we're going to be a family. I got her."

Grandma is completely unconvinced, "Yeah, you got her alright. You got her pregnant, out of school, and her life ruined. You got to change, son, and leave them streets alone! Ain't nothing good coming out them bad streets." While Grandma is lecturing, Earl's pagers are going off nonstop. Earl looks down at his pagers and stands up. "OK, Grandma, I mean Miss Frazier. I got to go and handle something. Thanks for talking to me. Rona, walk me to the car."

We head out to the front door to his car and he begins to laugh. I am unaware of any joke and ask, "What's so funny?" "Your

Grandma said 'I sell rocks/drugs.' I'm a supplier. If there was no demand, there wouldn't be a supply." "So she was right all along?" "No, she wasn't. I don't sell. I supply and there's a difference. Don't worry. I will never place you in harms way. I got this. Now lie down and rest while I go to 'straighten out this package.' I will hit you up later and take you to get something to eat." He plants a kiss on me and leaves.

Now I know why Grandma has been so short with me. She didn't raise me to be with a drug dealer/supplier or anyone in the "game." As much as I hated to admit it, she was right as usual. I really don't even want to have a baby with a drug dealer. I can't change the past but I can deal with the here and now. I am going to have a talk with him about our future. He is going to have to make some serious changes.

It seems as if after I became pregnant, I see very little of Earl. Other than the occasional phone calls, he doesn't come around as often. Grandma is having a field day with this. She feels he has "knocked" me up and gone to the next one. I've asked him why I don't see him as often and he assures me that he is setting some things up for us. He is going to surprise me. Days, weeks, and months pass. The baby is growing and Earl and I have grown apart. He has no time for us and is very short with me. I decide to take a drive to see him and surprise him. Maybe I was subconsciously checking up on him. After being cheated on by Drew, it's only natural that I would have trust issues. If my suspicions weren't warranted then my mind would be put at ease. If only it were so simple.

I pull up into Cambridge Square to his building and I see his Corvette at the building's entrance with his convertible top down. As I walk towards the car, I notice a female in the passenger seat. She looked awfully comfortable. No one was in the driver's seat. I approach the car and open the passenger door. "Hi, who are you?" "Who are you?" the random chic questions. "I'm asking the questions here. So what's up?" "I'm Nicky. Robert Earl and I are talking." "Is that so? For how long?" I demanded answers. "Not too long ago. Why? Who are you?" "His pregnant girlfriend." She looks surprised and confused, "Do you live in Sunland by the park?" "Yes, why?" "Nothing" she said. "So how do you know I live by the park?" I questioned. "My sister said she sees Earl's car by the park at a house. I asked him about it and all he says is 'he's straightening a package.'" "So he never told you that he has a girlfriend?"

Earl exits the building and looks startled to see me. When I lay eyes on him I immediately feel like putting hands on him. "Hey honey! What's up?" "You! So who is she?" I waste no time getting right to the root of things. "Listen, go home and stop tripping. You're pregnant." The random chic decides to chime in, "So you have a girlfriend *and* a baby on the way? You didn't tell me that!" Earl is never at a loss of words, "You didn't ask. Check this out, both of y'all. Rona, you know you are my number one and we are a family. Don't be stressing and jeopardizing my baby with this bullshit. Go home and lay down." He turns to the chic, "That's my wife and as long as you respect that we are good. Ok?" The chic sucks her teeth and rolls her eyes, "Yeah, whatever. Two can play that game." He responds, "It's not a game but real life."

He walks me to my car and begins to lash out at me in a tone I'd never heard before from him. "Listen, Rona, you don't ever run up on me *anywhere* about *anything*. You're going to be my wife and the mother of my kids. What I want done you can't do. You will have to kiss my kids in their mouth. I make love to you, but I fuck them. There's a difference! They don't get what you get. You're my main. She's sitting on the passenger seat while you drive. Don't ever question me or run up on me about *anything*. Now here, take this and go buy you some stuff," as hands me a wad of cash. "No, I don't want to go shopping! I want to know what you mean. Do you think that I am going to be played for a fool while you are doing whatever? Then you can have her. It's over!" I begin to walk to my car.

Earl grabs me by the throat and squeezes tightly. "You ain't going no damn where. You are mine! Now take your ass home before I snap! I don't know who you think you are talking to," he angrily states. "I will go home after she gets out of the car and you leave. She told me everything!" "She told you everything? Good, now you know! Now what? That changes nothing. We're still together and her and I are still together. Now what? Take your ass home and stop showing out!" I walk over to his car ignoring his orders and snatch open the door, "Get out of the car!" "I ain't getting out." I begin to forcibly remove her from the car and she begins to retaliate. "I will hurt you! Get out of the car! Every time I catch you with him it will be most certainly on." I warn her.

Earl runs over and snatches me off her and threatens her to not hit me back. He is visibly upset and wants this episode ended. He takes me upstairs and we begin to argue some more. He takes my car keys and tells me wait there until he takes her home. He leaves and I am in a complete rage. I've been disrespected to no end and I had no intentions of being there when he returned. I begin to look for the keys to the motorcycle or moped to plan my escape.

CHAPTER 10

GET A TOE HOLD

Sitting in his living room feeling beyond tried and disrespected, I decide that when and if he returns I will not be here. I'm completely stranded because he took my car keys with him. I go into the kitchen to look on the key rack to see if there was a spare. Nope! But, there are the keys to his little brother's, Mike, moped. I snatch up the keys, grab the helmet out, and head downstairs to get on the moped to get the heck from there. Filled with anger, rage, and completely in my hormonal feelings, I rode off on the moped five months pregnant.

Cambridge Square was less than fifteen minutes from Sunland Park by car, or less depending on the route taken. So I figured this was the best option at the time. I'm riding down 19th Street and make a right at the pink apartments across from the graveyard. Coasting down 31st and I make a left onto Sunrise Blvd by the Swap Shop Flea Market. Traffic is always thick on Sunrise because this is a main thoroughfare, which runs east to the Atlantic Ocean and west towards Alligator Alley—which is known as no man's land or dead man's land. I continue past 27th and catch a red light at the McDonald's by Dillard High. I'm a couple minutes from home. My house is just over the bridge two streets down. Unsure if I wanted to get as far away from the situation as I could or if it was the innate sense of wanting to escape the craziness of the outside world and find peace at the only place I knew I could be safe—home.

Impatiently I decide to make an immediate right and cut through the parking lot to save time and avoid traffic lights; my destination was just over the bridge on Sunrise Blvd. I hit the throttle and I fly through the parking lot and feet away I notice the reverse lights on a car backing out into my direct path. The parked car was backing out and there was no time to avoid it. Boom! The next thing I knew I took flight and was in the air. With quick thinking, I embrace for the impact and protect my baby by curling up. Before the thought process was completed, I hit the ground. I didn't recall feeling any pain or even the impact of hitting the pavement. Maybe it was the adrenaline.

I look down at myself to make sure everything is in tact. Touching my stomach I feel no pain and what little stomach I have is still there—check! My arms aren't broken but I notice I have concrete burns from the asphalt on both of my arms. The skin is completely gone off both forearms and elbows—check! I look down at my legs and they are skinned up pretty good too and my red flat shoe is off. I jump up to retrieve my shoe and take two steps and collapse. Now I am experiencing the worst pain in my life. It literally felt like electricity was being produced at the joint of my hip and pelvic bone. What is wrong? Maybe my legs are broken, yet I can walk, well, sort of. I jump up again and attempt to retrieve my shoe to the same outcome.

As I am taking off the helmet, my ponytail holder comes undone and my hair expands into an untamed Afro. A concerned white male approaches me, whom I later discover was the driver of the car that I hit. "Oh my God, you're a girl," he exclaims. "Yes and I'm pregnant. Please call the ambulance." He yells to some of the fast food workers, who were ogling, to call 9-1-1. "You came from nowhere flying!" he states to me. "Will you please get my other shoe?" "Ok, just relax until help comes. I've got insurance. Everything will be okay!" he assures me.

The paramedics arrive with the police and lights up the evening sky with their flashing lights. It's at this point that I start panicking. I don't want to lose my baby. It was in this moment that I didn't want to *not* be pregnant. At five months pregnant, I guess I'd accepted that I was going to be a mother. I begin to cry because I am afraid. I hate Earl and this is his entire fault. Had he not taken my keys, I wouldn't have been on Mike's moped. "Does anything hurt you?" the paramedic questions me. "Only when I try to walk. I'm pregnant! I don't want to lose my baby." "How far along are you?" "I'm five months!" He looks puzzled and concerned as he states what he is obviously thinking, "You're the smallest five month pregnant woman I've ever seen."

Upon hearing these words, I freak out completely! They rush me to Broward General Hospital. Someone had gone to inform my Grandma and they arrived at the hospital while I was being examined. Due to my being pregnant, they couldn't give me an x-ray to see if I had broken and/or fractured any bones. They do the ultrasound to check the fetus. Everything was replaying in my head up to this point. I was doing exactly as Grandma said—"making bad decisions!" I prayed to God to make sure my baby was healthy and fine. I decided that I was going to be a mother and I had to make changes. The family entered the room while the doctor was reviewing the images taken of my baby. Grandma, Barb, Sterling, and Earl had come in. The look on Earl's face was one I was beginning to become familiar with. He said nothing but his presence spoke volumes. His face was tight and I could tell he was gritting his teeth because the tension showed in the pulsating vein on the side of his neck and temple.

The doctor steps in the room and proceeds to give me the results of the images taken. "I have carefully viewed the images and kept the heart monitor on to see if there were any abnormalities.

Everything appears to be fine with the baby boy." Earl finally speaks after hearing the doctor, "Boy?" "Yes, you appear to have a healthy baby boy. As for your pelvic injury, that's a different story. At least, you've fractured your pelvic bone. It may even be broken, but without x-rays we can't say for sure. X-rays aren't an option because it could bring serious harm to the baby."

I hang on to every word coming from the doctor's mouth and respond with an affirmative, "Okay." "I advise you to lay in traction for six weeks, applying no strain or pressure to the pelvic area. This will allow the bone time to start fusing together and there should be less pain once this occurs." I question, "Lay in traction? You mean stay in the hospital?" "You can go home but you will have to follow the instructions given. You have approximately four months to heal before your due date. If your body responds by healing completely you *may* have a natural birth. There's a strong likelihood that you will need a C-Section, Caesarian birth, if your pelvic doesn't heal or isn't strong enough to deliver the baby naturally. So we have to allow nature to takes it course." Earl asks the doctor, "But is everything going to be okay with my son? Did she hurt him? He's not retarded or anything?" The doctor states, "So far, so good. There aren't any apparent causes for concern. But everything appears to be fine. " The doctor then addresses me, "I take it you want to go home. I will start the discharge paperwork. If you start to feel any pain, changes, or lack of movement from the baby come to the hospital emergency room at once. Follow up with your Primary Care doctor, also. Lastly, I don't recommend riding any more mopeds or motorcycles, even bicycles for that matter. Doing these acts places your unborn child in serious harm. Take care and take it easy!"

Grandma starts praising God and claims in Jesus' name that I will heal and nothing will be wrong with her first grandchild! They all leave out after ensuring that Earl will bring me home. He obliges and they empty the room. As the door closes, he begins to walk to the head of the hospital bed. Leaning in like he is going to give me a kiss, then he head butts me! The look in his eyes and face means he's beyond irrational. "If you have done anything to hurt my son, you are going to regret it. Please believe me. I told you to wait until I get back and you ride a fucking moped at five months in your pregnancy with *my* baby? Until you have the baby and I know he is fine, I'm done with you. You will make me hurt you *seriously* because you are too damn hardheaded!" he angrily spews his words without any concern for me.

I couldn't even defend myself this time. There were just too many things going on in my head, I was simply numb to most of the things occurring around and to me. After the contact with the pavement, the head butt was nothing. I was internalizing all the information that had been given me. I may have to be cut open and he is mad at me. I wouldn't even be in this situation if he hadn't been cheating. But, of course, Earl's smooth talking places the blame squarely on me. The nerve of this dude! I was not even in the space to deal with him and that situation. My life was fast becoming a movie and I'm starring in this unscripted, unrated independent film.

The nurse comes in and informs me that I am discharged. I dress with no assistance from Earl. The nurse sees me struggling and offers me assistance. I am unable to take any pain medication and the fight with the concrete has left me in serious pain. The concrete didn't knock me out, that would have been less painful, but gave me a long, drawn out beating. I felt every pain, scratch, and bump on my body. I literally hurt from head (butt) to toe. If the delivery would be worse than this, I have no idea how I am expected to get through this. The nurse helps me in the wheel chair and hands me my discharge papers. She rolls me down and Earl had left ahead of us to pull the car around.

The automatic doors of the hospital opens and I am rolled outside to the patient pick up area. Earl whips the car in and the nurse opens the door to assist me getting into the front seat. Once again, I receive no assistance from him at all. How disrespectful and inconsiderate! She buckles me in and I thank her. We begin to pull out of the loading area and I open the sunshade to look in the vanity mirror to assess any injuries to my face. Upon opening the lighted mirror, the mirror reveals a chic in the backseat. Not just any chic, but the same chic who was the reason for the argument. I slowly turn around in pain to see if the mirror is betraying me…

CHAPTER 11

GET A TOE HOLD

As I struggle to turn around enduring the pain of feeling every single muscle that I was using in my body, Earl speaks to me, "Do you have enough room?" "No." I proceed to scoot the seat back as far as it could go. I had every intention to make this trick as uncomfortable as I was. Earl addresses the trick/unwelcomed backseat passenger, "Baby, do you have enough room? Do you want to sit behind me?" Nicky states, "Do we have far to go? I'm not with this backseat action because there's no room." "I will drive fast and take her home. Give me about ten minutes, baby." The trick Nicky responds, "Okay, daddy!" I say to myself, "Daddy? Daddy?" Unable to keep my thoughts in my head I speak out, "I can not believe you! How are you going to bring this hoe to the hospital with you? I am so done with you! Just take me home and you can just forget about us! You tried me!" "What do you mean? I told you she was a friend. You're the one who pushed me to her when you got on the moped. It was over then when I told you to wait for me," Earl countered.

I am no longer in control of my emotions and I strike out at him again, "Fuck you! You don't tell me what the fuck to do! Your child is apparently in the backseat. What do I look like waiting on you at your house while you are with another hoe? You got me all the way fucked up! She can have you! I don't want your rock-slanging ass anyway! Take me home right now before I turn around and lose my baby beating this hoe's ass!" "You won't be pregnant forever and I will see you. Don't worry!" she futilely threatens. "Listen, you sloppy seconds slut! The only thing that is preventing me from putting a fist in your slick ass mouth is my baby! But please believe I will see you again and you won't be as lucky!" I promise her. "Both of y'all need to stop! Rona, you're having my baby and she's now my girlfriend. Y'all are going to have to get along. Nicky, if you cause harm to my baby then harm will be brought to you. Rona, I'm so done with you. I can't believe you almost killed my baby!" Earl stated.

We pull up to my house and I try to break the car in half by slamming the door as hard as I could. I struggle to walk in the yard by myself and the backseat-slut gets into the front seat. Grandma saw me struggling and came outside to help me. She sees the girl and gives Earl the "evil eye." Grandma wastes no time asking, "Who is that girl? Where is he flying off to?" "I don't know and I don't care!" "Sounds like he has made you mad." I begin to cry in complete pain from the accident and the emotional torture. I apologize to Grandma, "Grandma, I'm so sorry! I messed up! I've been so stupid and you were right all along. I'm pregnant and now he has another girlfriend. I'm so hurt!" Grandma always knew the comforting words to say to make you feel better, "Stop your tears! That may just be a blessing in disguise. He isn't any damn good anyway. Let him go!"

Grandma, the ever comforter, gets me in the house and places me comfortably in the bed. I lay there rubbing my belly staring at the ceiling. I begin to question how and why am I always the victim? My roots are too strong to be weak. Starting from the fight at South Plantation football field to now, I questioned how was I arriving at a place of victimization. Maybe Grandma was right when she would say a thousand times, 'focus on your books and wait on a man. You got all the time in the world for that." After seeing the disastrous results, I need to stop hearing her and start listening.

My due date was April 21st and the next few months I saw very little of Earl. However, everyone else would see him in the presence of other women. Even when he would stop by, every blue moon, there would be some random trollop in the car. If this is not the ultimate disrespect, then what is? Being alone in my first pregnancy allowed me much time to consider the future for my son and I. This is not the type of man I want to be around my son. What can he teach him other than negative behavior? My son deserves better than this.

My biological father, albeit the drug addiction, made his presence known. Unlike most kids with single parents, I had my father. It was my biological mother who abandoned me. I didn't have any "daddy issues" because I was blessed to have my father *and* grandfather under the same roof. I was somewhat bewildered as to how I am in these abusive relationships. I never saw my parents become physical with each other. Papa never disrespected Grandma with other women or raised a hand to harm her. These acts of disrespect and abuse just weren't organic to me but completely foreign to me like the visiting the moon.

This is probably what separated me from many of my girlfriends. Relationships, sex, and the attention of boys were important to them. They would seek out and pursue their lustful interests. I just wasn't as interested. I enjoyed the companionship while being athletic but the intimacy escaped me. It was an act performed simply to please them. I was more interested in an emotional/social level. Chivalry wasn't dead with me. I didn't pursue boys and I wasn't raised as such. No disrespect to the girls that did but I was never at a loss of suitors without pursuit. Spending time talking to me in person or by phone always drew me in. I think this started with my relationship with my Papa. My Papa and I would spend hours talking about his youth, Jim Crow, teaching history and valuable life lessons through his stories and parables. I was told at a young age that beauty fades but a wise mind will last you over time. Before I was even interested in boys, he would tell me what comprises a good man and otherwise. He taught me how men think and how women were viewed. I would listen intently to him because Papa had a low soothing voice that spoke with authority. I loved him to death and beyond. When he died in 1985, I was lost. It was at that point I began to be open to the attention of boys. On second thought, maybe I was just looking to fill the void left by his passing.

The phone rings and I am aroused from my thoughts. "Hello. Hello? Hello!" I answered the phone to no one on the line. After a long pause, the voice speaks, "Rona. Hello!" I begin to smile because I know the voice and I say, "Drew!" He answers, "I miss you! I just wanted to hear your voice." "Really?" I ask. "Do you think about me? Do you miss me?" I begin to cry and answer resoundingly, "Yes." "I never meant to hurt you! I messed up. But I hope we can one day be friends or maybe even more. I love you, okay?" Drew states. "I love you, too! I want us to always be cool. We were too tight to act like enemies. We both messed up. I forgive you and I hope you can forgive me," I asked. "Forgive you? For what?" Drew questions. I answer, "I'm pregnant!" There is a long pause and finally Drew speaks to break the deafening silence, "Please don't say that and whose is it? Oh my God! So is it true? Are you telling me truth?" "Yes, it's true and it's Earl's. I'm like five months and we've been broken up for over six months." I hear him sniffling and he begins to sob, "Rona, what have you done? Look at what you let him do to you. We could never be together again." "Why, is it because I am pregnant? You can't accept my son?" "Son? We can't be together because I hate him and I don't want anything to do with him. What if your son looks just like him? What are you naming him? Are you naming him after that fucker?" "I don't know," I replied because I truly didn't know.

We spend the entire night talking, crying, laughing, and argu-ing. Drew was my companion through the pregnancy. In spite of it all, he provided me emotional support. He also knew that Earl was dogging me and he still cared enough to not have me alone while pregnant. I told him what had happened with Earl and the random females, which certainly didn't help alter his opinion. He swore that when he came home that he was going to beat him up. Drew was away at college in St. Augustine College in North Carolina. He would go on to fulfill half of our dream. College was no longer in the cards for me but it was nice to know that Drew hadn't left me behind.

I looked forward to Drew's letters and phone calls. He could only call when he could get a "hot" phone card. The calling cards were only good for a couple weeks before the owner received a ginormous bill and it would no longer be good after the fraud was discovered. Hearing his voice and our talks reminded me why I fell for him in the first place. He was my friend and a great con-versationalist like Papa. Drew took my mind off Earl's absence and lackluster efforts. I would write Drew daily and receive his letters with joy. The phone calls became fewer and fewer. The long dis-tance calls were expensive and neither of us had jobs. Grandma had already stripped the long distance off my line after a big bill. Drew's letters and occasional phone calls became the highlights of my, otherwise lonely, days.

It was Drew who I shared the updates of my pregnancy. Earl was in and out. Weeks would go by without any communication from Earl. As my due date was nearing, I had a plan to start working and providing for my son. I was a month away from my due date and quite anxious and scared regarding the impending arrival of my son. Drew had befriended me to this point but the calls were now a rarity and the letters. The last letter received was explaining his lack of calling. Drew stated that he loves me and probably always will, but he couldn't fathom throwing a ball playing with a child that wasn't his. His deep disdain of Earl caused him to have a complete disconnect with the baby. He wished me the best and I knew by the tone of the letter that this was his goodbye.

As the tears are rolling down my face while reading the letter, I can't bring myself to hate or blame him. Drew thought that we would end up back together. If that wasn't in the cards, then he believed that there would be some other deserving guy who would treat me right. Drew said he tried to accept it but couldn't. I understand but it didn't make it any easier or hurt any less. I'd fallen back in love with him, or I probably never stopped loving him. His acceptance of me with a child would be a difficult "pill to swallow", especially with his ultra religious parents. They wouldn't cotton to their "golden child" having a ready-made family. After reading the letter several times I muttered out loud, "Goodbye Drew!"

CHAPTER 12

GET A TOE HOLD

"Hello, Rona speaking," I state as I answer the phone. "What are you doing? You don't sound happy to hear from me," Earl states. "Well, why would I be? What do you want? I haven't had the baby yet," answering him as I wipe Drew's tears from my eyes. Earl begins to laugh, "That's our baby and what do you mean 'what you want?' I want you! We are family. We are going to be together. I've been thinking, as soon as I get out I am going to show you. I'm going to marry you!" "Whoa! Whoa! What do you mean 'get out'? Get out from where?" I ask. "I'm locked up! These 'crackas' placed drugs in my car. They placed me on house arrest, and then my Probation Officer kept embezzling me for more and more money. I stopped paying him and he violated me. The pussy ass judge gave me a year and a day after my lawyer paid him off." "So you're in jail for a year and a day?" "No, I will be at the county for a couple weeks then they will ship me to South Florida's Reception Center. I'll be out in three to four months." "So you're going to miss the birth? I have to do this by myself?" "Honey, if I could be there I would. I've only got a couple of months and I'll be home. I'm coming straight to you and my son." "What about the other random females?" I ask. "They all knew I was going to be with you because you have my baby. I didn't lie to them or you. You got me."

71

Unbeknownst to me, this was typical jailhouse behavior. Get locked up and come crawling back to the one you were dogging while you were out. When his flashy ways no longer supported those "pigeons" they flew the coop. He talked me into coming to visit him before they shipped him off. He had his mother bring me back the car for transportation. I'd been laid up for months and it was no longer painful to walk. I was no longer crawling around, dragging my stomach on the floor. I'd been off my feet for about three months, just laid up rehabbing. Grandma didn't object to the car being there now because she felt I needed transportation. I'd been catching the city bus and rides. Grandma had given up driving after Papa was killed in a freak accident his car. Papa had been under the hood of the car working on his beloved Cadillac and it jumped into gear. He was killed right in front of the house and Grandma never drove a car since.

My pregnancy was without complications but with constant nausea and morning sickness, which lasted all day long until my delivery. I must say, this childbirth thing is rough. I would get up and drink a glass of water and I would literally throw the water right back up. God forbid, Grandma forces me to have breakfast and I awaken to the putrid smell of bacon or pork sausage frying. I would be up and off to the "porcelain god." I loved Big Mac meals with an orange soda, however, since my pregnancy the taste left me nauseous. While I was pregnant, I couldn't drink sodas or any carbonated drinks, for that matter. The taste was always off and the carbonated drinks did not sit well with my fickle tummy. Grandma had said to me that I was prettier pregnant and I broke into tears. I was so hormonally hypersensitive to everything. The slightest comments or remarks would be deemed offensive to me. In actuality, what Grandma meant was some women are worn out by pregnancy and for others they wear it well.

I've always had thick, coarse long jet-black hair, but while pregnant it grew even longer and thicker. My hair was filled with so much body and bounce. When I moved, so did my hair. It was at its healthiest before I had even started taking the prenatal vitamins. Like my father, I was of dark-skinned tone, but beautiful still. The pregnancy had lightened my face by several shades and I was told that my skin was glowing. I carried this pregnancy all in my breasts. My breasts rivaled Dolly Parton's. Heck, Dolly Parton had nothing on my breasts because I was a lactating machine. My derriere grew rounder and more pronounced. I did not have a very large stomach because I was basically all baby weight and not fluid.

At the six month in my pregnancy, things changed drastically and I blew up. Up until that point, the pregnancy wasn't obvious. People would tell me that I was small and would have a small baby. I did notice when I went to my prenatal appointments that many of the women were much larger than I was and fewer in months with their pregnancy. What do they know? As long as my baby is healthy, he can be big or small and that's quite all right with me. I decided to take the rollers out of my hair, which had been in for a couple of weeks. Since I hadn't a reason to get dressed or leave the house, I figured I'd primp myself up and go see Earl before he heads to prison. I get all dolled up and head to the county jail.

Entering the Broward County Jail is a nerve wrecking experience. The mood is of gloom, despair and intolerance of any bullshit! This was my first experience going to see someone in jail as an adult. I'd gone to see my dad as a little girl a couple times in prison. It was more of an open area with a concession stand with food and picnic tables strewn around the open area, but under constant watch of the friendly prison guards. My dad would even introduce us, his family, to the nice prison officers. That would not be the case at the Broward County Jail. The Broward Sheriff's Office (BSO) was rude, unfriendly, and spoke with a disrespectful tone. They would leer at you and I felt like I was being treated like an inmate. You enter through a walk through metal detector while being watched like

a hawk. You approach a desk with an officer reaching for your iden-
tification. He punches in the info into the computer and places the
id back on the table and yells, "Next!" There's not one "hello, how
are you, have a seat,"—not one obligatory salutation.

Looking around the waiting room I see all types of people but
mostly women of all types and from all walks of life. Some have
kids running around like wild animals and they are unaware and
inattentive to the unruly behavior of *their* kids. Some women are
looking like a million bucks: the fly hairdo, jewelry, and expensive
handbags. It's never a dull moment. Many officers appear to take
a man into custody who was here to visit an inmate. I overhear
some people saying he must've had warrants. I was unaware that
they check for warrants upon entrance. You are instructed to have
a seat and as you are waiting to be called for your visit and a team
of officers bearing handcuffs approach you. Please assist me with
understanding of why would you come to "cop central" with a warrant? If there was any inkling that I had a warrant, the Broward
County Jail is not where I'd be making an appearance. Then I hear
names being called for the next visiting session and then a loud
exchange of words drowns out the officer's voice.

Two different women, apparently both involved with the inmate in some capacity, began arguing and fighting. Before the officers could break it up, one of the girls had knocked the other girl
down with a chair. She gets up off the ground and throws a chair at
her before she could be subdued. They both are arrested and will
no longer be allowed to visit any inmates for a designated period of
time. Their banning would allow two other women to have visitation with him. I learned a lot just from listening to some women sitting next to me. They had a commentary regarding every act and
explained everyone's intentions from mere eyesight. According to
the women, since these two women have fought and been banned
he will now reach out to two more girls and have them take their
visitation slots. This, too, was a common occurrence. I wonder who

had been coming to see Earl before he asked me to come. The truth of the matter is there is no telling whom.

The funny thing about life is that you can never truly know enough or know it all. I considered myself to be a good student and maintained a high "B" average. School came naturally to me but there had been no subject or general education class that prepared me for the streets. I had no ideas to the living I was seeing first-hand. Grandma had shielded me from this living and now I was fully engulfed in it. I was feeling like a sacrificial lamb amongst wolves. My father had an extensive record for petty crimes due to his drug addiction. I would hear he was in jail and he would be released some time later. I saw none of it from this vantage point.

I may be a rookie in the streets but I can't say at this point and time I want to become a veteran. This is just appearing to be hard living: chaotic, complex, and difficult. If this is what street living brings then I don't want any part of it. I may not be built for this entire loud, rambunctious, classless, ignorant, and unsophisticated bunch. One of Grandma's golden rules she constantly stated, "Don't go outside this house and make me look bad!" Hard working, religious, homeowners, good parents and neighbors were how my family was known. They were well thought of in the community. We were expected to continue this expectation outside of the house. My parents were prideful people and did not believe in conducting business in public in a less than becoming way. There's a saying "when you know better you do better." Well, I've definitely been taught better and now I sincerely understand the meaning now.

An officer appears with a clipboard and begins to call names again. I hear my name and struggle to get up! I was now nine months pregnant and getting up and down is no small feat. We line up like cattle and are taken through a first set of doors. We are given the rules and the intolerance for insubordination speech. Breaking the outlined and defined rules can lead to revocation of visits. I was then buzzed in through another set of doors and we are instructed to have a seat at the glass and wait for the inmate's arrival. The glass is thick and a phone is attached to either side of the glass to talk. It all feels so clinical and impersonal. They ensure you adhere to the "no touching" policy by the thickness of the glass. You are able to barely see and hear him, because the glass is filthy and some phones don't work. I see some inmates walking on the other side of the glass peering in each glass to find their visitor. I am sure this is the highlight of their incarceration, their only contact with the outside other than phone calls.

Finally I catch a view of him. He looks good. He's much lighter and even heavier. He's picked up some weight and it looks good on him. Earl wasn't big in stature; he was like 5'10" and approximately 160lbs. He was slim like a tree branch. He looks at me flashing his rocked up, gold teeth smile. He walks to the glass and throws me a kiss. He then motions for me to stand up and turn around so he can look me over. Earl hadn't seen me in months. He'd call periodically but no in-person visits. I obliged. He shoots me the thumbs up sign and takes a seat while he picks up his phone. I do the same and attempt to get comfortable on the hard visiting chairs.

Earl was a different dude. He wasn't into the provocative clothing, such as the booty shorts and Luke dancer outfits. He preferred to see me in skirts and dresses. Knowing this, I wore a nice sundress to his visit. I really didn't purchase many, if any, maternity clothing. I generally just purchased my clothes sizes up. It didn't make any sense to spend the money on maternity clothing that won't get any use after the pregnancy.

CHAPTER 13

GET A TOE HOLD

Earl appeared happy to see me. He kept complimenting me on how good I looked, how much my hair had grown, and how pregnancy looks good on me. He was not short on compliments. I didn't disagree with him. Grandma had said the same. From what I've heard, pregnancy can wear you, and sometimes even take you out of the game completely. This wasn't the case for me; I was about to deliver my first child without one stretch mark. Earl thought that was great! He was not one to pay attention to the larger girls. He preference was petite and tone, and not thickness.

We spent the visit talking about our future and our child. This was a new beginning for us. I was drawn back in for many reasons. I was blessed to have a father and a grandfather in my household. I did not want to have my son denied the same. I'd accepted he would be in my life due to us having a child together and wanted to simply make it right for my unborn son. He stated he wanted the same and would be the man I required.

There were ground rules set and we both advised the other of what we required going forward. His incarceration allowed us time to communicate, by phone and mail, and share our feelings. I fell in love with this new man. Yes, he's rough around the edges but he has many attributes that I do like. Earl was a boss and answered to no one. He didn't work for anyone and was a go-getter by *any* means necessary. He was fiercely loyal and protective of his family. For all he knew a man to be, he was. The way he gazed and smiled at me made my heart skip. I left the visit with a renewed belief in he and I.

I enjoyed being outside and, being a native South Floridian, the weather allowed it all year long. Grandma and I were sitting in the front yard under the tree catching a breeze. I decided to share with her the news of Earl and I. I knew she was no fan of Earl but he was the father of my unborn child. "Grandma, Earl and I are back together." "I figured that. Be careful, gal. He's trouble! You know how I feel about him," Grandma warned. "I know. We are going to get things right and be a family." "You've made a deal with the devil. I've told you that a hard head makes a soft ass." "I know, Grandma." "You know so damn much and don't know anything. He has come crawling back because he's locked up. When he was out he was a ghost. And don't forget he was running around with another girl while you're pregnant. I've also heard some girls ride by here yelling, cussing, and carrying on. She better not try that mess when I'm outside."

Grandma had a valid point! I sat home alone through this pregnancy. Other than the communication with Drew, I was alone. He called sometimes but did not come as I, and others, felt that he should've. I'd asked him about this during our talks. Earl simply stated he knew he was going to end up with me. Due to my pregnancy, he didn't feel like I should be running about with him because I needed to rest. The answer satisfied my questions but not so much for Grandma.

Just then a car pulls up in front of the house and the tinted windows are rolled down. I am able to see it is Nicky in the passenger seat. "I've been looking for you," she says. "You found me. What's up?" "Did Earl tell you that I'm pregnant too?" "Why would he? It's probably not his!" The driver of the car decides to chime in, "Bitch, Earl is my sister's baby father. You better recognize!" Grandma jumps in, "Y'all heifers better get from in front of my house and don't come back. I'll be right back and I'm not playing!" Grandma gets up and goes into the house.

I knew she was going to get something to aid them on their way and I didn't want my Grandma fighting these "nothings" at her age. "I don't have time for y'all. I will see you after I have my baby. I promise you!" Nicky then hurls a 7-11 Big Gulp at me and hits me on the leg. I'm soaked from the exploding cherry soda. I jump up and run to the car and proceed to punch Nicky in the face and anywhere else I make contact. She is leaning towards the driver's side kicking and swinging at me, too. At this point and time, I'm angered to no avail and have no rational thinking. I'm able to grab Nicky's skinny leg and open the door and drag her ass out of the car. Before I can lay serious hands on her, I see a flash coming over my shoulder striking the robust sister who had gotten out of the car to jump on me.

"Didn't I tell y'all to get the hell from 'round my house," Grandma states as she is swinging a two-by-four. "Gone! Get! Don't come back! Leave my damn granddaughter alone or get your ass whooped." Nicky yells "Come on. Michelle! We will be back, bitch! It's not over! You're going to lose that baby. I promise." Then Nicky's lard ass sister, Michelle, then threatens, "We gon' beat that baby out of you!" When this threat was verbalized it made a permanent enemy of them both! After hearing this I became enraged and dove into the car to begin to beat both of their asses. I was yelling the entire time, "I will kill you! I'm going to kill you!" Grandma grabs me and pulls me out of the car. I was so mad at that moment because that was the ultimate threat. To even state that they had any intentions to bring harm to my unborn child was jeopardizing their safety for *life*. It is on for life! I will take them out! Word is completely bond! They screech off yelling expletives and threats.

The level of disrespect to bring the heat to my house in the broad open daylight is mind-boggling. Miss Nezzie comes outside and asks, "If everything is okay? Do I need to call the police?" Grandma tells her everything is fine but if they return she is going to jail. We take our seats back under the shade of the tree.

"Rona, you know I love you. I tried to raise you right. Never let a man make a damn fool out of you! Never! Now I'm just telling you! Where's there's smoke, there's fire. Who is that girl?" "I don't really know. She was the girl in the car with Earl the day I got hit on the moped." "Well, she knows you! Something has to be going on for a woman to come to another woman. She wants you to know about her," Grandma states her wisdom. "Yeah, that's pretty bold." Grandma disagrees, "No, that's disrespectful! Bold my black ass! That's pure disrespect." I agree, "You're right, Grandma! I didn't know she was pregnant too. He didn't tell me. I told him he had to be honest and open with me." Grandma begins to laugh, "Ain't no man can give you what they ain't got! It isn't in him. He's a no-good snake—the devil!"

My pregnancy changed me in many ways. I initially resisted the reality of the matter, which is that I'm now responsible for another life. Once I accepted I was going to be a mother, I knew that I would have to be the best me that I am capable of. Unlike a tennis match, I can't strategically plan my attack. Life isn't scripted and there are no films of matches to review. I just had to be ready at all times.

My cousin Dawn from Ohio called and stated she was coming down for my delivery. I was now in the last month and the additional support was welcomed. She flew in and I shared with her all that I had been going on with Earl and I. I told her that we were back together but I would no longer be disrespected. Going forward, he's going to have to fly right or get left. Dawn was a couple years older with no kids but experience in the dating area. She supported me and shared the excitement of my delivery.

Lying across the bed talking with Dawn and I wet myself! I get up and shower to freshen up. That's strange! That hadn't happen to me before. Maybe it's the pressure from the baby. My belly had definitely dropped and I felt pressure often. I kept wetting myself and just kept cleaning myself up. Hours have now passed and it's still occurring. It was a Thursday and I was planning to watch "The Cosby Show." Grandma was cooking salmon patties and fresh homemade biscuits, which were my favorites. As she was cooking, I mentioned that I was uncontrollably wetting myself. Grandma became frantic, "What? We need to get you to the hospital because you are in labor!" I wasn't trying to go anywhere until I ate dinner and watched my show. This is exactly what I did since I was in no discomfort or pain.

After dinner and TV, I get ready to go to the hospital. I was ready to meet my child for the first time but I wasn't convinced that I was in labor because I had no pain. None! I kept getting asked if I felt anything but I didn't. According to TV, a woman in labor is screaming at the top of her lungs. This would not be the case for me. Dawn accompanied me to the hospital carrying my bags. I'd had my bags packed for over a month in advance; unsure if the baby would come early nor not. My due date had been the 21st and today's date is the 23rd. It could be time!

The old folks say, "The way a child comes into the worlds says much about their life." Other than the lingering morning sickness, I had no pregnancy concerns. I didn't gain an enormous amount of weight. I did notice in the latter months of my pregnancy that the baby felt like he was going to kick out of my uterus. The sex of the baby was known but I only prayed for a healthy baby. I was going to receive the blessings the universe had given me.

I was admitted to the hospital after being examined. The medical staff prepped me for delivery. I am shaved, given an I.V., and all types of monitors are placed on my stomach. Is it truly possible that the moment is finally here? I didn't have a master plan or any schematic or blueprint. Motherhood would be dealt with in the moment. So many thoughts are going through my mind. My mind is racing as fast as the resounding cadence of the baby's heart rate filling the room. Placed in a gown and now I am assigned a room. The day has worn on me. It is now nearly midnight and I settle into the hospital bed comfortably. Dawn had settled in the chair swaddled in a blanket. She was supposed to be watching over me and supporting me, but not so much. I guess the day had worn her out by flying here and she fell fast asleep. I joined her and we both drift off to sleep.

I went to sleep as a teenager planning my future to attend college to make my family proud. Langston Hughes asked, "What happens to a dream deferred?" Hughes questioned life choices as I have. That life would not occur at this time. I will awaken to being a mother, responsible for someone else other than me. Selfishness is no longer a practiced art. My life would no longer be mine. I restfully sleep until an uncontrollable force causing my body to push awakens me. I was without warning or comprehension of what was happening; I called out to Dawn, who was no longer in the room. She had left the room and fallen asleep in the waiting room due to the much more comfortable couch. It was as if my whole body was having convulsions. I reached out to ring for the nurse and she arrived to inform me that I was in full labor. She wasted no time wheeling me in to the delivery room and the delivery would occur with no help from me. It was if my body was expelling this being as a fully ripened mango falls from the tree.

CHAPTER 14

ON YOUR TOES

As quickly as it began, it was over. They wheeled me in and my legs were placed in stirrups. My doctor hurriedly placed the gloves on and informed me that the baby is here. There was no time to react. I simply did as I was instructed. I was petrified; to simply say I was scared was putting it quite mildly. Staring up at the bright lights and seeing the medical staff in my peripheral view all gowned and gloved up, I prayed as Grandma has taught me. After my accident on the moped, I wasn't too fond of hospitals; they just didn't bear good memories. "Breathe! Breathe! When you feel your next contraction, I want you to push until I tell you to stop and relax," the doctor orders. "Okay, but my body keeps pushing and I can't stop it!" The doctor says, "Then push! I have the head." I am pushing and crying, as I am about to receive my blessing. "Relax! Breathe! Now push again. Push!" I begin to scream at the top of my lungs because I can feel the baby passing through me. The doctor then holds up the baby and says," "You have a healthy baby boy!"

He hands the baby to the nurse and she wraps him in the standard hospital blanket—striped blue, pink, and white. She then places him in my arms and I couldn't stop the tears from flowing.

Life as I had known it would no longer be the same. I was wrought with so many emotions. This beautiful baby boy I was holding allowed me to experience a love I had yet to ever know. I gaze lovingly at him while welcoming him into and as my life. "Hello, Robert Earl Jackson, Jr. I've been waiting to meet you. I love you so much and my job is to keep you from being a negative statistic," as I tell my baby through my tears of joy.

I was abandoned as an infant, that's how I ended up in the care of my paternal family. As a young girl, I envied the girls who had a mother. Please don't get it misunderstood, Grandma is a hell of a woman and I couldn't have asked for a better mother. She loves me unconditionally and no less than a child she bore. But, there was a generational gap that separated us an ocean apart. Grandma is an old school disciplinarian and doesn't care much for this new generation. Her opinion is the kids these days are too "fast in the pants and smelling themselves." In other words, growing up too fast for her liking. Grandma was not progressive and compromising with a child was not in her nature.

The story that I had been told, and believe, is that I was left at six days old by my biological mother, Carolyn, and have been in the care of my paternal family ever since. She returned when I was eight or nine years old and took me to Bartow, Florida. She became locked up shortly thereafter and my family then lawyered up and sought successful custody. The ante was raised and they legally adopted me. Game over! Checkmate! My last name was changed and I was official. I would not be in her presence again.

It was quite common growing up to know friends without present fathers. However, this was uncommon to have an absent *mother*. As a child, I yearned for this idealized mother. My idealized mother would come looking for me, being beautiful, loving, caring, and providing a reason for her absence. This would be a dream, a fairy tale and not reality! The older I became the less I dreamed of the reunion. I no longer desired the relationship with my biological mother and grew to deeply appreciate and honor the authentically loving relationship I had with the only mother I will ever need and know—Grandma. I thank God for Grandma! There is no telling where I would be without her.

I am holding the love of my life in this hospital bed and I couldn't ever fathom leaving him! I had never dreamed of being a mother but I knew looking at him I was up for the challenge. Having my son was a life-changing event immediately. I had to have a course of action to provide for him. His father wasn't present and he left his turncoat mother with his money. It was if the minute her son and I had a disagreement, she became my archenemy. After the accident, she came to my house to make it known, in no uncertain terms, that I was just a "dumb young girl who didn't deserve her son *or* his baby!" Our relationship was irretrievably broken from that day forward. I refused to play into her hand by asking her for money. This would not occur! I would get a job and work. Then I could provide for my son without dealing with her.

Leaving the hospital and taking my bundle of joy home was the beginning of a new life for me. Grandma had prepared my room for us and family and friends awaited our homecoming. He was such a beautiful baby. He was chubby and weighed nearly 8lbs. at birth. I wasn't sure whom he favored, but he was a cutie pie nonetheless. I held him and looked upon his face knowing that my life had changed forever more. The carefree teenager who spent hours on the tennis court, talking on the phone, and hanging at the mall with my friend is no more. The stakes had been raised and the game has now changed. This little person in my arms is now my life. I would face death a thousand times before I would allow harm to come to him.

Earl would call daily to talk and I kept him abreast of his son's daily actions. He was a proud father; I'll freely give him that. I could hear the smile on his face as we discussed our son. He impatiently waited the day he would be home to hold his son. He only had a few months remaining and all he talked about was coming home to his son. His son was his pride and joy. Interestingly, he would always say "my son" and rarely "our son." I didn't pay much attention to it because I knew he was happy to become a father. Maybe I should have been more mindful of his words.

The birth of Robbie invigorated and motivated me. I was going to make sure that he was provided for and I refused to beg Earl's mother, Miss Cat, for money or handouts. I got a job at the Galleria Mall one month after having my baby. I was hired at the Cinnamon Shoppe, which I loved passing by because of the sweet smell of cinnamon that filled the air. I took the job because it was ideal and practical since it was on the bus route near my house. I no longer had my car since Miss Cat claimed it needed to be serviced and she never returned it. Once again, the car was in her name and she exerted an iron fist over his possessions. She felt I had no need for a car because I should be home with my new baby and not running in the streets.

Luckily, I didn't have to worry about babysitters because my half-sisters were in the home. My father had married and had four girls with his wife, Diane. As for the story I've heard, my father introduced her to drugs and she became strung out. In her addiction, she walked away from motherhood when the youngest was under a year and the oldest at five years old. The word had gotten to my father and he went and got them. He attempted to raise them on his own, but eventually placed them in the care of Grandma, too. Grandma reached out to their maternal grandmother to come get them and she was willing to only take the oldest, Amy. Out of four granddaughters, she was only willing to take one of her *daughter's daughters*. Grandma opened her home to the remaining. Although we were raised as full-blooded sisters, there was always an underlying, unspoken division: me versus them. But when it came to Robbie, we all joined in loving him, especially Aisha. He practically lived in her arms while I worked.

The job went well and I was trained to be a cashier and make cinnamon rolls. I learned every aspect of the job and was kept on the schedule and worked many hours. I would be no stranger to hard work. I inherited my work ethic from my grandparents. I was in a position to care for my son and had even saved enough to purchase a car. It was not as nice as the IROC Z but it was mine. The car was $300 and was an older Falcon Wagon. It was a much older vehicle but ran very well. Aesthetically, it left a lot to be desired. The paint needed updating and the backseat floor was missing. It was like a Flintstone vehicle in the backseat floor. Even this was okay because Robbie would be in a car seat. I was making progress. I may have been young and naïve but I was most definitely determined. I possessed the drive to fight for a good life for my son.

I worked nearly everyday and would also pick up overtime. With having live-in babysitters, this freed me up to work like an ox. Also, living at home with no bills allowed me to stockpile my money. Earl will be released in less than a month and I plan on securing a place so we can be a family. You never know how strong you are until your back is against the wall. My pride wouldn't allow me to beg his mother for money. Secondly, I came from a family who are no strangers to work. Getting and keeping a job came natural to me. My baby had everything he needed and soon we will all be together. I'd decided to give the relationship another chance for the sake of my son. I grew up with my father and he deserved to have his father in the home too.

Robbie is sleeping so soundly and I watch over him lovingly. I decide to use this time to pen his father a letter informing him once again we need to be clear that there will be no more friends and cheating. As much as I love my son, I refuse to be a fool for anyone. If his intentions were not going to be genuine, he could just go right on about his business. The game has changed now because we have a child involved. I wanted him to have this manifesto and accept it before we take a major step to live together. I poured my heart out on the lines of the paper. I am a good girl and I deserve good love in return. And without cheating, disrespect, and physical altercations! I want to be loved and treated right. This would not be a request but a demand.

I was willing to move beyond the past indiscretions and his complete abandonment during my pregnancy. That was my reality. Being the optimist, I believed it could only get better. We had a rocky short path and I was praying for a smoother course. There was no way I was going to have that around my son. He would not grow up thinking it is acceptable to degrade and abuse *any* woman. The manifesto needed to be received and agreed upon before his release. His tone with me when he called would tell me where he stood and how he received it.

CHAPTER 15

ON YOUR TOES

The phone rings and I answer, "Hello, Rona speaking." An automated voice states, "You have a collect call from Robert Earl." I accept the call and Earl speaks, Hey honey!" "Hey." He hears the lack of excitement in my voice, "You don't sound happy to hear from me." "I am a little tired." "Tired from what?" Earl asks. "I worked today. I was waiting on your call so I can go to sleep." He understands and states, "Ok, well go to sleep then. Kiss my son for me and you too." I agree and we end the call.

I fall asleep and awaken to someone shaking me. I open my eyes to see Earl holding Robbie and smiling. He appeared to have been crying. He was obviously teary-eyed and he looked very well. I couldn't believe my eyes and questioned if I was dreaming. If so, please don't wake me. My family has been reunited for the first time. I am elated. He told me that when he called earlier, he was being released. He wanted to surprise me and sneak in on me. "Pack your stuff and my son's stuff. We're going to a hotel until we find a place. Get all his stuff." "Okay, are you sure you want me to pack all his stuff or just for a few days?" I question. Earl confirms, "Everything! He's going to be with me. He won't need his stuff here. He won't be here much, if at all."

I abide to his demand and we pack up and head to the beach to get a suite for a week. It was happening, we are a family. We get the suite and settle in. He then proceeds to tell me in the morning we are getting married—just like that and straight like that. There would be no bended knee, no heartfelt speech professing his love and asking for my hand and heart in marriage. Earl could be flighty and his mind could change by the morning. If we become married or not, matrimony wasn't a deal breaker for me. The commitment is most important, married, seriously dating or otherwise involved.

The day has been exceptionally long and the day wasn't over yet. I am quite certain Earl will want sex. Unless I was on my menstrual, he was definitely expecting it tonight. It had been some time since I had been sexual. Probably since I conceived Robbie or the one time after that. Something tells me the drought is over. I prepare to shower and succumb to Earl's sexual desires. Even though we had a child together, Earl and I had only had two or three sexual encounters. There was an attraction beyond my inexperienced sex life. He enjoyed simply being with me, talking with me, and simply keeping his eye on his prize.

Earl wakes me up bright and early once again holding Robbie. "Honey, get up! Get dressed, we gotta go." "Go where?" He replies, "To the courthouse. Downtown. I've got to handle some business." It had seemed like it was only an hour before that I had fallen asleep. I was pooped and really didn't want to be up with the chickens. I'd taken off a couple days from work. I just didn't think telling them that my boyfriend was getting out of prison would have gone over well. I mustered the strength to get out of bed. Earl dressed Robbie and we headed to the courthouse.

We arrive at the courthouse and we head in. Earl goes to the info desk and asks where the marriage license office is located. Did I hear him correctly? Did he just say "marriage license?" He was serious about getting married. I thought we were going to the courthouse to register for his probation or parole. "Earl, what's going on?" "We are going to get married," he said. "Are you serious? Are you sure you want to do this?" I ask. Without hesitation he responds, "We're here aren't we?" This is surreal. I'm getting married. Wow! We fill out the necessary paperwork, face the Justice of the Peace and are pronounced husband and wife after the marital vows are recited. "You may kiss your bride!" declares the Justice of the Peace. We share our first kiss as husband and wife. We are now officially the Jacksons.

Earl surprised me with our wedding bands. There was no engagement ring due to our engagement being less than twenty-four hours. I looked down at my left hand bearing the gold band symbolizing eternity. Gazing into Earl's eyes, I could see a sincere happiness. He smiled ear-to-ear displaying his gold front. It was just the three of us against the world. There were no other options other than making it work now. Failure just wasn't an option! As we left the courthouse, hand-in-hand as husband and wife, I was taking in this new life. New baby, new husband, new resident and I'm feeling a new me. Let's see how long this feeling last as we head to see both out parents.

We head to see his mother, Miss Cat. I'm actually looking forward to his announcement. It goes without saying that there is not an ounce of love lost between us. Any woman in her son's life has to bow down to her to get along with her. If you are a woman, like myself, who is independent and assertive is a certain recipe for dislike on her part. I was taught to be respectful of my elders, but I don't tolerate her disrespect respectfully. I've not seen her since the birth of Robbie and since my schedule doesn't work for her, she hasn't seen my baby much; with Earl being home now this will most definitely change. Miss Cat was left with monies to assist me but she made it clear that I would not be running around doing whatever on her son's money and in his car. She wasted no time after Earl was locked up that she had his money and was in charge of it. The joke was on her because her hate just made me great!

We arrived at Miss Cat's and we all go in. Earl calls out his mother, "Ma!" "I'm here in my bedroom. Let me throw on my robe, I'm coming. Do you have my baby with you?" Miss Cat questions. "Come see, Ma." "If you don't have my grandbaby I am going to be mad," Miss Cat stated. She comes into the living room with her robe on and hair wrapped. She was just off work and was preparing for bed. She'd been working at night and usually slept all day. "What is it, Earl?" Earl extends his left hand to show her his wedding band, "Look, Ma! We got married!" Earl stated with glee. Without speaking a word, her face made it quite obvious there would be no congratulations. Her face showed her disapproval and outright disgust. She rolled her eyes and stated, "I am too tired to deal with this mess!" As quickly as she appeared, she disappeared back into her bedroom.

I'd tolerated her antics solely due to my upbringing. Disrespecting an adult, even a disrespectful adult, was not something that my family would tolerate! Respecting your elders was another topic not open for discussion. This was the *only* reason I'd not given her a piece of my mind. Miss Cat should be thankful for my parents. As far as I'm concerned, I am married now to her son and not her. I'm done with her. I only need to please the person I took the vows with and not his mother. It's a wrap! No longer will I force a relationship with her. Point blank period!

Earl turns to me and hugs me while kissing me passionately. I believed this was his way of apologizing for his mother. Her reaction did not rain on his parade. He was happy and kept flashing his gold smile. Regardless of his mother's rudeness, he was obviously happy to be my husband. This was the beginning of our life together raising our son. "Come on, honey. Let's go see Grandma." "Okay, let's hope that goes better." "They will be okay. We are family now and they have no choice but to come around because there won't be a divorce," Earl assured me as he looked me into my eyes with a look that made me a little nervous. Earl continues, "'Till death do us part. If you ever try to leave me I will kill you! You hear me? I will do a quarter. Do you know what that means? Do you hear me?" I am unsure how to feel, respond, or act and asks, "What are you talking about?" Earl replied, "You are my wife for life. Ain't no divorce. If you leave me then your Grandma better pull out her black dress. Come on, let's go!"

On the drive to Grandma's I hadn't said a word. I didn't know how to feel about what my husband had just told me, several times, with a straight face. I wasn't very familiar with divorce since my grandparents had been married over sixty years when he passed. My father had been married once and never divorced, although the separation has been greater than the years married. My dad has been separated for greater than twenty years and never filed for divorce. For some reason, I just didn't take him seriously about killing me. However, I am kind of feeling some kind of way about bringing that up now and the way it was presented. I guess the honeymoon is over before it began.

We arrive at Grandma's house and she isn't home. I can smell food cooking but she is nowhere to be found. The stove is turned off but still warm to the touch. I wonder where she is and the phone rings. I answer the phone, "Rona speaking." It is Aunt Pearl on the phone and she asks, "Hey Rona, this is your Aunt Pearl. Where's Mae? Is she back from the hospital, yet?" I have no idea as to what she is talking about and ask, "Hospital? What's wrong with her? What happened?" "Barb fell out at work. They rushed her to the hospital. I just got off work and was going to go see her if they kept her." "What hospital?" I ask. "Broward General. If Mae isn't back yet they must've kept her. I am going to go there," Aunt Pearl stated. "I will see you there, I'm heading there now." "Okay, Rona, see you shortly!" Aunt Pearl ended the call.

I hung up the phone and head to the hospital. We arrive at the hospital and are informed that Barb has been admitted. We take the elevator to her room. Once on the east wing of the 5th floor, we find her room number. There are warning notices on the door. You cannot enter the room without a gown and facemask. Since Robbie was with us, I didn't think we should enter. Barb had always been the picture of health and as strong as a man, and now she is in a room with "Contagious" warnings. I stayed in my head trying to figure out exactly what is going on.

A nurse approaches and begins placing the facemask and gown on to prepare to enter the room. I decide to get some clarification for the warning signs. I decide to ask the nurse, "Excuse me, ma'am. Why are those signs on my Aunt's door? Do I have to wear this stuff?" The nurse replied, "Yes, you must wear these items. You don't want to bring outside germs into the room and you don't want to get any of her sickness." "Okay, will you tell her I am outside but I have the baby with me? Will you ask my Grandma to come here for me?" The nurse agrees, "Sure, I'll do that for you."

I stare at Earl looking to him for some possible answers to all the questions running through my head. He looks as puzzled as I am. I embrace my baby and begin to cry. Barb was my female role model. She is the epitome of an independently strong woman in both stature and spirit. As I stand staring at this door that gives the appearance of someone with leprosy, the door opens and Grandma appears looking completely and emotionally worn.

She hugs me and says, "I wondered if you had heard." "Heard what?" Grandma looks at me in complete silence with a long pause before she finally answers, "Baby, Barb is sick. They say she has pneumonia. I just don't know. It ain't good. I don't care what them doctors say, my God is a healer and in the healing business." "I just don't understand. She's going to be fine, right?" Grandma always has the sage wisdom needed and states, "It's in God's hands. She's been asking for you. Get yourself together and come back to see her." I start crying uncontrollably. Earl takes the baby and Grandma cradles me in her arms. She always has the words to soothe me, "It's going to be okay. Don't you worry! The only thing promised in this life is death. We none don't know the day or hour, including those doctors. Go home and get yourself together. I'll tell her you that you had the baby and had to come back." I reply, "Tell Barb that I love her! I'll call her when I get home." I left the hospital completely numb. Everything had happened so suddenly. Still confused and not sure as to what exactly Grandma meant. Was Barb going to die? Earl had no words; he only could comfort me by holding me as we headed to the parking lot. We decided to head back to Grandma's and wait for further updates.

Whenever I got in hot water with Grandma, I'd run to Barb for refuge. A couple years back I had even moved in with her for a couple months. Barb had a heart of gold and opened not only her home, but also her closet and all else to me. Barb was about 6'2" and I couldn't wear her pants but her shirts were fair game. I could not stop thinking about her and how much she means to me. When I was younger, she was my aunt; as I grew older, she often referred to me as her little sister. I get to Grandma's house and sit in silence until the phone rings. "Rona speaking." It is Barb's voice but it sounds unusually weak as she speaks, "Hey Li'l sis. How's the baby, Rona? As soon as I get home we are going to go shopping for him. Kiss and hug him for me." "He's fine. Are you okay? I'm worried about you," I ask as I begin to cry, "What's wrong?" Her weakened, yet soothing, voice spoke ever so gently, "Don't cry, Rona! God is going to heal me and I will be back as good as new. I still mean what I said, too. Once I get home, we need to discuss your plans for school. I'll take care of him while you go to college. When you graduate, you can have him back. You hear me?" "Yes, I love you!" "I love you, too. Mama will be home soon. Make sure she gets some rest. She's been here all day. I'm tired and going to get some rest. Call me later and I'll see you when I come home," Barb ended the call.

Earl asked if I was going to wait on Grandma to come home and I would. He decided to take the baby to see his aunt and he'd return after his visit. The house phone had been ringing off the hook with the concerned, the well wishers, and the plain old nosey asses calling to inquire about Barb's health. Grandma made it home and she sat in the car talking with Aunt Pearl before getting dropped off. I hadn't even had a chance to tell Grandma I was married because Barb's sickness had stolen my joy. How can I be happy when Barb is sick?

Grandma enters the house and plopped onto the living room couch looking obviously worn and asks, "Where's my baby?" "Earl took him to see his aunt." "Okay, but it's not good to have him around a lot of people. He's still a baby," Grandma advises. "I know. I have something to tell you," I nervously stated. "Please, Lord, don't let it be no more bad news. I don't know how much more I can take." "Earl and I got married this morning at the courthouse. We came to tell you but you weren't here. Are you okay with us being married?" Grandma clears her throat before speaking, "Well, he wouldn't have been my first, second, or even last choice. But y'all have a child together so I can understand. Don't be no fool! Don't let your left hand know what your right hand is doing. Keep you a 'rainy day fund' that he doesn't have access to or know about, just in case of emergency. Pray for the best, but be prepared for the worst. That's all I can tell ya!"

CHAPTER 16

ON YOUR TOES

Work was a welcomed distraction, although Earl didn't care much for me working. The money was good, location convenient, and I needed a welcomed distraction from worrying about Barb constantly. I threw myself into work while being a good wife, mother, daughter, and niece. I wore many shoes and the fit was all-different. Life can be changed at any moment and I was going to seize all moments.

My manager, Freddie, brings me out of deep thought and informs me that the owner was coming in shortly. Freddie warns me, "You know he wants to talk with you. So if there's something you need to tell me, you need to do it so I can help you." I am completely oblivious to his question, "Freddie, I haven't done anything. I was just off for several days. How could I do something wrong when I was off?" "He can watch purchases from home. His computer is linked into the registers. If the money isn't right he knows immediately. You know he personally pulls the registers every night," Freddie lectures. "So, I don't steal!" I protested. "Well, I'm just letting you know. Something ain't right. I can't help you if you don't…" Freddie notices the owner coming into the store and heading into our direction.

Freddie acknowledges, "Good morning, Mister Rubenstein, sir. How are you doing, sir, on this fine day, sir? Freddie is really laying it on thick and his tone changed from authoritative to a seriously submissive servant. Mr. Rubenstein ignored Freddie's question and asked his own, "How's the sales? Are these rolls fresh?" "It's been slow due to the rain but it's stopped now so I'm sure it'll pick up. Yes, sir, the rolls are fresh, sir." Mr. Rubenstein then turns and rudely states to me, "Your register was short about twenty dollars last week. If I'd looked in your pockets, would I have found it?"

You can't be serious, I think to myself. I took over the register that day without counting. Freddie had told me he hadn't rung up anyone and the draw should be balanced. The implication that I had been accused of theft really rubbed me the wrong way. What about the days I am tipped and I place those monies in the register? Where are the complaints about the register being unbalanced due to overages? I think all these thoughts to myself but I stand there in silence. "I am deducting $20.00 from your next check. I am going to watch you extra careful. Stealing won't be tolerated! Now get to work!"

Is this *really* happening to me right now? I'd never taken anything from the registers. However, this would change. Since I'd been accused of stealing then I will play the part. After he left, Freddie approaches me to find out what was said, "What did he want? I take it you're not fired since you're still here." "He accused me of stealing! He said my register was $20.00 short last week. He even asked if he would find the missing money in my pockets." Freddie stated, "He doesn't believe you're stealing because he would've fired you or removed you from the register. He has you on the schedule every day and on the register from opening to closing." I fired back, "I've worked my butt off here. Never missed a day from work. I work late and never complain. And the thanks I get is to be accused of stealing! He even said the sales are highest when I work the front counter last week. But it's ok and quite alright!" Freddie attempts to console me, "Just keep up the good work. Everything will work out. I told him you're the best worker I got."

I felt disrespected to the core, the nerve of him to accuse me of stealing. Well, from that moment on I decided I would make him right. I was going to do just as he accused me—stealing. All of my co-workers had the fear of God in them when it came to the owner. He was deemed as "Big Brother." He knew all and seen all without being present. After my years of experiencing my dad on crack, I was not one to intimidate easily. My dad was like "Dr. Jekyll and Mr. Hyde" on drugs and when he was around I "walked on eggshells." After him, anyone else was simply a peanut to an elephant. I wasn't afraid of Mr. Rubenstein, nor did he intimidate me. He was more of an annoyance than anything else.

I implemented my plan to compensate me for the false accusation. As long as the register didn't come up short then no attention would be drawn. I already knew the price of every item and all the combination prices by memory. When a customer would come in and order, I would ring up only a coffee regardless what they ordered. Then I would give the customer their correct change, place the coffee money in the drawer and place my money to the side. When the coast was clear, I'd take the money and place it in my underwear to conceal the stash. Just in case he ever came to check my pockets or purse. He was going to learn to never falsely accuse me of stealing. I left daily with hundreds of dollars concealed on my person. My register was always balanced and drew no unwanted attention. Freddie was often out of the store once all the baking was done and I usually ran the store by myself. Therefore, only I knew the true sales.

I carried on with the scheme for months. I was so well compensated that I held a couple months worth of checks not cashed. Even this didn't draw suspicion from "Big Brother" because Freddie had heard through the grapevine that my man was "the man." Freddie was not even sure why I was working in the first place. Little did they know that I was self-made while Earl was jailed. He was back building his "paper" and I had stockpiled a considerable amount of cash.

To give you a sense of the money being taken, how can a very busy gourmet cinnamon roll shop make only $20 on a Saturday? The irony of $20 being made while I had more than twenty times that amount by doing as I had been accused. When I came in to work on the next day, Freddie said it must've been really slow yesterday because only $20 was made. Wow! Opening at 9am and closing at 10pm with only twenty dollars made is shocking. I had gone overboard and needed to stop before I got caught. Those meager monies would sure cause Mr. Rubenstein to visit more frequently. The gig was over and I was done. My point had been proven.

After work, I decided to go visit Barb. I decided I would bring Robbie and her some cinnamon rolls. Barb was now at home in a hospital bed placed in her living room. Under hospice care, she had a nurse around the clock. I hadn't seen Barb since her illness. I'd heard from other family members that she had lost a lot of weight. After being hospitalized for several months, she came home with hospice care. I decided that I would wait for her to come home and then I would go visit. I really didn't know what to expect. As I entered the living room and saw her, I couldn't believe how frail she appeared.

I walked over to her and placed my head across her chest and cried out, "Lord have mercy!" "Rona, don't cry! God is going to heal me. I don't need this. You have to be strong! God is going to heal me. How's my baby?" I go get him out of his carrier and place him at the foot of the bed. "Here he is," I state while still crying. Barb begins to cry and says, "Rona, he is beautiful! My great nephew." She then asks the Hospice Nurse to get her checkbook and says to me, "Take this check and buy him something from me." "It's not necessary. He has more than enough. He's already spoiled." Barb wouldn't hear any of that, "Then put it in his piggy bank." Barb writes out a check and even her handwriting was unrecognizable. Her voice had changed from clear and direct to barely audible. She was wasting away and the decline was very sudden. Barb barely resembled the caramel beautiful stallion she had been. I promised to come see her more often.

A few days later, she had been hospitalized again. Earl and I went to visit her and Barb could barely speak. She simply moaned in pain. I called out for the nurse. I began to weep and ask her what she needed and what could I do to ease her pain. Barb stated, "Apple pie and ice cream. Daddy brings me apple pie and ice cream at night." It was obvious that she was now out of her mind. Granddaddy had been dead for nearly three years. He couldn't have brought her dessert as she claims. Or could he? The nurse enters and begins to admonish Barb for pulling out her IV tubes and loosening others. I implore of the nurse to help her and she gave horrible bedside manner. I begin to rip into the nurse and was asked leave out the room while they replace the IV tubes. Barb is crying out in pain and I hugged her trying to soothe her discomfort. I told her that I'd be back later tonight. Earl, once again, comforted me as I left in tears. This is primarily why I despise hospitals to this very day.

The old folks say when "one comes in the family then one goes out." Robbie was born in April, the very month that Barb became sick, and five months later in September Barb died. In 1987, we gained Robbie and lost Barb. Barb never left the hospital from her last admission. Even to the very end, she believed that God would heal her and restore her. May her sweet soul rest peacefully!

CHAPTER 17

ON YOUR TOES

I called in to work to ask for some time off since my aunt had died. To my surprise, I was told that I hadn't provided enough notice to cover my shifts. Well, excuse me for not having the ability to foretell my aunt's exact date of death. "I can try talking to Mr. Rubenstein for you. Come to work and when he tells me what days you can have off, then I'll let you know. The part-time girl called in today, we need you to here to cover. What time can you be here?" I snap, "Freddie, I'm done! My aunt is dead! I have no intentions of coming to work at all. So you and Mr. Rubenstein can fire me. I care not!" I begin to cry after realizing that my aunt is gone and I continue, "He cares only about his money being stolen and my aunt has been stolen from me. Bye, Freddie!" "So what do you want me to tell Mr. Rubenstein?" "Tell him that I'm tired of stealing from him and I quit. You can mail my last check," and I hang up the phone. The job didn't matter and I'd stacked a nice nest egg. Though Freddie thought I was being facetious and sarcastic regarding my being tired of stealing; it was the absolute truth. It was no longer a challenge and the point had been proven. Plus, Earl was completely capable of providing for us and he wanted me home with the baby anyway. I just needed time to process the loss.

For a period of time, this marriage thing was working. We'd moved to Hollywood off of Taft Street and were a family. Earl went out and about and handled his business while I tended to the domestic duties. I was settling into this "wifey" thing. Constant phone calls to Grandma on how to cook this and that was the daily norm. I couldn't even boil water without burning the pot. Earl was a tad better cook but over time we both improved our cooking skills. We began to cook together and share the techniques given by our mothers. These would be some of my fondest memories with him. Before the outside drama transformed our inside foundation. I guess there's always a calm before the storm.

Earl moved me out of Fort Lauderdale to Hollywood to be able to do his dirt, as I would later learn. I hadn't been in contact with many friends and hadn't been to Lauderdale in months. I talked to Grandma all day everyday, though. The "cabin fever" had been getting the best of me and I decided to go visit Grandma and catch up with some friends. Once there I'm informed that Earl has been out and about with various women. There had been several sightings but all with the same theme—another random woman. I gather as much information as possible to confront him. I even ride around in the city to see if I can catch him red-handed but to no avail.

After a long day filled with more information than I was prepared to process, I take the drive home to prepare to confront Earl. I truly thought that was behind us. Why did he want to marry me to cheat on me? That's the resounding question I need to have answered. I get home and get Robbie fed, bathed, and off to bed. I wait for hours and hours on end, so I decide to page him 9-1-1. This would surely get his attention. He rings the phone but I don't answer. This goes on for about an hour and the calls stop. Finally I hear the keys at the front door and it's show time.

Earl bursts through the door obviously agitated and without his wedding ring. "What's wrong? Why did you page me 9-1-1 and not answer your phone?" "I didn't want to talk to you by phone. Where have you been? Who have you been with? Why did you marry me to cheat on me?" I relentlessly questioned him. "Is this why you paged me 9-1-1? I thought something was wrong, that something happened." I angrily respond, "Are you deaf? Something is wrong and your cheating is what happened. Why is it I'm being told how my bedroom looks and how my bathroom is decorated?" "Don't question me about shit! I take care of you and don't question me about shit!" "How does Vicki know how the suite we lived in for a week look and the description of the place? She's my friend, well—so-called friend—and she's around saying y'all messing around," I demand answers. "That's why I want your ass to stay home. Every time I turn around somebody's telling you something. As long as I take care of you and home, what else matters?"

He then walks over to me and jacks me up while yelling in my face, "You are *my* wife. Those are my girlfriends. They don't get what you get. You are the mother of my son, you can't do for me what they do and kiss my son in the mouth, bitch!" I was not done and continued, "I am not going to be married to someone cheating on me. They can have you! I'm done!"

The honeymoon was officially over and reality set in. Earl then begins to beat me like a man! I withheld my screams for not wanting to wake Robbie. As I lay on the ground, he mercilessly punched and kicked me. I got into a fetal position and attempted to protect my face. Aware of my defensive posture, he grabbed my hands from my face and proceeds to punch me in the face. I see nothing but white stars and start to scream and yell at the top of my lungs. He starts choking me while ranting, "You ain't going no damn where. If you ever try to leave me I will do a quarter. You hear me? Don't question me about shit! I take care of you, bitch! Don't I give you everything?"

I begin to try and scratch his eyes out so he will release his grip from around my neck. He releases and begins to punch me and slap me in the face. "I don't give a fuck what anyone says. You are my wife and if you try to leave me I will kill you! Your Grandma will pull out a black dress. You hear me? I'll do a quarter, bitch! Twenty-five years will be the time for murdering your ass. You want to die?" I begin yelling, "No! Get off me! Leave me alone! Stop hitting me. Stop! Stop! Get off me!" Earl grabs two handfuls of my hair while pulling me close to him and says, "Every time you try me I am going to beat your ass. You think you're tough! Bitch, I'll kill you and raise my son without you. You are mine and if you try to leave I am going to do a quarter. Now go put the baby back to sleep and take your ass to bed!"

The fighting and yelling had awakened Robbie. I went into his room and picked him up crying as I held him. I rocked him back to sleep with a sobbing lullaby of "I'm so sorry, I'm so sorry!" I was sorry at the moment for many things, but mainly for having his innocence jeopardized by my unwise choices, or lack of having a choice in the matter. I settle him down and he fell back asleep soundly. He was still tired from the all day visiting. I go into the bathroom to assess the damage and fix my hair. I literally heard my hair being pulled out at the root. Staring in the mirror and seeing the reflection, those few strands of hair would be the least of my worries.

I looked like the "Elephant Woman." Like, seriously, I couldn't believe my eyes. I had knots across my forehead and swelling the size of golf balls. The redness in and around my eye was a good indication that I would have a nice "shiner" in the morning. I couldn't even cry after seeing myself in that condition. I stood there just shaking my head in disbelief. I'm sitting in the living room nursing my wounds after mustering the strength to clean myself up. I rigorously am icing my forehead and eye.

I hear the front door open and I don't even look to see who is entering. It is Earl and he comes in bearing gifts: a necklace, bracelet and gold earrings. He places them on for me. He moves the ice bags from my knots and now closed left eye and gently places a kiss on the injuries, which hurt to the touch. "Honey, I'm sorry. I love you. Don't make me do that again. Okay? I won't hit you like that again, okay? You're still beautiful. Do you love me still? You love me?" as the abuser ask me. I don't say anything because there are no words I could speak at this time that wouldn't aggravate the situation. Earl begins to remove my clothing and have sex with my body. Not my mind because it is a thousand miles away. I feel nothing. I am numb. I lay there with my eyes closed, one without any effort, and pray. All I knew to do was just pray that I am given the strength to endure. When you have a prayer warrior for a grandmother, you know the power of prayer. I drift off to sleep and feel Earl pull me closer to him as he settles in to go to sleep.

The next morning I awaken to the smell of breakfast cooking and Robbie's angelic laughter. I lay in bed for a moment to gather my thoughts. That's when the recollection of last night's events comes forward. I hurt from head-to-toe, but everything pales in comparison to my eye. I couldn't even open my eye upon waking. Earl enters the bedroom with an ice pack for my eye and breakfast prepared. "Good morning, my beautiful wife. Eat your breakfast and then put the ice on your eye. Do you want to eat in bed or come out to the kitchen with us?" "How bad is my eye? I don't want Robbie to see me all beat up. I'll just eat in here." How crazy is it for the abuser to beat the hell out of you and then nurse you back to health? The one responsible for my injuries is also my doctor and nurse. From that day forward, I could never trust him. That was the foundation for the brick wall that would separate us from that day forth.

Earl spent the day at home with us. His beeper beeped incessantly but he would only return particular calls. Some of them were obviously women based on his tone and short answers in code. I knew the difference between his business calls and his "getting busy" calls. The minute I thought that I could make a life with him, the seconds changed the thought for a lifetime to simply day-to-day. He was trying to make up for last night by staying home watching movies and going swimming with Robbie. It was such a vain attempt to erase such a life-changing act.

The brutality of his punches silenced me. For fear of ever being hit like that again, I submitted. He beat me into physical submission. My spirit hadn't been broken or taken; it may have been misplaced but not taken or broken. I couldn't allow him to beat the spirit out of me. If I'd lost that then I'd lost it all. So began the chess match. There would be no more verbal attacks because they perpetuated serious violence and rage. I didn't take heed to the "kill you" threat but I didn't want to be his punching or choking bag. For now, I will get along for the sake of getting along. He won't know how I feel anymore. My feelings would now be off limits to him. They didn't truly matter to him anyway.

CHAPTER 18

TOE THE LINE

During the next year the physical violence escalated. Earl could no longer control me by mere words. There comes a point in time that you get sick and tired of being abused and used as a punching bag. It was a continuous cycle of Earl giving me a direct order and my intentional disregard that often resulted in physical violence. I'd come to know his triggers. I learned him. Spirited discussions would often lead to him punching me over a difference of opinion or perspective. Call me crazy or it was that "Sunland Park" in me but he never knew my retaliation. Some times I would take a swing first knowing the impending blows were coming and then I would ball up in a fetal position and protect my face. This never ended well but the days of him beating me with no fear of retribution were long gone.

Physical brute strength wasn't the most rewarding course. No, I had to outsmart him and often times I did just that. He would beat me badly for whatever reason and I would wait for him to fall asleep. I would then line up pots and pans, lamps, and any other household items that could be used as a weapon. Once I had my weapons positioned, I would commence to beat his ass with what-ever I put my hands on. When he was most vulnerable, I'd attack his ass for a black eye or busted lip. Sadly to say, those injuries became the norm. He had underestimated me. He'd wake up in laughter sometime after seeing the arsenal lined up or my being in full combat mode. I know deep down inside he respected my acts of war but loathed them at the same time. It didn't matter how he responded to my attack because I was ready for war!

Two years into the marriage and I'd decided not to bring any more kids into this marriage. I'd taken safeguards by going to the clinic and getting on birth control pills. Upon Earl discovering them, he threw them away. I knew this to be a mode of control. He wanted more kids and he'd even requested a daughter now that he had a son. This was not my plan. Pregnancy would prolong my exodus. I knew now this would not be lifetime but my early death. Be it by staying and him beating me to death or him killing me for leaving. I'll take door number two, Alex; I am willing to take my chances. I did not want my son to think that it is acceptable to beat the hell out of a woman. Only boys carrying a man's name do such and I was in the business of raising a man. I'd lost all respect for Earl as a man because he was simply a boy carrying a boy's name.

I no longer had any contraceptives and shortly thereafter I get pregnant. This was an unplanned pregnancy. I did not feel that I was capable of being the mother the child deserved. Emotionally and spiritually I was in warfare. I was literally in a fight for my life. I was often left alone for long periods during the day while Earl handled his business in the streets. I'd come quite close to Libby, who I met while we both were pregnant with our first child. Our firstborn were both boys born days apart. We kept in touch and she was often my confidante. She was no fan of Earl's treatment of me, specifically the violence, but she did respect how he attempted to compensate me with the material possessions. The father of her child wasn't present and she did everything alone. The fact that Earl did take care of me well was something she wanted in her own life. Libby would be the person I was closest to because I dare not breathe a word to my family about the abuse.

I couldn't even wrap my mind around having another child. Robbie was not quite two years old but walking and talking. He was potty-trained and no longer used bottles or pampers. Now I would have to start this all over again. I'd also enrolled in the Licensed Practical Nursing (LPN) program at Broward Community College (BCC). Having another child would impede that and I sought out Libby's assistance to help me with this situation. I would have no discussion with Earl; I was going to abort the pregnancy. Libby would take me and Earl would be none the wiser, or so I thought. I made the appointment and was told the preparation for the procedure and cost. Libby would deliver me and pick me up since I'd opted to have anesthesia for the procedure. Earl wasn't usually home during the day and when he was it was only briefly. He probably wouldn't even notice that I had gone out. I would come home and sleep it off while Grandma had Robbie.

Truth be told, I had no reservations about terminating the pregnancy. The state of the marriage was abusive and uncertain. Another child would tighten his hold on me. One child was a do-able situation. Subconsciously, I didn't picture a future with Earl. I knew and felt this but went along with the program for the sake of getting along. Our future was bleak and the honeymoon period was long gone. I had Robbie to take care and protect above and beyond anything or anyone. He was my primary concern and not Earl. The decision for me was a no-brainer. Robbie made me feel loved and depended on me for his needs. Conversely, Earl beat the love out of me and attempted to control me with dependence on him.

I became a shell of a wife to Earl and blossomed into being the best mother to Robbie. Robbie had changed me after his birth. I no longer sought outside validations of love from a man. Robbie now filled the void. When I gave birth to my little man, I could no longer chase a man but would raise one. All of my time and efforts were placed on teaching my son what he needed to know in order to have a fighting chance in this world. He was both my gift and blessing and that's where I placed my focus. My focal point would not be on a loveless marriage. I reaped few rewards from the efforts sown with Earl. I was faithful to him while he conducted himself in a faithless manner. I truly tried to love him and he literally beat the love out of me.

The day had arrived and as planned, Libby picked me up and we took Robbie to Grandma's. I kept the conversations short with Grandma so that we could make the appointment on time. I arrive and begin filling out the paperwork, pay the fee, and was placed in a room to wait for the doctor. It wasn't until I was sitting in this clinical room that the reality hit me. I was *killing* my child. Wow! Looking at the pictures of gestational stages of pregnancy, I see an image of my child based on the length of my pregnancy. I was barely six weeks and I see a zygote resembling a lima bean.

The doctor enters the room and brings me out of my thoughts. "Hello, Corrona, is it?" "Yes, but I go by Rona." "Rona, we are about to start the procedure. Based on your last menstrual cycle, I would say you are five to six weeks. I am going to check you quickly and then get you sedated." The doctor places his latex gloves on and instructs me to lay back and place my feet in the stirrups as I relax. "Do you have any questions for me?" "Yes, how long will this take?" "The procedure is approximately five minutes. Due to you being so early, it will only be a few minutes. Everything appears to be fine." I think to myself, if only that were the case. Looks are very deceiving and everything isn't fine. "We are going to sedate you now. You have a ride, correct?" "Yes, sir." The doctor instructs, "Count from ten backwards to one." I feel the needle pierce my skin and tears well up in my eyes as I count, "10, 9, 8…"

I drift off and recall the conversation with Libby on the way to here. Libby asks, "So you're going to do this and not tell him? You're bold! You do know Earl is going to go crazy *when* he finds out." "He won't find out! I'm not telling him. This is my body and my life! I have no intention of bringing another child in this marriage. I can make it with one." Libby is confused and questions, "What do you mean? You're leaving him? He may have his faults but he does take care of you. You want to lose that? He's not a bad man." I reply, "He's not a good man, either. Earl hits on me. I'm not going to have a man beating on me. I don't care what he buys me or how much money he gives me." Libby advises, "You can cancel that thought because everyone knows Earl ain't letting you go." "He may not let me go, but I've let him go," I state matter-of-factly. "You know he loves you. He loves you to death." "No, he doesn't! How can you hurt something repeatedly that you supposedly love? I love Robbie and I would never beat him to hurt him. That's the problem; I feel he's trying to love me to *death*. I don't want that kind of love."

I suddenly feel someone shaking me and calling my name. I open my eyes to bright white lights. I wasn't all too sure where I am or what was going on initially. The nurse takes my blood pressure and it all comes together. I look under the cover and lift the hospital gown for assessment. I am wearing a sanitary napkin as long as the "The Love Boat," so I guess it is over.

I awaken wanting to continue the conversation with Libby because it had been on my mind. I needed clarity because I was feeling like she was on Earl's side or was it just me? Or could it be the anesthesia? We're going to continue this discussion on the ride home. Libby was a new friend and hadn't been tested to be tried and true. I trusted her and shared more of my intimate details of my marriage with her than my family. She knew Earl through me and would often tell me they crossed paths in the streets. But this was different, it was almost as if she was defending him while questioning my position.

The nurse states I can get dressed and leave. I stand up and notice the room was spinning and I was still quite loopy. The nurse assisted me and placed me in a wheelchair to roll me into the guest waiting room. They had given Libby my aftercare instructions, antibiotics, some pills that would close my cervix, and birth control pills. I could barely keep my eyes open. There would be no discussion with Libby. I could only recall bits and pieces. I could hear what was going on around me but I was not an active participant. In my brief moments of clarity, I kept asking for Robbie. I kept saying over and over, "I want my baby!"

We arrive at my house and Libby helps me into bed. Home sweet home! I just wanted to sleep away this incident. If I am lucky, I won't remember any of this once the anesthesia wears off and I'm lucid. I immediately get into bed and fall fast asleep. I'm hearing Libby speak but it's all gibberish to me. I hear the front door close and I'm off to sleep. There would be no sweet dreams. I keep having reoccurring nightmares of "someone", unknown to me, trying to take Robbie. Over and over, this nightmare keeps repeating itself. I am fighting this unknown person trying to take my son. I am kicking, fighting, and screaming and my son is not taken. Before I could relish in the success of the struggle, the figure reappears and again attempts to take my son.

Grandma was big into dreams and would often have me look up the meanings in her dream book. I needed no dream book. I knew the source. It was my subconscious feelings of guilt for having the abortion. Yet, I fought like a gladiator to keep Robbie from being taken. This unborn child had no one to fight for him or her, not even me. Lord, please forgive me for what I've done.

CHAPTER 19

TOE THE LINE

I am suddenly awakened to being slammed to the floor. I am being hit and kicked. This unknown figure is really trying to take my baby. All of a sudden I am being choked. I open my eyes to Earl on top of me with his hands squeezing tighter and tighter around my neck. I start seeing white and my head is then slammed against the floor. The force of the floor brought me back, however, I didn't have the strength to fight back. I was too weak to defend myself. What is going on, I think to myself. I yell to Earl, "Stop!" at the top of my lungs. I continue, "Get off me! What did I do? What's wrong with you? Why are you hitting on me?" Earl is yelling in my face so loudly that he is spraying me with his saliva, "I'm going to fucking kill you, bitch! Whose baby did you kill? Who were you pregnant from? Because I know damn well you didn't kill *my* child!" "What are you talking about?" I ask in attempt to gather as much information as possible. "You think I am playing with you, don't you?" He begins to punch me mercilessly and says, "I am going to fucking kill you, bitch! You've been fucking around on me and got pregnant! You fucking whore! Didn't I tell you that you belong to me and if you ever cheat on me I will kill you?"

I am trying to get him from on top of me so I can deflect some of the blows to protect my face and head. There are so many things

114

going through my head and emotions right now. I've got to out-smart him so I don't allow him to seriously hurt me, while I am thinking that Libby betrayed me. How else would he know? "I never cheated on you! I should have because you've never been faithful to me. I don't want any more kids. I am not happy and I don't want any more kids. How do you know? Who told you?" I question him defiantly. "I know everything about your dumb ass. You think you are so smart, don't you? I know every move you make." "If you know every move I make, then why didn't you stop me? Why didn't you say something? Why are you so mad now if you know everything? You should've known before I went, Nostradamus." I had to have known that my sarcastic tone would not go over well with him, but I truly didn't give a fuck!

Earl kicks me with all his might in my side. I am wrenching in pain. I no longer cared about his feelings. I spoke my mind in the heat of the moment, which was never the ideal time. He beat me physically but I always gave him a verbal lashing. Everything I felt that I dared not speak would spew out of my mouth. He hated this about me and would cause him to fly into a rage.

"I hate you just as much as you hate me. I feel like you feel. You love me then I love you. You try to be sneaky and I'm going to beat the shit out of you. You're so smart and dumb at the same time. You really thought I wouldn't find out?" Earl continues. Then he punches me in the mouth. I can taste the blood dripping from my nose and now my lip. This doesn't quiet me and I state, "I didn't tell you because you would've made me keep it. I want to go to school. I just didn't want to have any more kids right now." I am now crying and have been beaten into submission and just want it to stop. I cry out, "I'm sorry! I'm sorry! Please stop hitting me! I'm sorry! I'm sorry! I won't do it again. Please stop hitting me, please!" Earl always enjoyed when he had got me to submit. I guess this made him feel more like a man. He smirks and says, "You don't have anything else smart to say? I know you're not going to do it again. What you killed, you will replace. I want a little girl, anyway. You're going to have all my babies. You're going to stay pregnant. I like you better pregnant anyway. You are usually too sick to put up a fight with your hands *and* mouth. You're mine! You don't tell me you're not having my babies, dumb bitch! Take off your clothes and I am going to make you pregnant again. I start yelling at him through the tears, "No, I can't have sex! No, don't! Please don't!"

My pleas went unanswered and unheard. As I lay looking at the ceiling wondering why was this happening to me? What did I do so wrong to deserve to be mistreated so? Earl was winning the battle. He had broken me down. My self-esteem was in Australia—down under. I felt as if I was a voiceless being. I had no control over my body. He laid claim to that, but he knew it would be much more of an arduous task to control my mind and completely break my spirit. I knew that if I didn't kill him, he would kill me; this is just the fact of the matter. My son needs me and we're not going to be free until he stops breathing. He has no soul.

He finished his deed after ripping my clothes off of me, and rolls over and goes to sleep. I lay there for a while completely paralyzed. I get up and head to the bathroom to assess the damage *this* time. I look in the mirror and it's worst than it's ever been. My nose and lips were swollen and bleeding. Lord have mercy on my soul! This man is trying to kill me. I become completely enraged as I stare at the damage to my face. This has to stop! I cannot continue to be his punching bag. It will stop tonight! I'm going to kill him. I go back into the bedroom and go to dresser and pick up his gun. I take the safety off and stand over him while he slept. I was at a point of no return. Robbie isn't here and this ends now! I strike him across the head with the butt of the gun. "Wake up! Wake your woman-beating ass up! I want you to hear me out for once. My words will be heard as to why I am going to kill you." Earl sits up laughing and says, "So now you're going to shoot me with my own gun?" "Damn right! I'm tired of you beating on me. You're trying to kill me! So I am going to kill you first! Look at my face!

Look what you did to me! I don't deserve this!" Earl refusing to cede power, "Honey, put the gun down and come to bed before I get mad. I'm not going to tell you again either."

I know he won't tell me again because he's going to die! I pulled the trigger and nothing. I pulled the trigger again and the gun is jammed as I try feverishly to fire it. Earl lunges up and grabs the gun. As we struggle for the gun, it discharges in the ceiling and he grabs it from me. He empties the gun of the remaining bullets and places it on the dresser. He looks at me and states, "Get your ass in bed. So you were going to shoot me? I like that. You showed me you still have fight in you. Don't worry, I'll eventually break you or kill you in the process. Now get in bed!" I refuse, "I've got blood all over me. I need to clean up." He isn't having it, "No, come to bed. I'm not taking my eyes off you. From now on, when I sleep, you sleep. You won't catch me slipping any more."

I get in bed but I don't sleep. I never had a distrust of female friends, but first Vicki messes with Earl and then Libby sells me out. There was no other way Earl found out about the abortion. Libby must've told him, but why? I've never done anything to her to deserve this. This would explain her tone with me on the way to the abortion clinic. I am done with her. She cannot be trusted. Needless to say, I am going to confront her. It has to be Libby because no one else knew. I told no one *but* Libby.

Earl would often say that I had no friends. I defended my friends but he may actually be right. Earl didn't care for Libby and she claimed to not like him either. How is it she gets to a point where she chooses to be loyal to him and disloyal to the person she supposedly liked? The only conclusion I could draw was that they, too, was probably messing around. I put nothing past him anymore and now Libby has a great, big question mark hovering above her. The heaviness of the day begins to wear on me after staring at the ceiling for hours. I recite the Lord's Prayer and drift off to sleep.

The next morning I hear pots banging in the kitchen. It's Earl's usual "I'm sorry for beating the heck out of you" acts of kindness. I am not amused or changed by it. I sit up and I'm hurting all over my body. Everything single thing aches and hurts. Earl walks into the bedroom and tells me, "Good morning, honey! Take a shower and breakfast will be done soon." I look at him without speaking a word. I am sure he sees the hate in my eyes, how could he not? Maybe he tolerates it, like I tolerate his professions of love.

I shower the remnant of the day before off. Standing under the showerhead I begin to cry. My tears are the struggle to accept this living as my reality. I refuse to have my son model his father's behavior. There was no way that I would allow that to happen. I've got lumps, bumps, and knots all over my body! Cuts, too, because the running water reveals the scrapes and carpet burns unseen but most definitely felt. Things have to change for the better. They must!

The breakfast talk sickens me. Now I have to endure his terms of endearment and how beautiful I am. Not to forget, how much he loves me. Blah, blah, blah! I've heard it all before. The same mouth he gives pleasantries with is the same one he uses to speak death upon me. I'll play the role until I hatch an exit plan, I will simply grin and bear it. The beatings are becoming worse and my fight is lessening. He's breaking my spirit. I have to devise a way to get away from this *alive*.

I am missing Robbie but I hate for him to see me when I have been beaten. Earl states, "I will go and pick up my son. Stay in the house until you heal. Keep ice on your face so it will go down. I better get him now and get that out of the way so I can handle some business." "What are you going to tell Grandma when she asks where I am?" "I'll just tell her that you are getting your hair done. I love you, honey. I'm sorry. I just get so mad at you because I love you so much. Stop making me mad and we will be all right. Just do what I tell you to do." He then leans in and kisses my sore swollen lips and heads out the door.

CHAPTER 20

TOE THE LINE

Months pass by and there hasn't been an incident of violence since our last episode. I do believe that when I pulled the gun on him it got his attention. You can only beat a person so much until they start to fight back for their life. Our tolerance of each other probably has to do with my attention on school, also. I'd started taking classes at BCC; I had too much on my plate to be bothered with Earl. My focus was on Robbie and Earl didn't even bleep on my radar. We'd been cordial and since I stopped talking to Libby, he didn't have any issues with me regarding something I'd told her. Earl had implied that Libby tells him what I told her in confidence. I don't know if this was the honest truth or simply his way to break our close bond. Just to be safe, I pulled the plug on the lines of communication.

School was good for me. It put me closer to my goal of independence and provided me with some socialization. I was not allowed to have visitors or friends stop by. My only mode of communication had been the telephone and Libby had always been an available ear and someone I thought I could trust. I'll just continue to talk with Grandma. I'd do better to confide in her because she'd never betray me. But how do I even begin to tell her that Earl has been beating me? She'd not only warned me but didn't raise me to be anyone's punching bag. I really missed her, although I talked with her daily but my visits to see her was far and few between. I'd kept so many battle wounds concealed from her. I didn't dare allow her to see me all battered. Since there had been a lull with the beatings, I'd come by to see her more often. Grandma always had a way of bringing hope to a seemingly hopeless state.

We sit in the front yard and catch up. Grandma states, "This breeze sure feels good under this tree. Come back Robbie, don't go out the gate." I run over to get Robbie and close the front gate. I state, "It does. I've missed you." "I miss you too, Rona. I'm glad you stopped by. I've been dreaming of fish again. You sure you ain't pregnant?" "Ma, I hope not! I don't want any more kids right now. My marriage isn't strong enough to bring in another child in this world." "What do you mean not strong enough? What's going on? He better not be touching you," Grandma states sternly. I pause and want so badly to tell her of the beatings but I am far too embarrassed and scared to alert the family. Plus, Grandma has endured enough hurt with the loss of Papa and Barb. "I just don't think having another baby is a good idea. Too many issues," I state.

I have Grandma's full attention and she's completely tuned in. She asks, "What kind of issues? Talk to me. What's going on?" I confide in her, "I just don't trust him, that's all. Just can't trust him." Grandma starts chuckling, "If you are waiting on a man you can trust before you have a baby, then you ain't never having a baby." That excuse sounds better than the complete truth. I didn't trust Earl but I just couldn't bring myself to tell her everything. We laugh and watch Robbie play in the yard. We talk about the family goings-on and the neighborhood gossip. Some things never change. Nothing gets past her and she barely leaves the house, except for church and her part-time maid work. But she knows everything going on in the streets. She is truly the "Wizard" if this was "Oz."

After spending several hours being brought up to speed on everything, I get ready to go home. Earl has paged me five times and I've seen him drive by also. I guess it's hard to trust me when he never gave me a reason to trust him. "Grandma, I'm going to take Robbie home and get him fed so he can get ready for bed." "Alrighty! Let me give him a hug before he goes." Grandma walks over to him as he is bending over looking between his legs. He falls down and gets right back up and does it again. Grandma yells out, "Rona, look at him! You sure you are not pregnant? This boy is looking for a baby. And I've been dreaming of fish. I tell you now, you might need to start trusting that man." Grandma laughs as we hug goodbye, but I didn't find much humor in it.

On the drive home I am thinking about Grandma's premonition. I hadn't waited after the abortion and I hadn't been taking the birth control pills. I really hope that Grandma is wrong and it's one of my half-sisters. I mean there are four of them and I believe at least one is sexually active. We never discussed it but they all had boyfriends or guy friends. That doesn't necessarily mean anything because I had many boyfriends and I wasn't sexually active. That was often the reason for the break up, being pressured to do more than "hunch" and kiss.

I was closest to Aisha, the "knee-baby." It was her with whom I took care of and took the big sister role seriously. Aisha was my heart and I groomed her and gave her more access to my room growing up than the others. Ebony was the middle but acted more like the baby. She sucked her thumb and was Grandma's constant shadow growing up. Her lungs were made out of steel and she cried like a fire truck siren. Nikki was the baby and the dreamer of the bunch. She would place towels on her head as a kid and throw it around like it was flowing blonde hair. She lived in her own fantasy world, which may have been her coping mechanism being the baby of five girls. Amy was the oldest of the four. She was the one I was now closest to. She was closer in age, yet still a couple years younger.

Amy lived with her maternal grandmother whom they called "Hitler." She would only take Amy to raise and leave the others with Grandma. She had a nice home and didn't want to take custody of all the girls and have her lavish living turned upside down. She didn't appear to hurt for anything, nor were we scraping for meals. We always had everything we needed and some of the things we wanted. After all, there was five girls and Sterling to be clothed, fed and kept busy in extracurricular activities. We never went without. Amy had the same but with more freedom. Her grandmother worked a lot and was very much a partyer. Amy would have the run of the big home to herself. She was given things to keep her occupied, and we were provided things we earned: good grades, Christmas, or birthday gifts. We were taught to value what was given due to the effort made to attain it. On the other hand, Amy had no value to things because it was often handed to her on a silver platter.

My sisters had grown into cute girls. Amy, a beautiful dark-skinned beauty with "good hair." Ebony had beautiful thick hair and was nice and tall like her mother. Aisha was the caramel cutie with the "round-the-way-girl" style that kept them coming for her. Nikki was the Barbie doll, tall like Ebony, with the biggest most beautiful dark eyes and long lashes with the pouty lips to match. She looked like a model with a head full of gorgeous black hair. We didn't look alike. Nikki, Ebony, and Amy all looked alike and could go for triplets. Aisha looked more like her mother, Diane. My features were a combination of my biological mother and father, but it was often said that I looked like Grandma. I had the thick hair and full lips like my dad's side, but the high cheekbones and hue of my skin from my mother's Indian descent.

I get home and Amy calls. "Rona speaking." "Rona, what are you doing?" "I just left Grandma's and I am about to bathe and get Robbie ready for bed. Amy states, "If you're not doing anything, I was going to come spend the night. But you got to come get me.

You know 'Hitler' isn't going to take me no where." "I will come now. You better be packed and ready when I blow. Be ready, Amy, I'm not playing around or waiting." Amy agrees, "I got you, sis, see you when you get here."

I turn back around and leave the house again with Robbie in tow. I know Amy quite well and she's trying to get out the house. I am fine with being used a pawn because I can get some extra studying done while she plays with her nephew. I can't stop thinking about Grandma and her fish dreams. She is usually right. I'm going to pick up a pregnancy test on the way back. I arrive to Amy's and blow the horn and she's not ready as expected. I lay on the horn so much that I awaken Robbie, who was quick to fall asleep on a drive.

Amy finally appears with her overnight bag. "Hey, Robbie. You're getting big. Hey, Rona. Why are you blowing the horn like you're crazy?" "Because it's been a long day and I need to stop by the drug store and get my baby to bed." Amy questions, "What do you need from the drug store?" "Grandma dreamed about fish." "So you're pregnant?" "I don't know." "What are you going to do?" "If I am pregnant, I will do what most pregnant women do and that's have a baby!" "But I thought y'all weren't getting along. So you're not leaving him?" "I don't know what I'm going to do. He's been better. So I don't know." "Well, you know he isn't letting you go nowhere. Everybody knows that." "So I've heard."

I stop by Eckerd's and grab a pregnancy test. I am praying and hoping it isn't me but I hadn't had my period since the abortion. It has been nearly three months ago. It is also said that stress could cause you not to flow and stress was definitely a constant companion. Earl hasn't been pulling out, as if he had been purposely trying to get me pregnant, as he said he would. If I was pregnant, I was definitely not going to have another abortion. I would just have the baby, Robbie would have a playmate and then I would be done. After arriving home, I get Robbie bathed and fed. He falls asleep at the dinner table and I put him to bed. Amy immediately came in and jumped on the phone while bunking up in the living room. I place the pregnancy test on the bathroom counter and retire for the evening.

CHAPTER 21

TOE THE LINE

I awaken in bed gathering my thoughts while listening out for Robbie. I can hear his movement in the living room. I look over to my left and notice the bed hadn't been slept in on that side. Earl didn't sleep here last night. I get up and place on my bathrobe to go check on my baby and my bedroom door opens. "Hey honey!" Earl greets me. "Where have you been?" "Here!" he replies. I am not convinced, "You didn't sleep here." "When I got home you were sleep. I stayed up with Amy watching television." This sounds strange and I ask, "All night?" "Yes, I kept checking on you. You need your rest with our baby and that's why I didn't wake you. I saw the test, too, take it now." "Where's Robbie?" "In the living room with Amy watching cartoons. Go take the test!"

I go into the bathroom and take the test and, once again, Grandma and her dreaming of fish is correct. I am pregnant! Earl is grinning like a Cheshire cat. He did exactly what he wanted to do. There was no way I was going to have another abortion. So we're having a baby! Earl kissed and hugged me, assuring me that everything would be fine. He offered to take Amy home and he would take Robbie with him so I could get some schoolwork done.

As expected the morning sickness came and accompanied me to the delivery room. This pregnancy was much more difficult. I stayed sick and nauseated out of my freaking mind. There were days I couldn't even muster the strength to even get out of bed. I ended up completing the semester and decided to wait until the baby's birth to continue. It felt like another failure and a hard pill to swallow. I'd done so well by completing the semester on the honor roll. My diversion and escapism was over. I was left to deal with the harsh reality of life with Earl's antics.

During my pregnancy, Earl was so sweet and attentive. I'm not sure if he just felt sorry to see how sick I was or if he truly had a heart beneath all that deceit. I would spit nonstop and he even purchased me a stainless steel pot to use. He placed it next to the bed for me. It was those hit and miss moments that would draw me back in. There was no physical violence but I also did nothing but lay in the bed for months. There was really no reason to be upset at me. The pregnancy had me worn.

It appeared that Earl loved me more pregnant. He knew that I wouldn't pose any resistance to any of his antics because I didn't have the energy. He was free to roam about the cabin, or in his case, he was free to roam like a dog looking for a bone. I was too sick to hear any of the street gossip; I pretty much only talked to Grandma. I had many friends but Earl had successfully placed a wedge between us, with exception to my family. For whatever reason, any friendships I had threatened us. I simply saw this as another method to control me. We spent more time together and, on this day, we would do dinner and a movie. We laughed and talked like when we first met. It was this side of him that drew me in and allowed me to believe that he would do right by me.

His mother had Robbie for the night and we headed home. I missed my baby whenever he wasn't with me, which was rarely. He was my "safety blanket." In addition, she believed in "roots" and voodoo. I didn't trust her and didn't want her sending anything back for me through my baby. The distrust was mutual; she didn't trust me and I felt the same. "Let's go get Robbie," I said. "No, let my mama keep him tonight. He's probably sleep already." "I don't care. I want my baby! I miss him. Doesn't she have to go to work early in the morning?" "Yes, but I'll go get him or she will bring him home. I am going to take you home and put you to bed. I've got some business to handle at the house. I got some people coming by." Now this was very strange because Earl rarely allowed people to come by the house. He didn't allow unwelcomed guests or men entering his house when he wasn't home. Now "people" are coming by and it's very strange sounding to me. He must have some level of trust with them.

We arrive home and I prepare for bed. This "newfound" Earl was trying to make me feel more of an equal. He'd started giving me the money to handle as I saw fit. He would bring all the money to me and then ask for some if he needed pocket money. Earl was without any habits, like drinking or smoking. He was simply obsessed with making money and women—these are his habits.

His pager is blowing up. I heard him on the phone in the living room as I crawled into bed. It was a short call and then he called out for me in the bedroom, "Honey, I need $100." "Look in that nightstand and that money you gave me last night is there. Mark on the paper in there that its negative $100. It should be about $3,000 on the paper, right?" "Yes, did you put that other money up?" "Yes, I kept $3,000 like you told me available in the nightstand and everything else is in the safe. Earl takes a $100 bill out and tells me he will be right back before his "people" get here. I lay in the bed thinking about the past, present, and future. I am now going to be a mother for the second time. All of the possible escape routes now have to be paused. I'm stuck for now. However, the course of this pregnancy will determine my course of action after the birth. Many thoughts cloud my mind and I still have unresolved guilt regarding the abortion. I aborted a child to only end up pregnant months later. Karma possibly?

Sleep doesn't come easily and I can hear voices in the living room. Earl must be back with his "people." I wonder what he is up to. He enters the bedroom and appears surprised to see me still awake. "You're still up, honey? Why aren't you sleeping yet?" I reply, "I am not sleepy yet. I told you that I miss Robbie." "One night won't kill you. Do you need anything from out there?" "No. Who's out there? What are you doing?" "We got some business to handle. That's why I am asking if you need anything from out there before I go back out there. Don't come out the room. Stay in here! Go to sleep, it's late. After we finish, I got to 'straighten a package.' I might not be back home tonight. But I'll get Robbie in the morning and be back before you get up."

There was something going on. Earl goes back into the night-stand and takes some more money out. "What did you do with that $100 bill you just took?" I ask. He is annoyed with my questioning and answers, "Someone needed it. It wasn't for me. Stop asking so many questions. What you need to know, you already know. Now go to bed and stay in here!" The timid Rona was gone. My naiveté was a thing of the past. Entirely too much had been put past me because I didn't know what was going on. Now I snoop and ask many questions. I ask questions, I rarely get truthful answers, but I ask anyway. Waiting for a while, I eased to the door to listen. Earl didn't close the bedroom door all they way when he turned off the lights. He thought he was leaving me "in the dark" but I was going to look and listen to the business in the living room.

I could see Earl and two other guys. I knew one was Darnell, his "do boy." The lighter-skinned guy I couldn't see his face but I recognized his voice as being familiar. They were in the living room wiping down guns and loading them with latex gloves on. They were all dressed in black garb and had ski masks pulled back like knitted caps. Earl was doing most of the talking but I couldn't hear what was being said because Jam Pony DJs was blaring out of the speakers in there.

Whenever Earl was dressed like this, something was most definitely up. There were several guns being loaded but Earl had only his beloved Uzi. The streets talk and I'd heard the whispers of Earl "handling" people who crossed him. The "handling" usually means they are not seen or heard from again. Earl has admitted to me that he has not one issue with taking care of someone who crosses him. That's when I began to believe that he'd kill me, if I didn't kill him first. Just then, Earl gets up and heads to the bedroom door. I don't have time to get back in bed without being caught; so I do exactly as he instructed me *not* to do and open the bedroom door and walk out.

"Whoa! Whoa!" Earl states as he turns around to tell his "people" to "tighten up." He is not done with me, "What are you doing?" He is clearly mad as hell with me, I can see it all in his face. He continues, "Where are you going?" as he pushes me back to the bedroom. "I need some water. What are you doing" asking as I push his arm out of the way and enter the living room asking, "Who is in here?" I walk in there and quickly scan the scene. I see diagrams, bullets, guns, and one bulletproof vest. Now this is very interesting. Darnell stands up in an attempt to block the view of the arsenal.

Darnell speaks to me, "Hi, Rona." "Hey Darnell." I can see scrambling behind him, but no identifiable face yet. I walk towards the kitchen and see the third person. I knew I'd known that voice and I speak, "Orion?" He was somewhat surprised to see me, "Hey Rona! Long time no see. I just saw Sterling the other day." Darnell immediately begins to cut the conversation short between us, while Earl is watching this interaction like a hawk. "Ok, we will be outside," Darnell states as he grabs the filled duffle bag. Earl immediately addresses Orion, "How do you know my wife?" Darnell's face warns of the possible altercation if Orion doesn't answer correctly. Orion speaks, "I didn't know she was your wife. I grew up with her and Sterling. She used to be a tomboy and played football with us."

Earl is not pleased, "Well, she's not a tomboy anymore. She's my wife and don't talk to her. I don't want any dude in her face unless he wants to die." Earl raises his fingers to mimic a gun blowing out one's brains. Orion says, "No disrespect but we go way back. That's my home girl. I haven't seen her in forever. I just asked her cousin about her. I thought she was in college or playing professional tennis." "Now she's *my* girl and I got her so you don't need to ask about her anymore. Are we clear?" Darnell intervenes, "Hey y'all. Let's go. We got something to do. We can finish this later." Earl is glaring at Orion and concludes, "We are finished and I will meet you both outside." They walk out the door and he turns to me and spits in my face. He drew back to hit me but, unbelievably, he caught himself and grabbed his Uzi heading to the door. He glares at me and states, "You're going to get that dude killed. You're so heardheaded. You don't listen!"

CHAPTER 22

REMOVING THE PEBBLE FROM MY SHOES

A few hours later, Earl wakes me up visibly shaken. I open my eyes to him looking scared out of his mind. I ask, "What's wrong?" "Honey, get up! Get your car keys. Let's go!" Earl orders. I look toward the window and notice there's no sun shining. I have no idea what's the problem. I ask, "What time is it?" "About 3a.m. Hurry, you drive. Take me to the One-Stop. Let's go!" I am awakened to complete panic mode. I jump up and put my slides on heading to the door. Unsure as to what is going on, I begin to get my wits as we both hurriedly get into my car. I ask, "What is going on? Is something wrong with Robbie? Where are we going?" Earl is deep in thought and simply staring out the window. He finally speaks, "Nothing is wrong with him. You need to pick him up in the morning. Drive to the One-Stop." I ask again, "What's wrong?"

After a long pause Earl finally speaks, "We went to 'bust a lick' and they got shot. I need to go peep the scene. I couldn't find them and I didn't want my car to be seen. I just knew this shit was wrong from the beginning. I was set-up. This dude got me for a package and I found out who he was and rolled up on him. Orion and Darnell got out of the car to rob him and got shot." I am in shock, "Oh my God! Where are they? Are they ok?" I am gripping the

131

steering wheel nervously while my legs are shaking uncontrollably as I drive. Earl yells out, "Damn! This is all fucked up. I hope they are dead." I am completely confused, "You hope they are dead? Why?" He turns to look at me with a piercing stare, "Because a dead man can't talk. I don't know your *boyfriend* Orion that well and that means he will talk. Darnell knows better than to talk but you can never trust a nigga." I now know and hear the gravity of the situation and ask no further questions. I don't want to know anything else.

I drive to the One-Stop and it is off a major road, Sunrise Blvd., just west of I-95. It is in the bad part of town in the northwest section of Broward County. The lower income people were housed in poorly maintained small apartments. All type of illegal and illicit activity occurred in this one hundred yard stretch of blocked in corridor. The city had closed in the entry to Sunrise Blvd. and the street was now a dead end—no man's land. The irony of the street closure, it is caged and boxed in with no exiting into freedom.

We arrive there and the street is lit up with flashing lights of police cars, fire trucks, EMT, and headlights of the onlookers. Based on the sheer number of emergency vehicles, something major had occurred. It was if this was a scene out of a movie. I was an unwilling lead and I merely wanted to exit stage right. Earl is surveying the scene intently, "Don't turn into the parking lot. Just drive by slowly." He then reclines his seat back and continues taking in the scene. "Do you see anyone in the police cars or being worked on?" he asks. "I can't tell. It's too much going on. Oh my God!" I state. He tells me, "Go down the street and turn around. Drive by again but slower this time. I need to see if I can find them. Damn! They fucked up and there are witnesses. Damn!" We drive by and are unable to see either of them. The street is being blocked off and they're many onlookers and uniformed persons. Whatever has happened is very serious.

Earl decides that we are going to look suspicious if we drive through once more and he advises, "Drive to Darnell's house!

Let's see if he made it home. His house is close enough for him to make it there blasted." We drive to Darnell's house and there's no sign of him, not any lights on. Earl decides to just lay low until he finds out their whereabouts. We go home and he grabs a few things and heads out the door. He stops briefly to say, "Get Robbie from Mama's. I'll call you. I have to lay low for a minute. Got some things to handle. 'Straighten a few packages!' Don't talk to anyone! You hear me? Especially your big mouth Grandmother."

Earl leaves and I leave out behind him to go get Robbie before Miss Cat has to go to work. What in the world have I gotten myself into? The drive allowed me some time to process what I was just told. I didn't sign up for this. This will not be my life. It may be my reality but not much longer. There was no way my children would be subjected to this street living mentality. It was at this time that I decide that enough was enough! He and I would have a talk. This gangster street lifestyle was going to endanger and jeopardize our children's future. But what do I do? How do I get out of this? Where do I go? Who would I run to?

Arriving at Miss Cat's house, I just wanted to hold my love tightly in my arms. Based on her demeanor when she came to the door, she knew what was going on. She didn't even question why I arrived three hours earlier than she was expecting. Earl told her everything—good, bad, or indifferent. I saw the concerned look on her face. She was her usual short-worded self when it came to me but she lacked any attacks with her double-edged sword of a tongue. She was worried and clearly preoccupied with something far greater than her disdain of me. No matter what her beloved Robert Earl did, she had his back come what may. She was not the mother who imparted the ideals of morality and good living. She was his partner-in-crime. The Titanic would be on the bottom of the ocean and she would still be trying to stand guard on the deck. She created this shell of a man. He's a clear representation of her shortcomings.

As I place Robbie in his car seat and I strap on my seatbelt, I look in the rearview mirror and see Robbie's angelic face smiling at me. It was then I knew what I must do. I'm out! I was going to have this baby and then I'm leaving straight from the hospital. If I didn't have the strength and courage to fight for myself, I'd find the courage to fight for him and my unborn child. The game plan is to start stashing money away and leave this crazy lifestyle after my child is born.

The drive back home was filled with devising my exit strategy. I couldn't continue living like this. I'm not built for this. I do not call this "good living," in spite of the material trappings. There is a price to pay for it all. I now refuse to sell my soul for the appearances of high living. The money from the streets is fast coming *and* going. The life is fast living. Just stop this ride because I want off. Never in my wildest dreams would I think this would be my life. I refused to accept this as life.

I get home and get Robbie fed. I wash him up and put on some cartoons for his entertainment. The phone rings and breaks my thinking. "Rona speaking." "Rona, is Earl there?" "Who is this?" "This is Darnell. I *really* need to talk to him." "He's not here. Are you ok? Where are you?" Darnell responds, "I'm locked up in the hospital under guard. I got shot but I made it out. He didn't. Just let him know I'm going to ride, he's got his keys. I knew what time it was going in. I'm just lucky I made it out, I'm the only one." I state, "I don't understand." "He will know what I'm talking about. It's Gucci! I'm going to ride *alone*. Make sure you tell him that *I'm riding solo*. He'll understand. I gotta go now." Darnell hangs up the phone and I am left trying to figure out the code he was talking. Solo? Riding? Making it out? So, Orion didn't make it? Gucci?

I am standing there trying to make sense of it all when the phone rings again. Maybe it's Darnell calling back to make sense out of the gibberish. "Rona speaking." "Rona, go get your husband from Amy's house!" Grandma says. "What? Go get my husband from Amy's house? Why is he at Amy's house?" I hear Grandma sigh before she spoke, "I wasn't going to tell you until you had that baby but they've been messing around." I yell so loudly that Robbie starts crying, "What?" "Yeah, something about he gave her $100 to get her hair done and she didn't get her hair done. She bought some guy a birthday gift." I am just confused, "When did he give her the money? So they've been messing around too?" Grandma replies, "I don't know for sure but I know he's been giving her money. She called over here saying Earl wouldn't leave her house and her grandmother isn't there. She said she was going to call the police." "Why didn't she call me? Why is he giving her money? He did ask me for a hundred dollar bill last night and left. He must've got it for her. So he's messing with *my sister* too?" Grandma attempts to comfort me, "You got that baby there and one on the way. Stay calm! I'm going over there. I'll call you when I get back."

CHAPTER 23

REMOVING THE PEBBLE FROM MY SHOES

There was no way I was going to sit home. I grab Robbie and head to Amy's house. The drive seemed like eternity as my mind raced to the conclusion that "something in this in this milk ain't clean." When Earl told me he stayed up all night with Amy, it just didn't feel right. My antennae went up but the fact that she was my sister left me with no signal. That wasn't a thought I *ever* entertained. For some reason, I was livid at *only* Amy. If this is true, it will be the nail to forever seal the coffin.

The betrayal from the women I trusted the most placed me in a state of distrust of women and I remained guarded for forever more. If you care to psychoanalyze it, it began with my abandonment from my biological mother. She left me when I was a baby. Throughout school, I had associates but I really didn't hang with the girls. It was always something going on with the girls, mainly drama. With the boys, it was all fun and games with no drama, jealousy, or envy. Libby was the next kink in the armor. Even though I'd never confronted her, I knew she snitched me out to Earl. I cut her off! Now run and go tell that! Now it's my sister, whom can I trust?

Earl was a master manipulator. He was good at reading people. He quickly honed in on their vulnerabilities and weakness by using money. He had more of it than everybody else I knew. He always said, "Everything and everyone has a price." I guess you could say he was good at assessing value. There's no doubt in my mind if Earl had decided to be legal and go in to a legit business, he'd be a force to be reckoned with. But for right now, hell hath no fury like a sick and tired scorned woman. May the force be with him because it will be needed.

Turning into Amy's driveway and I pull in behind another car, which is probably Grandma's ride. I don't see Earl's car or any police. I wind down the windows and leave Robbie in the car. I get out and go into the house without knocking. The lecturing voice of Grandma is coming out of the kitchen and I head to the direction of the voices. I hear Grandma demanding answers, "What is wrong with you, gal? I know you're better than that. That's your sister's *husband.* Are you out of your mind?" Amy responds, "Ain't nothing wrong with me. I'm not crazy! Rona is the crazy one for staying with him. What about that? He beats her up and she stays, having another baby. He's making her look like the crazy fool."

I run into the kitchen and proceed to beat her lights out. At this point and time I have no regard for being pregnant. Pregnancy or not, she was going to get fucked up! It's one thing when the betrayal comes from the outside, but within the same bloodline? That's such a hard pill to swallow. I whooped her ass with all my might. She attempts to defend herself but she's no match for all my bottled up emotions. She better thank God and her guardian angels that Grandma was there.

Grandma pulls me off of her and yells, "Stop it, Rona! Let her hair go, Amy! Both of y'all stop right now! I will not have this. Amy, you are damn wrong. Rona, now you know. Let God and let go! She's still your sister. Stop before you hurt that baby." I respond angrily, "She's *not* my sister! She's a *whore*! She's a husband thief. I brought her into my house and she does this? You wait until I have this baby. Every time I see you I am going to jump on you. You're the lowest of the low! You can have him. I'm done with him. I'm done with you both! Y'all deserve each other!"

Grandma pushes me from her and stands firmly in between us. Amy has nothing to say. She even has a smirk on her face. She knows I wouldn't dare take a swing at her with Grandma in between us, regardless of the situation or the depth of the anger. I start to have some sharp pains down my side. I grimace in pain. Grandma notices and tells me to go home and lay down. Heeding her advice, I walk out of Amy's house *and* life.

Let me get my baby home and away from this foolishness. I check on him and his face just lights up with a smile when he sees me. I need to relax and get him home. It's been quite a day and it's not even noon yet. I'll feed and freshen up Robbie before his nap. How lucky is he to not have a clue as to the chaos around him. He doesn't deserve this. Nor did he ask for any of this. He deserved better than this and I was going to see that he gets just that. As I come around the corner to my house, I see the street is filled with police cars. As I get closer, I see they are at my house. I am suddenly overcome with fear. Did Amy call the police on Earl? There's no telling what they had on him. There are so many cars that the driveway and front yard was filled with marked and unmarked police cars. There were more unmarked cars, which tells me that these are either detectives or the feds. Either way, no bueno!

I get out of the car and am met by several police officers that prevent me from immediately entering my home. The officer asks, "Do you live here?" "Yes, what's going on?" "Who lives with you?" I find it difficult to even say our relationship status, "My h-h-husband." The words don't easily roll off my lips or tongue. The officer pulls out a photo and asks, "Is this him?" I stare in the face of the man I've become to hate and confirm by saying, "Yes, it is." "We have a warrant for his arrest." "For what?" The officer replies, "Murder. Come in and I want to ask you some questions."

I follow the detective into my house and I see Earl in the backseat of one of the unmarked cars. He is yelling out something to me but I couldn't hear him clearly through the closed windows and doors. I walk right past him just leering at him. Feeling no concern for his arrest, it was simply karma for all the wrong he has done. Walking through my front door, I see evidence bags and my house in disarray like there had been a fight. The front door was unable to close completely due to being barely on the hinges.

We take a seat and I have Robbie sitting in my lap. The detective pulls out another picture, "Do you know him?" I look at the picture and the face is familiar, "Yes, I do." "How do you know him?" "He's a classmate. We grew up together." "When was the last time you saw him?" "He was here with Earl." The detective asks, "Were they friends? Did they have any problems? 'Beef?'" In my head, I am recalling the exchange between Earl and Orion regarding me, but it wasn't that serious. Or, so I thought. I answer, "Not that I am aware of." The officer states, "Orion is dead. We believe your husband killed him. We have witnesses that saw Orion and Darnell attempt to rob a guy. We believe Robert Earl Jackson was the getaway driver. The victim was armed and shot Darnell. They got away. Orion ran back to the getaway car and witnesses heard gunshots and the care drove off. It is our belief that Jackson shot and killed him. What we are trying to figure out is why? They rode together and planned this robbery together, but in the end he was killed as he tried to get away from being shot at by the victim."

Oh my God! That is not the story Earl told me. Earl killed Orion. I know why he did it. I am sure Earl was going to make him pay for questioning his stern command to not speak with me. Earl trusted no one and their lives had no value to him. Earl killed Orion! I become paralyzed with fear and hugged Robbie so tight that he began to cry. The officer asks, "Would you know why he would've wanted him dead?" "No." The officer concludes, "That's all I have at this time. If you hear anything or have any questions, here is my card." "So he is being arrested?" The officer states, "Yes, we have a signed warrant for his arrest with the charge of murder."

Here I was rushing to become an adult as a child. I couldn't wait to be grown and on my own. Not knowing this would be the life I was recklessly running to. If I had known this, I wouldn't have been in such a rush to grow up. I wanted no part of this lifestyle. I am seriously done. Drugs, police, murders, and guns—I don't have a part in a "New Jack City" movie. This is real life and I'm changing the channel. I was almost twenty-one years of age, and since Earl had come into my life it has been turned upside down.

The confrontation I'd expected to have with him regarding Amy seemed miniscule now. I'd have to save my children, and myself. As soon as I have this baby I am gone. Done! This marriage is over and this nightmare. There is no way I am going to subject my innocent children to Earl's street living. As I look at Robbie playing with his Tonka truck, I now know what I must do. It's time for me to "straighten the package," as Earl would say. This has been a whirlwind the past few years. As much as Grandma instilled her old time wisdom in me, I was not prepared for this new school. Like David against Goliath, what I am facing is monumental and seemingly impossible. However, with the faith of a mustard seed…

There were so many decisions and moves I needed to make. I ran to the only source that could give me the much-needed strength to preserve—God. I fell on my knees to pray, I could also feel Robbie kneel next to me and I looked over to find him mimicking me. I pray out loud, "Dear Father God, I come to you in need of strength to endure. Good Lord, I am not asking that you move my mountain but *do give me the strength to climb.* I am crying out to you because I don't know where else to go. Lord help me keep it together for my son and unborn child. I need you! Help me get out of this marriage in one piece with my life, Lord. I pray and ask in your name, Amen!" I hear Robbie repeat after me, "Amen."

CHAPTER 24

REMOVING THE PEBBLE FROM MY SHOES

Earl had been locked up for months without bond and I continued to progress in my pregnancy. I'd now been informed that I was having a girl and my due date was the 21st of December, which is weeks away. I was ready to have this baby because I had been suffering from morning sickness for nearly the entire pregnancy. The pregnancy kept me with no energy and constantly praying to the "porcelain god." I'd been more peaceful in Earl's absence. I could get used to this. I'd gotten used to this. He was gone physically but called daily.

Earl could sense something had changed with me. He could tell in my tone. There were no more "honey, sweetheart, baby" references. He was no longer any of those things. Earl had shown himself to be an abuser, dealer, liar, cheater, and now murderer. I believed nothing he said. There would be no more lies accepted as truth. He wanted nothing more than his freedom and I basked in his incarceration. His incarceration was my freedom. I never again wanted to change places. I was moving forward and his voice would take me back. For this reason, I took his calls sparingly.

The phone rings and I answer, "Rona speaking." It is automated voice stating, "You have a call from an inmate. Press '1' to accept call and charges or '9' to decline." I accept the call. Earl speaks, "Hey, honey!" I respond dryly, "Hey." Earl starts laughing, "You're not happy to hear from me? Is this how a wife treats her husband?" I am angered, "Do you really want to question about treatment of others? So I guess fucking my little sister and killing my home-boy is the royal treatment?" Earl is bothered by these statements and says, "Whoa! Whoa! Have you been talking to them 'crackas?' They are the only ones saying that. Have you?" "Every time I turn around somebody is telling me about something you are doing or have done. So I guess everyone is lying on you." Earl answers, "Because they don't want to see us together." "After I have this baby there are going to be some changes. You fucked my little sis-ter. That's the lowest of the low." "Listen, I am coming home and everything will be ok. I'm married to you for life—good or bad. 'Til death…" The automated caller states, "You have less than one minute remaining." Earl says, "Honey, I'm going to call you right back. Please accept…" The automated caller ends by saying, "This call has been terminated. Goodbye!"

The phone begins to ring but I don't answer it. There's only so much I can tolerate of him. I despised him. No longer afraid of a beating from the honesty of my sharp words. My voice would no lon-ger be silenced. Those days are over. Where there is no trust there could *never* be love. I don't trust someone who is purely unadulter-ated evil. He's the devil! I'd been burned one too many times. The kitchen was far too hot and I had every intention of getting out.

I didn't dare to tell Earl of my escape plan. He's locked up and would be none the wiser. His intention is to keep me close and, especially my mouth closed. Since we are married, I could not be forced to testify against him in the murder trial. When it comes to Earl, co-defendants/witnesses don't fare well when they are even suspected of being capable of turning state's evidence. I'll let the court system handle that because I want no part of that. I believed he did kill Orion and he threatened me with death constantly.

While awaiting the delivery of Elisha, I'd started getting out walking more and met a new friend Theresa. We would walk the trail at Sunland Park and share our stories. Theresa was an overweight, fairly decent-looking woman with coke bottle glasses. She was no looker but had a heart of gold—or so I believed. She had a couple of kids and was a single parent. She was now walking daily in an attempt to lose the baby weight from her last child. It was good having someone to talk to and who could relate to and understand my struggles. In the short time that I had known her, she offered me a bedroom in her apartment if I ever needed it. Her seemingly kindness won me over with her.

Past men had abused Theresa and they used her up and moved on. She knew not the love and protection of a good man because this was foreign to her. She sympathized to a certain degree with me, but, like many other women, they are willing to turn a blind eye to many things due to the seemingly lavish living. This was a common occurrence. I couldn't bear being treated like a second-class citizen, or even worse, or a piece of property regardless of the Gucci bags, wardrobe, jewelry, and luxury vehicles. It's like I didn't care about the materialism if I'm being victimized. Try keeping the material possessions and treating me the way I deserve to be treated. I can go shopping for myself. Theresa understood this, well, in a way.

Theresa states, "Do you really want to leave all that? 'Cause it sounds like you do but girl..." "You can't put a price tag on your happiness. He is literally killing me. After I have this baby I am leaving." Theresa asks, "Where will you go?" "I am not sure but far away from him." "Well, you know I don't have it like you got it but if you need the other bedroom in my apartment it's yours." "Thank you!" I reply. Theresa states, "I'm serious plus I could use a roommate to keep me company since I don't have a man to do that." "I just might do that."

I don't think Theresa could truly understand where I was coming from. I didn't want the material possessions but the things that money can't buy. Theresa says, "Well, you can do what you want but I wouldn't go anywhere. You got it too good. He takes care of his kids and you. You don't even work. You stay in a new car and look at all that jewelry." I contest, "All those things mean nothing if you have no respect! Even self-respect! I have two kids now and I don't want them in this lifestyle. They deserve better than that." "But he's locked up, right?" Theresa asks. "Yes he is." "Well, you have a break from him. How long will he be in?" "I don't know. I don't want a temporary break, but a permanent break. He is a good father but he feels he's a good husband because he provides for me. But he can't give me things and think he can do whatever he wants."

Theresa heard me but she still wasn't convinced that it was bad enough to leave by saying, "I hear you but if he paid my bills he could do damn near whatever he wants. You need financial security! It's hard out here! Guys just want one thing. That's all they care about. Make a baby and provide no support. You don't know how good you got it." I respond, "Everything isn't as it appears. He pays and does everything for control purposes only. I don't care how much a man buys and provides it doesn't give him the right to beat on you. I'm tired of being his punching bag. The only time I am halfway safe from physical abuse is when I am pregnant. Well, sort of." Theresa states, "If you are really serious about leaving, like I said, you can come to my place. He doesn't even know me or where I stay."

I think that may be a viable option and I state, "That may work. I don't want to go home to my Grandma because that'll be the first place he looks for me." "But he's locked up and he can't come looking for you." "Yeah, but that doesn't keep him from sending his henchman for me. He has made it perfectly clear that if I leave him he will do a quarter and my mom better pull out her black dress." Theresa begins laughing and says, "Child please! That's just tough talk to scare you. He's just talking. How is he handling being locked up now since he's so willing to go to prison for life?" "He wants out and has lawyered up. Earl hates being incarcerated. I'm also aware that his Mom is heading to Haiti to see someone to help get him out. I bet he is worrying her like crazy." Theresa inquires, "Why is his mother going to Haiti? Who is there that can help him here?" "Girl, I don't know."

I realize that I may have already said too much. In this lifestyle, you learn that you acquaint yourself with some but trust none! Theresa appears to be cool but I've not known her long and she really doesn't get it. She hears me but doesn't really *feel* me. Theresa, like other women, is sometimes drawn in with the financial aspect that seems to buy "blind eye" passes for the blatant disrespect. That has never been, nor will ever be me.

Whenever I go against Grandma wishes I ended up in dire straits. She warned me about Earl from day one and loved me enough to accept/tolerate him. I knew she was watching for fissures like a hawk. This would be the reason I concealed much from her. Partly because I didn't want her to go to jail for "offing" him if she knew he had been beating me. Mainly because I wanted nothing more than to prove her wrong while wholeheartedly knowing she was dead right. If only I had not been so quick to "smell myself" and listen. If I would've, could've, should've...

CHAPTER 25

REMOVING THE PEBBLE FROM MY SHOES

My pregnancy was just a couple weeks away from my due date of December 21st. To say that this entire pregnancy had been filled with many struggles, sadness, and sickness would be an understatement. I struggled with the state of my life. Unhappily married to an abuser with a son and another on the way. Although he is kinder when I was pregnant, I believed that was only because he felt like he had me under his complete control. There was no need to worry about me because he had me cuffed. His treatment meant nothing because his façade of a loving nature belied pure unadulterated evil. Simply put, he's the devil like Grandma has always said.

I wore a mask. I concealed the pain with the love I had for my son. He, and only he, held my heart. There was no place for his father. A mother-son bond is an unconditional bond of love and respect. The love I had for my son made me despise his father even more. He deserved so much more. I love my son and couldn't fathom bringing harm to him, intentionally or unintentionally. I could never take a closed fist and punch him in the face until his eye closed shut and blackened like his father did to me—with the same hand he gave to me in marriage. To have and to hold? To love and respect? Through good and bad? Those vows have been irretrievably broken. He was now my nemesis, enemy, abuser, and undeserving husband. I could not live my life under the constant fear of continued abuse and disrespect. What's love got to do with it? It's about respect.

Morning sickness kept me home and usually in bed. This pregnancy was rougher than my first. I was constantly sick and unable to keep many things down. At one point, the doctor had me on beets and liver three times a week to raise my iron level. The pregnancy broke me. I was so sickly that Miss Cat was even nicer to me. So much so, I'd moved in with her the last month of my pregnancy. Everyday I was drilled about when I was going to have her grandbaby. No one was more ready for me to give birth than I. I had stuff to do and I had to first have this baby before I could start making steps to get out of this hopeless situation.

Drew and I had started communicating again. Talking to him reminded me of all the things I believed were possible before I got off track. I still cared deeply for Drew, in spite of everything, and we always could talk. What we had seemed a lifetime ago and our paths were no longer parallel. Since graduation from high school nearly four years ago, he'd graduated college and was now back home working as a probation officer. He was doing well for himself.

I, on the other hand, had only an incarcerated accused murderer as a husband and two kids. Everyone expected I would be a success story. I was always a good student and a gifted athlete. I was supposed to be like Drew, a college graduate. At best, a professional tennis player. I was supposed to be *the* Serena and Venus Williams. Life can be a trip. You can do everything right and make one bad decision and change the course of your life.

The communication with Drew filled a long-term emotional vacancy. Not that my son did not make me feel loved, but this was a different kind of love—an intimate love. Earl and I never shared the level of intimacy that Drew and I had. Although I cared deeply for Drew, there would be no future for us. The best we ever had would be behind us. Drew clearly admitted he loved me but could not easily or probably ever accept Earl's kids. He said he hated him and couldn't see himself calling his namesake "son."

I couldn't blame him, these were supposed to be *his* kids. I appreciated Drew stating his honest opinion and I didn't have any unrealistic expectation from being lied to or led on. After all, Drew came from a very religious background. I am not sure that they would condone our relationship now that I have two children. Drew, the golden child, dating a married woman with two kids would be frowned upon. His parents had invested too much time and money for him to not do anything but be the best *and* be with the best. I was no longer what would be best for him.

Drew gave me a much-needed ear and reminder of who I am. I'd lost me in the chaos of being in Earl's world. Well, I want off his planet. His planet is not conducive to my sustenance. He also chastised me for not being the woman he knew. He never knew me to be weak, passive, and a victim. The stories I shared with Drew only deepened the hatred he had for Earl and reminded me of the person I no longer was. I was known to be a fighter and now I have laid down and nearly accepted defeat. I needed that motivational speech.

The pregnancy had me as a ball of unresolved emotions. My emotional state was a continuous ebb and flow. Like the waves at the beach, they would come crashing in flooding me with anger, rage, hatred, and despair. Once I've wallowed in the tears, they roll back like a rescinding wave. Logic and rational thinking stands on the shore until another wave or flood of emotions wipes everything out. Regardless of the pendulum-swinging emotional state, there was a constant, which was my hatred of Amy. My hatred for her grew with every nanosecond.

She had committed the ultimate sin and every day of her existence, in my presence, would be hostile. There were no words and Amy's unforgivable act created a division amongst them: Amy, Ebony, Nikki, and a strained relationship with Aisha. Aisha was the only one of them I had a semblance of a relationship. It eventually caused her and I to become estranged. Before this occurred, she did share with me her feelings and personal experience with "evil."

Aisha states, "I just feel like we are sister's and you are mad at her. You are mad at the wrong one. Why not blame him?" "Earl is a dog and I don't put anything past him, but Amy...that *was* my sister." "Maybe she didn't know how to tell you." "If she would've told me, how can I be mad at her for being my sister? But she chose to roll with a dog and now she has fleas." Aisha states, "Well, I didn't know how to tell you because I thought you would try to fight me, too, like Amy." I am surprised by this and state, "Why would I do you like that for telling me? You know me better than that, right?" "I never thought I'd see you and Amy hate each other so I don't know. But the last time he took me home, he asked if I wanted to get a wine cooler and kick it. You know? He was trying to see if I would go for it."

I didn't expect to hear that. I thought I couldn't be surprised anymore by anything that has anything to do with him. I was wrong! I respond, "Wow! Thanks for telling me and I am not mad at you. Thank you for not betraying me." "You deserve so much better. Why do you stay with him?" "You're right and I'm in the process of making some changes. You will see!" I didn't trust her enough to tell her what I was planning. She had shown me shaky loyalty and I couldn't trust her completely because of her support of her sisters. Aisha says, "Please do. Enough is enough." "Ok, I love you, little sis." "I love you too, big sis. Call me later and hurry up and have that baby."

Aisha too! He's evil, pure evil. Amy is more of a whore than I previously thought. Aisha is several years younger than Amy and she didn't go for the "okey doke" but told me about it. I was incapable of feeling nothing but hate and disgust towards her. My hatred of her caused people to choose teams. Amy's team was the obvious "husband stealing whores" and her sisters chose to stand behind her or just simply against me. Either way, this was the beginning of the end of any true sisterhood. I didn't expect anything different though. There had always been an unspoken division. It was like "Animal Farm," we were all equal (sisters) but some of them are more equal (sisters) than others (me).

I was too pregnant at this point to be fighting Amy, but I had every intention of making up for lost time the minute I have this baby. It really doesn't matter when or where. She deserves to get the beat down for being such a dirty little low-life whore. I mean, who does that? Like, really? While pretending we are so close as sisters. I wasn't one to share my closet, nor my no-good husband. Even though she wasn't raised under the same roof, we had the same genes.

How simple life was and I rushed to become an adult. Now I'm an adult and only now know what Grandma meant about growing up too fast. I am existing in a chaotic state and bringing another life into it. Peace and harmony, what is that? I'm working on finding it for keeps. I'm not putting out anything positive into the universe. I'm in despair. Darkness and gloom has befriended me. I've got to change my present situation. That's it in a nutshell and by any means necessary!

The phone rings and I look at the clock. I know it's Earl calling and I care not! I don't even want to hear his voice. In an attempt to circumvent his dear mother from accepting the call, I take the phone off the hook. I'm not in the mood to hear any of his lies and future broken promises. He can go straight to hell where he deserves to perish. He's evil and I want no dealings with him. If I'm lucky, he'll get found guilty of the murder charge and go to prison for life. I would then be free. I am no longer willing to play the role any longer. I'm demanding my liberation now!

CHAPTER 26

REMOVING THE PEBBLE FROM MY SHOES

I awakened to tightness around both sides of my abdomen. My due date has come and gone. In addition, so has Christmas and New Year's Day. I've just resolved myself to the fact that I'm an elephant and will carry this child for a year. This child is obviously going to come when it wants to and quite stubborn with it, too. Every technique and "old wives tale" to induce labor has been tried to no avail. It was unusually cold this January in Florida. There had been an unusual frost in 1990 and the cars were covered with ice. This was by far the coldest winter ever.

As I get dressed and prepped to exit my bedroom, Miss Cat burst into the room. "Rona, are you up?" "Yes, I'm in the bathroom." "You're still having morning sickness? I have never been sick like that." I inform her, "I was getting dressed. I'm not sick this morning." Miss Cat continues her barrage of questions, "You ain't in labor yet? You ain't felt anything yet?" "I didn't sleep well. My sides hurt all night long." This has her attention and she shows faux concern by saying, "Come here. Let me see you." I come out of the bathroom to be inspected by her. "It's still kind of hurting right now." Her faux concern continues, "Your stomach has dropped. You're in labor. Let's go to the hospital!" "Let me get dressed first and I am hungry too. Take me to have breakfast first because there's no telling how long I will be there before they send me back home."

I am in no rush. I'd accepted that I would probably have the baby in April. That is a year from conception. It is like carrying an elephant, which usually takes over a year to birth. Miss Cat is rushing me but I'm going to take my sweet time and get all pretty to come right back home. I dress and take the rollers out of my hair. I even apply lipstick, which is a rarity. There's no doubt I will be runway ready in the infinite waiting room. I'd given up on having this baby once the New Year came in. My due date was December 21st and here it is January 5th. Heck, April is right around the corner.

Much to Miss Cat's impatience and unconcealed joy, we get into the car and head to the nearest fast food restaurant to order my breakfast. She really didn't want to make this pit stop but I was adamant there would be no labor room visit without breakfast first. I guess there is a pattern with me eating before birth. I did the same thing with Robbie. Miss Cat complied and I dined on my breakfast while en route to Broward General. It didn't take us long to get there and we arrive at the hospital.

The formalities had been done and due to my passing my due date by weeks, it was determined that this baby must be delivered immediately. I could see the concern on the face of the nurse assigned to me. I was really going to have this baby. I am shocked! Maybe I won't carry the baby for a year. The nurse instructs me, "Undress and place the gown with the split in the back and remove any undergarments." "My bra too?" The nurse answers, "No, you can leave on the bra. Just remove your underwear. We have to hurry. I will be right back to get you shaved and prepped for delivery." I am concerned and ask, "What's wrong? Is something wrong with my baby?" "Your baby is full-term and you're well beyond your due date. If this baby isn't delivered right now, there's a serious threat of sepsis." I quiz the nurse, "Sepsis? What is that?" "Since the baby is full-term it can have a bowel movement placing the baby, and you, in harm's way. If that happens, we could lose the baby *and* you. The fecal matter would be like poison in your bloodstream. There's nothing wrong, we just have to get this baby delivered stat."

I begin to cry. Here I am again having another baby I didn't conceive by myself, yet I go through labor alone with no one to hold my hand or give encouragement. I begin to pray because that's all I knew to do. Grandma taught me to trust man for nothing and pray to God for everything. I begin to pray out loud, "Dear God, I am afraid! Please be with me and make everything all right. I have faith that my baby and I will make it through. Be with me, good Lord. Lay your hands on everyone who has a part in this delivery—great or small. Amen!" I place the gown on and the nurse re-enters the room to shave me. I must say, this was awkward, uncomfortable, and kind of painful. I hadn't shaved, nor even seen, my pubic region for many months. My hair would get tangled in the razor and hurt. We get this necessary evil done and I'm placed in bed to wire for monitoring.

All types of wires were attached to machines and an IV was inserted to induce labor. The heart rate of the baby filled the room. I am now such an emotional sort. I cry, not due to any present discomfort, due to the joy of knowing my baby is almost here and fear of the now doubled motherly duties. What doesn't kill you will make you stronger, it is often said. You must remain strong because it is your *only* option. I'm told that contractions will be beginning soon in an attempt to get my water to break naturally. Shortly thereafter, the nurse breaks my water bag. Ladies and gentleman, we have full labor now.

Miss Cat enters the room and immediately I begin having the worst contractions, short and very intense—much like her. "How much longer you think we have before I meet my new grandbaby? I am ready to hold the baby," Miss Cat asks. "I don't know but I hurt so bad." I leaned forward to feel between my legs, it had become very damp down there. I freak out, "Oh my God! Something is wrong. I'm bleeding. Call the nurse!" "That's normal, you're in labor." Her words do not wipe out my concerns, "I didn't bleed with Robbie. Everything went to almost perfection with his delivery. He was due April 21ˢᵗ and I went in to labor on the 23ʳᵈ and delivered him on the 24ᵗʰ. I had no complications and very little assistance was required on my part. He came into this world like he had a job to do, but this one right here..."

The nurse enters the room to check how far I've dilated. She can see I am in discomfort and stroke my arms and reassure me it will be over soon. "I am bleeding and I hurt so bad," I tell the nurse. Miss Cat chimes in, "Tell her it's normal and it didn't hurt when she was making it." The nurse is even taken aback with the statement and gave Miss Cat an awkward look. I wasn't having any of it. I'd tolerated her in the past and I thought we were making strides. Game over! It's not going to happen at this moment. I yell at her, "Get out! I want her out of here! I feel like I'm dying and you're taking pot shots. No sympathy, empathy, or affection. Get out! I could die and you won't have the pleasure to witness it!" The nurse intervenes, "Rona, calm down! Stay calm. I'm taking you to the delivery room. Ma'am, please wait for her in the labor waiting room." Miss Cat declines, "I'm not going anywhere! That's my son's baby. Why can't I stay in here? I'm not getting out!" The nurse responds, "Then you can stay in here while she is in labor. But you're not allowed in delivery because the mother doesn't want you there and your presence could cause stress. I don't think it's healthy for the baby or the mother."

The nurse removes all the wires and monitors but keeps the IV in tact. I am now being wheeled to a room a short distance away. I'm screaming out in pain and I look up to the extremely bright lights. I'm placed on a delivery table and instructed to start pushing through my contractions. The doctor is in full medical gear and orchestrating every move. I close my eyes and attempt to just breathe. I am in so much pain. I am told to push while experiencing the most *horrid* pain I could ever feel. Like, really? I'm in so much pain I can barely breathe, no less push.

It seemed like this went on for an eternity. So much so, I had no further strength or desire to push anymore. I was done. I needed to get some sleep and I'll try this again in the morning. Labor was hard work. Completely drained and I'd thrown in the towel. The doctor states, "The head is almost out. Push, Rona." "No, I'm done! I'm tired! I need sleep! We can try this again later." The doctor instructs the nurses, "Grab the x-ray board and apply the restraints."

The nurses are like synchronized swimmers as they applied restraints on my wrists simultaneously. A metal board was handed to the doctor and the nurses made sure both legs remained in the stirrups. He walked on the side of me and placed it on top of my stomach and proceeded to push down. After enduring this for a couple fabricated forceful pushes I yell out, "Ok, I'll push! I'll push! Please stop!" The doctor says, "Push, Rona!" as he pushes down even harder once more. He places the metal board down and goes back to look between my legs while stating, "Push harder once more!" I began to scream out in pain with all my might. I could feel the release and the doctor tells me, "It's a girl!"

CHAPTER 27

AS IMPOSSIBLE TO GRASP AS A PAIR OF SNEAKERS HANGING FROM A TELEPHONE WIRE

I didn't hear any cries and the doctor holds her up to provide me the first look at my baby girl. I notice she is bluish-colored. I immediately ask, "Why does my baby look like a smurf?" The doctor informs me that it's only temporary and due to a lack of oxygen. He taps her on the buttocks and she begins to cry. It's music to my ears. Thank you, God, for a healthy delivery! By far, this was the most intense pregnancy and delivery to date. While they were cleaning her up to hand her to me, I'd fallen asleep.

I woke up in the recovery room hours later as I was being rolled to my room. I was still kind of groggy; I realized I hadn't seen my daughter up close and personal. Being beyond tired, I needed to get some rest because I had a lot of work to do. There's nothing like sleep after having a baby; it is the best sleep in the world. Closing my eyes I drift off to sleep again. I've endured many trials during this pregnancy, not to mention carrying this stubborn little girl had beaten me down. I needed to rest because I would need the strength to walk a new unchartered path alone.

The nurse bringing my daughter in the room interrupts my sleep. Now introducing Elisha. I found that name in the bible and

Earl wanted the kids to have his initials. Problem solved! As the nurse hands me my daughter I checked her hands to make sure there are ten digits on her hands and feet. She is a tiny little something weighing 7lbs. 1oz. and with the cutest cleft in her chin and deepest dimples in both jaws. She had a distinctive blue vein that you could see over her left eye. Elisha is such a cutie.

Having this adorable little girl, I knew I had to be an example of a strong, black woman. I didn't want this precious little doll thinking it was acceptable to be disrespected by a man openly and continuously; or to be beaten like a man, and made feel less than human. She was not going to witness this. I didn't witness it but endured it. She would be shielded from this abuse. No one deserves to be treated so badly by a person who claimed to love him or her. As John Locke states, we enter into this world as a blank slate. It is our environment and experiences that shape our being. If this is so, I must get away from Earl and all his negative behavior.

The hospital stay was a couple of days. I was told that I'd be probably discharged in the morning. I was able to bond with my daughter. I attempted to breastfeed her but she wouldn't latch on. My breasts produced enough milk to hydrate a small village. Dolly Parton had nothing on me. I carried my pregnancy in my breasts and butt, mainly in my breasts. My body was resting but my mind was racing. I had to act on my master plan. As soon as I get released from the hospital, I am moving out. It was now or never.

The phone ringing interrupts my thoughts and I struggle to reach the receiver on the nightstand. "Rona speaking." Earl speaks, "Hey honey! How are my girls?" "*She* is fine," I dryly respond. "You gave me my little girl. As soon as I get home we are going to work on our third." "You're out of my mind." "Why is that? You're my wife." I answer sarcastically, "Having another child would require sex with you which won't ever happen again. As far as being your wife, that's only temporary." Earl begins laughing, "You must be on drugs in there with all the tough talk. I'll be home soon. My lawyer is working it out and I go to court in a couple days. I should be home right after court." "So you're getting out? How? Weren't you charged with murder?" Earl says, "Don't sound so happy and what's with all the questions? You know these phones aren't clear. Anyway, who does she look like?" "Your mama…" "Does she?" I start again, "Your mama just walked in." "Did she? Let me speak to her."

As they talk my heart is racing. Oh no! He's getting out. I'd hoped that I'd be moved by the time he got out. I've no time to spare. I'm going to call Theresa to see if the offer was still on the table with her second bedroom. Once Miss Cat leaves, I'll call Theresa. I hope this visit is short. She is a seasoned pro in talking in code. I'm sure she was reporting all within earshot but I hadn't broken the code. She hands the phone back to me and I speak, "Hello." "I cant wait to get home to my family," Earl states. "Yes, I am sure *they* will be happy." "That includes you. You are my family." I boldly say, "You don't have a home to come to." "We will finish this conversation when I get home. I see right now you've forgotten what happens when you run that big mouth of yours."

I was waiting for him to show his real side and not this loving husband bullshit. I do not relent and say, "I guess you've forgotten that I'm not pregnant anymore." Miss Cat interrupts and defends her son, "Rona, what's wrong with you? Why are you talking to my son like that?" "Because your son ain't no good. He's pure evil! He's the biggest mistake I've made by far." Miss Cat continues, "You need to wait until he gets home and talk about it." "What I need to do is get as far away from your son as possible," I state. Earl is laughing and sends his threat, "You will pay for all that. I'll see you in a few days." I counter, "Or maybe *not*!" "What's that supposed to mean?" Earl asks. An automated voice breaks the conversation, "You have 30 seconds remaining on this call." I get my last point in, "You and I are no more. It's over!" Click! The call terminates.

I hang up the phone *and* the marriage. I really don't know if it's the hormones or my decision to end this nightmare. The rose-colored glasses were off and the sleep has been wiped from my eyes. Now I am left to deal with the extension of his evil, Miss Cat. She begins to speak while mean mugging, "You shouldn't act like that. What's gotten into you?" I counter, "Your evil son! You refuse to see any wrong doing on his part. He has disrespected me for the last time. Would you stay with a man who slept with your sister?" My question is met with a long pause as an answer. I demand she answers, "Answer me! Would you? Would you tolerate *that* level of disrespect?" She finally answers me, "You don't know that to be true. I don't believe it. You're talking crazy."

She would not have any shelter from my bottled in feelings. I wasn't raised to be disrespectful to anyone's mother, regardless how much she deserves it. What she will get is my unbridled feelings. Without any further delay I unload on her, "Of course you don't believe that your evil son does any wrong. It's sad what you've raised. And you are *supposed* to be a woman? Your son is a reflection of you! Goodness doesn't beget evil. Evil begets evil! I've had it with you just as much as your son." Her face shows pure hatred of me and, maybe even, amazement that I expressed my mutual dislike. She plays the only card she has and says, "Earl will deal with you when he gets home. I saw the baby. Instead of raising hell, you need to rest up because I'm not getting up in the middle of the night. You are on your own until Earl gets home. Unless you want to just give the babies to me."

I completely ignore that idiotic statement. I am over her and the dumb remarks. I respond dismissively, "I'm tired and going to get some sleep. I have a busy day tomorrow." I am sure Miss Cat was ready to go as much as I wanted her out of my hospital room. She agrees, "Do that! I am going to go back to the nursery and look at my baby. When they release *her*, I will come get y'all if I don't have to work. I don't think I have to work. Just call me and let me know when they are going to discharge *her.*" I agree and wait for her to leave so I can get my escape plan in action. I pretend to close my eyes and drift off. There are a few minutes before I hear the door close. Finally, I hear the door close and I lace up my boots to get this plan in action!

CHAPTER 28

AS IMPOSSIBLE TO GRASP AS A PAIR OF SNEAKERS HANGING FROM A TELEPHONE WIRE

I can hardly sleep after talking to Theresa. She still had the offer on the table and she would pick me up from the hospital. Grandma has Robbie and I will go get him and we're on to a new chapter. I'd been dreaming of this day for a while. The time had come for me to get my life back on track. Feeding LeLee while looking into her face, she has no cares and is unaware of the chaos she has been born in. I needed to give her a life she deserved and preserve her innocence as long as I could. I will forever keep her safe.

I decided to call Grandma to have Robbie ready for me in the morning. Grandma answers, "Hello." "Hey ma!" "Hey baby. How are my babies doing? I wanted to come up there but I had Robbie. I can't wait to see y'all. Who does she look like?" "I know and I appreciate you getting him. I know he is safe with you. I think she looks like herself. She's light-skinned like Earl's family but she looks like a doll." "Does she have hair? I sure hope so. She didn't come out like you did, did she?" Grandma begins to laugh and is then interrupted by her calling out to Robbie. Grandma yells out, "Boy, get out of that! Come here. Your mama is on the phone.

Come and talk to her." I then hear the sweetest sound to my ears, "Hello! Hello!" I smile and happily respond, "Hey Robbie! This is mommy! I miss you!" I begin to cry and continue, "You are going to meet your little sister tomorrow."

I hear rumbling and tussling, as if the phone is being grabbed for. Grandma gets back on the phone and says, "He was smiling then he tried to run off with the phone. You're crying? What's wrong? You miss Robbie, don't you? You're never away from him this long." Grandma always could read me no matter how much I tried to hide from her. I tell her, "I love you so much, Mama. I'm so sorry for *everything* I put you through." I begin to cry uncontrollably. Grandma always had sage wisdom and a nurturing spirit that always made me feel better. Grandma speaks, "I know you do and I love you too. Just pray, everything will be ok! I've already forgiven you. You're young. You've got to live and make mistakes to learn. God has blessed you with two little 'flowers', now tend to them so they will grow up in the right way." "Yes ma'am. I'm coming by after I get discharged to let you meet Elisha and get Robbie."

Unlike Miss Cat, Grandma was available to assist me because she knew I could use the help. Grandma states, "Rona, with the new baby your hands are going to be full. I can keep Robbie. You know I don't mind." "I know but I'm leaving Earl for good. I'm going to the house and pack up. He's supposed to be getting out in a few days. I plan on being gone when he does," I reply. "You know this is always going to be your home. Come on home! I'd been praying for God to lead and protect you," Grandma says in her motherly tone. "I'm going to stay with a friend girl, Theresa, until I get my own place. Your house is the first place he will come. I'm not going back and I don't want that trouble at your house. I've put you through enough." I felt like I had brought only sadness and disappointment since I had been involved with Earl. For this, I was truly saddened and sorry. I had no further desires to bring any hardship at her door. I had to turn this all around and make her proud of me.

Grandma lovingly says, "Rona, don't cry! Be strong! Read the 91st Psalm everyday and several times a day. Pray for protection." "I will, Grandma, but I'm not afraid of him anymore! I'm sick and tired of him! You were right. He's evil! And him being with Amy was the very last straw. I'm divorcing him!" I wholeheartedly state. Grandma exclaims, "Praise God! Thank you Jesus! You know I will help you in any way possible. Anything that Grandma can do for you, I will. I'm behind you all the way." "If I don't get away he's going to kill me. If I leave he may try to harm me, too. But that's a chance I am willing to take. I'm tired of him beating on me and disrespecting me." My statement surprised Grandma and I could hear it in her voice as she asked, "Beating on you? He hit you?" Even I was kind of surprised I said it too. But I would no longer be silent and without a voice. However, this was the woman who loved me as her own and would harm anyone who hurt her family. I can't be completely forthcoming with her.

I realize I may have said too much. Grandma is a lioness to her cubs, so I better clear this up. I answer, "He might as well. The names he calls me and the things he does feels like a striking blow. I don't deserve this and I wasn't raised like this. I messed up by even getting involved with him. He's such a snake! He can't be trusted." "You live and you learn. If you raise a child up in the right way, they may stray, but eventually they find their way back, Rona! That's why you have to raise up your two right. You see now what I'd been warning you about." "I do. I better rest before Elisha wakes up to be fed. I got a long day tomorrow. Good night and I love you, Grandma. We'll see you in the morning." Grandma ends by saying, "Read the 91st Psalm! I love you too! Get on your knees and pray!"

I believed in God because I had no choice! Grandma made sure we were in church several times a week with choir rehearsal, the Junior Choir, and even Vacation Bible School. She would make sure that you had the Lord in you. I believed in God but I also believed that faith alone without works meant nothing! I ask that the Lord be with me in all that I do but this situation was my doing and would have to be my undoing as well. I am filled with hate and anger. It's hard to be a vessel with the light of God when you are filled with raging darkness and gloom. I was broken and really couldn't focus on much, other than getting away from him. My faith was being tested and I was praying that my works would give me a positive outcome.

The resounding words of Grandma's insistence that I read the 91st Psalm stayed with me. I opened the drawer next to the hospital bed and, lo and behold, there's a bible. I open the bible to Psalms and find the 91st chapter. I read it and begin to weep. It speaks to my broken soul and I begin to pray. The anger and rage towards Earl is fueling my destruction. It's all a process. I am still in the anger stage and it honestly feels comfortable. I do know for me to truly move forward, I'd have to let go of the emotional baggage. That day, however, would not be today! Earl is very conniving and calculating. He plays minds games. I can't let my guard down with him. If you play with a snake and end up getting bit, whose fault is it? Does the blame lie with the snake or the snake handler?

Drifting off to sleep while tears drop onto the pillow, I am a little scared. But I have to get away from this. I've got two kids that I'm removing from their home to live with someone else. I am making this move with a newborn that is just two days old. I am tired of pretending and lying to myself. I want people to know what he is and why I am leaving him. He doesn't treat me right. He's a woman beater and the lowest of the low. Sleep eventually comes and I am seeing the verses of Psalm 91 in my dream.

The morning comes and Elisha slept soundly through the night. She was awake in her bed just smiling and playing. The old folks say they are playing with angels when this occurs. She must've known that I needed some rest. Thank God for sending his angels to keep us through the night. The discharge nurse enters the room and tells me she is processing my discharge papers. Light, cameras, and action! I call Theresa and there is no answer. She is an integral part of this power move and I can't contact her. I am beginning to worry. Did she back out or change her mind? If that were the case, I couldn't blame her. I mean, this was a lot to take on with of someone you just met. I don't want to call Miss Cat, but if Theresa can't pick me then I wouldn't have much of a choice.

The nurse gives Lelee her final checkup. She has no obvious signs of distress or lack of progression since birth. She is free to go home. I begin to get dressed and look over my post-pregnancy body. I am pleased and think I have done well maintaining my youthful figure. My stomach is nearly flat but hideously darker than my natural skin tone. The same thing occurred with Robbie and it does lighten up in the coming months. I am not complaining because I don't have one stretchmark. I look at myself in the mirror and I recognize the reflection. She isn't a familiar stranger. I like the looks of her!

There had been many times that I didn't even recognize my reflection and that was a harrowing experience. I'd gotten to a point in time that I could no longer look at myself in the mirror. I no longer knew the woman I saw with the sorrow-filled and pained eyes. If the eyes are the windows to the soul, then mine were of a blizzard-like cold. The fire had not produced any heat or light, it was simply a glimmer of light barely existing. I had been victimized by the billowing winds of an abusive life.

The reflection was now familiar. My eyes had life in them. My face glowed, hair was thick and long, and my skin was clear. The stress hadn't worn on me physically, but spiritually was another story. I look myself in the eyes and say several times, "I will not, won't stop climbing that mountain until I reach the top." This would be my war chant! Whatever comes my way, I will stand. I dress Lelee and pack up my things.

I pick up the green little bible and turn to Psalm 91 and read it. The Psalm is one of protection from evil. I say a short prayer and I hear the door open. Theresa comes through the door. I begin to smile and look towards the heaven and give thanks to God. God is so amazing! He can turn a hopeless situation right around. I go to Theresa and hug her and begin to cry while giving her thanks for coming. She was my angel and she didn't even know it.

The nurse hands me a message while heading pass the nurse's station. The phone has been busy and Miss Cat left a message to call her at work if I needed a ride. Perfect! She's not at home. Now I can pack up my things without detection. Mainly gathering Lelee and Robbie's daily necessities, then I'd go by my house and pack up some things. Luckily, Theresa had a large car. I'd pack as much as I could in both of our cars. I am still thanking God for favor because my plan is coming together.

CHAPTER 29

AS IMPOSSIBLE TO GRASP AS A PAIR OF SNEAKERS HANGING FROM A TELEPHONE WIRE

The nurse wheels Lelee and I out as Theresa headed to get her car. It has become warm since I've been in the hospital. It was unseasonably cold the day I was admitted in the hospital. Lelee is bundled up and looking around. She did not make a sound and simply took in the new world she had been born into. Her and I are much alike. We both are discovering a new world. Her world changed by being attached by an umbilical cord that had been cut. My world changed by the cutting of the vows in this marriage. We both were now discovering a new world independently *and* together.

We are all loaded in Theresa's car and we head to Miss Cat's house to get my car and pack. My heart was racing because I kept imagining the worst scenario being he would be there when I arrived. I pray the Lord has mercy on my soul. I know that I'd eventually have to deal with him, especially since I've released the filter and now spew out my thoughts and feelings. There was no way he was going to let me get away with that. He was far less forgiving than I. I would bottle things up and then implode. He was more like an explosion on contact. There was nothing to occupy his time other than being all up in his head. Those words I beat him with would surely be met with a closed fist.

Finally we arrive at my house and Theresa is smitten with my living conditions. From the outside, I can see how she would have that misperception. We live in a quiet upper-middle class neighborhood with nicely manicured lawns showcasing beautiful homes. Luxury vehicles and boats parked in front of the homes gives the impression of a perfect world. I didn't know any of my neighbors and Earl preferred it that way. I open the garage and enter the cold, dark home. I used to love this house and now it no longer feels like home. I'd become detached from this house of horror. Theresa came in to help me grab some things but instead ogled and stood in amazement of the house.

She takes in the furnishings and states, "Girl you are crazy! You're leaving this? I figured you had it good but this is like some 'Better Home and Gardens' house. Are you sure you want to do this?" I have no time for her confusion and state, "Please take this stuff to the car for me. We have to hurry. Just don't stand there. I can't be here but for a few minutes because Lelee is in the car." She states, "That's the problem with y'all girls who have it good. You run from them and women like me only dream of having a man to take care of us like this. I'll be right back." I tell her, "Check on Lelee, please. Make sure she is breathing and still sleep." The house phone begins to ring and I contemplate whether or not I should answer it. I decide to pick it up, "Rona speaking." "Is this the lady of the house," an unfamiliar voice asks. "Not anymore," and I hang up the phone. Theresa comes back in and looks at me with disgust. I don't expect her to fully understand because she doesn't know the full story. I don't even attempt to make her understand. I refuse to be mistreated for the sake of having a man. I'd rather be alone than unhappy.

"It smells so good in here. I bet y'all don't even have roaches," Theresa states. I respond, "Roaches? Of course not! Do you? Please don't tell me you have roaches." "I've seen some before. Living in apartments with nasty people, you can't help it," Theresa states. "I've lived in apartments and not had…never mind! Well, I'll call an exterminator and get it sprayed," I state. "I don't have money for that. I'll buy some Raid," says Theresa. "I'll pay for it. Once we get there, lets sit down and talk finances. I really appreciate it. I'm going to help you," I assure her. She questions, "How? You don't have a job and you can't work because you just had a baby." I respond, "I've got money saved. Trust me! I got you. I'm going to let things die down and will be moving out in a couple months." Theresa concludes, "the baby is still sleep and so is her mama. This is a *really* nice home and you're crazy. But, ok."

I've no time to entertain Theresa's disbelief. She's right, in a sense. I am crazy to allow this haphazard living to become my reality. I'd been crazy from the first time I found out Earl cheated on me. The first time he hit me, I must've been crazy. I'd also been crazy to allow him to call me out of my name. Now I am getting out of his home. In record time, I'd grabbed Robbie's necessities, toys, and clothing. LeLee's things were at Miss Cat's house since I'd been with her the last few weeks. I've no attachment to this house or possessions. The only joy was mainly the times I spent with Robbie here. There was some times shared as a family but the majority of the time it was Robbie and I. The house became the place of my confinement. Theresa sees a nice house and I see it as a prison of love.

I place as much as I could into my trunk and front and I turn the key to the ignition. I lock my seatbelt in and place the gearshift into reverse. As I roll out of the darkness of the garage and into the brightness of the outside. I have one more stop and Theresa follows me to Miss Cat's. There are no words to express my mood. This was a time of newness. I had a new beginning with a new family and a new attitude. I had no idea what to expect going there, but I was less scared than I ever was determined. Whatever belies me, I'll handle it. Miss Cat isn't very smart. I think quickly on my feet. I'll just tell her I'm staying with Theresa for a few days to help me with my babies. She will object, of course, but she can't stop me. She will simply report all to her beloved Robert Earl.

The minute we pull up to her house, I needed to tell Theresa the game plan. I just want to prepare Theresa in case we encounter Miss Cat. In the event we do, she will be in the know. Simply put, she'll know that I am using that lie in case of emergency and stand by without looking shocked. I turn into Miss Cat's neighborhood and I think of how beautiful the neighborhood is, too. From the outside, it looks like a middle-class area with nicely maintained yards. She was living amongst the well doers and on the inside of the beautiful neighborhood lived a woman who was rotten to the core. She blended in well but she was more of the lower class echelon. Simply put, she was from the street and about that life. She upheld her son in all of his wrongdoings and even attempted to justify his mal behavior. If this had to be the last time I laid my eyes on that short, red-haired, Jheri Curl wearing, gold tooth smiling serpent, I wouldn't have not one regret.

Miss Cat only appeared to have a change of heart to play kind with me the last couple of weeks of my pregnancy. It was not authentic! I am sure her son put her up to it to keep me close and not talking to the authorities. She was standing in for him as usual and the masks were off and the games are over. It has been friction between her and I from day one. It was made quite clear that her son could do no wrong in her eyes. They had an undeniable and seemingly unbreakable bond. There is nothing with wholeheartedly loving your children. Because God knows I love mine, *but* not to their own detriment. You cannot turn a blind eye to their wrongs. You have to be able to call them on the carpet and this has never occurred with their relationship; and this is why he is the way he is. He has no respect for authority or any others, for that matter. Unbelievably, I am now thankful for the well-deserved discipline

I received. I have home training and I guess everyone does not, specifically him but my children will.

Coming around the corner and onto Miss Cat's street and I could see her car was not in the driveway. Sweet! I pull into the driveway and Theresa pulls in behind me. I tell her this will be quick as I knock on the front door. No one answers and I turn the knob to an open door. Earl's little brother and sister were constantly losing their house keys and the door would often be kept unlocked for them. Great, no one is home. Most of Lelee's things were already packed up and neatly separated. I'd be able to get everything in one load. If I'm lucky, I will be even able to load her bassinette. I'd worked myself up to this day and it's smooth sailing thus far. The universe is tilting my way.

Once we are all loaded up, we head to Grandma's. I think I was able to pack up so quickly because I miss Robbie immensely. Running off pure love, I've packed up my things from two homes. Did I forget to mention that I had a newborn baby girl two days ago? I may have been weakened physically but mentally and spiritually I was strong. I begin to speed through Lauderdale Manors to get to Sunland Park. Once I get to Sunrise Blvd, I begin to tear up with joy. Grandma's house could be seen across the park. My heart begins to race because the wait is nearly over. It was him who I fought for and now I was going to introduce him to his little sister. Theresa is following me but I am speeding and turning off Sunrise Blvd to 16th Avenue like a Nascar driver.

I can see Robbie playing in the front yard with his bowlegs. The mere sight of him recharges and soothes my soul. Turning onto 15th Terrace I could see Grandma sitting under the tree like a Queen on her throne watching over her kingdom. When Robbie catches sight of my car, he darts toward the closed gate before I can even stop the car and park. He makes a mad dash out of the gate and smiles at me ear-to-ear while screaming, "Mommy!" I yell back, "Robbie!" as I get out of the car running to meet him. "I missed you so much!" I pick him up and hug him for dear life. I weep as I had dreamed of this moment. Robbie is no longer smiling when notices my tears and is concerned as he states, "Don't cry mommy! No cry mommy! You're a big boy, mommy, big boy don't cry!" I begin to laugh. He has always been able to calm my spirit. His mere presence alone soothes me. I tell him, "I've missed you so much! Did you miss me?" Robbie responds, "Yes." "How much?" He stretches his arms wide apart with the biggest smile and says, "This much!" We laugh, hug, and kiss before I take him to Theresa's car so he can meet his sister. Hand-in-hand, we walk to the gate to meet the newest addition to our family.

CHAPTER 30

AS IMPOSSIBLE TO GRASP AS A PAIR OF SNEAKERS HANGING FROM A TELEPHONE WIRE

Theresa had unfastened Lelee and handed her to me. She was awake and the brightness of the sun caused her to grimace. Robbie's hand is still in mine and we head under the shade of the tree to speak with Grandma. I give Grandma a kiss on the cheek and take a seat. I introduce my kids to each other by saying, "Robbie, this is your little sister Elisha. You are her big brother and it's your job to *always* take care of her and protect her. *Never* beat on her!" I begin to cry. Robbie is looking at his little sister with a big smile. He reaches out and grabs her by the hand and says, "Hi baby!" He then leans in and kisses her face.

Grandma wants to get a closer look at her first great granddaughter and states, "Let me look at her. She's a little thing. You shouldn't have her out. You shouldn't be out and about, either. You're still open from having the baby." She then turns to Theresa and greets her, "Hello, I'm Miss Frazier." Theresa addresses her back, "Hi, I'm Theresa, nice to meet you. You are right too. She is doing too much. She'll mess around and have a setback." Grandma agrees, "That's right. Go in there and get the baby out of this air. You need to lay down too." "I know, Grandma. I've done everything

I needed to do. I came to show you the baby and get Robbie. I'm moving in with Theresa for a little while and then I will get my own place. The first thing I am going to do once I get settled in is divorce Earl.

The words were exactly what she wanted to hear but she much rather have me home. She started by saying, "Wait a minute! Just come home. You know I got the room for you. Your old room is empty. We are family. Family sticks with family. Plus, I can help out with the babies." "Ma, he's locked up now but may be getting out soon. He may be on his way home now. The first place he is going to look for me is here. Also, I don't want him coming around here bothering you." "What about taking care of the kids? You're leaving him but what about taking care of y'all? You can't work right now." I advise Grandma, "You always told me to keep an account he doesn't know about. You always said to 'not let my left hand know what my right hand is doing.' That's why those Landmark Bank statements come here with my name on it. You know the ones I tell you to keep in your safe deposit box?" I see the approval upon her face and she simply says, "Hm."

The sage wisdom she has imparted upon me has not been lost. I may not have used it all the first time but when I needed guidance the most her words were always my guide. I continue, "I've got a nice amount that he doesn't know about. Enough for me to raise my kids comfortably for a couple years." Grandma laughs out in joy and says, "You ain't never been a complete fool! Good girl!" Grandma packs up Robbie's things and we load up to head to our new home. I hug Grandma and a ringing phone interrupts our good-byes. Daddy comes to the front door and informs me that Earl is on the phone for me. "Daddy, tell him I'm not here or just left." "Ain't! Give me $20 and I will tell him whatever you want," Daddy states, as it is obvious that he is looking for money to get "high." Grandma saves the day and says, "I'll handle it! Rona, be safe and call me after you get some rest. Take the kids in and call me later." She turns to Theresa and says, "My name is Mae Frazier. I'm listed in the phone book. Keep an eye on my babies. All of them." Theresa agrees by saying, "I will. Yes ma'am."

Theresa now takes the lead and we head to her house. As I am driving, I begin to experience sharp pains in my abdomen. My body is letting me know it needs rest. There's no question that I've overdone it. I will get rest at Theresa's. I have to. Then it dawned on me, Grandma has a block on her phone. How was Earl able to call her house? He must be out and he probably knows that I've packed up. There's no turning back from here. Theresa lives in the northeast section and that wasn't his stomping ground. He doesn't know where Theresa lives or her existence, which is a good thing.

The pain and discomfort was still with me as I unloaded my possessions. I had to unload then because it wasn't advisable to leave anything packed conspicuously in a luxury vehicle. She didn't live in the best neighborhood but there are far worse places we could live. For this, I was thankful and chose to see the glass as half full and not half empty. We would make due for now. The most important thing was that I was out and away from Earl and his people. I told Theresa that I needed to rest for a bit and then we could talk business.

I retreat to my room and get in to bed. My beeper is buzzing like crazy. I look down at it and its the house number with Earl's "911" code behind it. Great, he's out of jail. I got out in the nick of time. I roll over to my side and place Lelee next to me with Robbie behind me. We fell asleep in our new home and are as one. I'd had every intention to pray before my nap but fell fast asleep. I was worn out and seriously needed to rest. The babies even fell out quickly and remained sleep as long as I did.

When I awakened the day was over and most of the night. Apologizing to the babies, I jump up to feed them both. They'd missed lunch and it was now past dinnertime. Going into the kitchen to prepare Robbie something quick and LeLee's formula,

I turn on the kitchen light and there's roaches scurrying about the kitchen. I'm completely disgusted, nauseated, and grossed out. I made her bottle but I'd rather run out and get Robbie something to eat.

After feeding my baby, I look for Theresa and she's not in the apartment, but in the parking lot courting. She'd been telling me about this new guy from Pompano named Walter. She was obviously smitten with him based on how she talked incessantly about him. I don't think it was as deep as she made it out to appear. I believed it was more like he was giving her much needed attention. She was attention starved and obviously willing to settle for some attention. I open the bedroom window to call out to her. I can see her standing next to a nice truck with rims and blaring old school music, which was drowning my calls out. My efforts were in vain, so I grab my shoes to go outside to see if she will grab Robbie something to eat from the fast food restaurant down the street. I exit the apartment to the parking lot and approach Theresa and Walter all hugged up with another guy, who was the driver of the truck.

I walk up to her and speak, "Hello. Theresa, can you go to grab us a bite to eat or watch the kids while I run to pick it up?" Suddenly the driver walks up to me and yanks my hair. "Ouch, why did you do that?" The driver responds, "All that's your hair?" "Yes, and why would you do that? That hurt!" The driver reaches out for my hand and kisses it. He then speaks, "Hi, I'm Jerome. It's nice to meet you. You're beautiful! What's your name?" "Rona," I then ask Theresa, "What's it going to be?" Jerome steps in to answer for her, "She can watch the kids and I'll run you there. I'm hungry anyway. Come on." Theresa gives me a nod and wink to show her approval and states, "Yeah, I got the kids. Go ahead." I tell her that we will be right back and I go to grab my purse. Jerome stops me, "You're not going to get away from me. I've got money. Just hop in."

I get into the truck and we head to get the food. Jerome appears to be tall, well dressed, and with the most beautiful big white teeth I've ever seen. He had to know this was his best asset because he smiled a lot. The drive allowed us to talk a bit. I was honest and told him I was just getting out of an abusive marriage. I figured he'd run for the hills rather than take on a married woman with a newborn and toddler. He didn't run. He told me he had just gotten out of a long-term relationship with his high school sweetheart and they bore a daughter, which was his only child.

Even though I'd just met him, I could tell he was a genuinely good guy. How refreshing and new. We got the food and head back to the kids. We exchanged numbers to keep in touch. We both were in the rebuilding stage and it could be good to have someone to lend an ear. I'd lost that with Drew. My ready-made family was too much for the high school love we shared. In addition, I'd no time to attempt to rewrite history. The past is the past and the present is here and now. I was open to getting to know this new friend once I got settled into this single life.

Back in the apartment with the kids, I get them fed and bathe for bed. This may not come soon since we slept the day away. My pager is blowing up and I turn it off. It's obvious Earl is out and looking for me. I've not one intention of going back. Like it or not, I am now a grown woman with two mouths to feed. The marriage is not conducive to my overall well being and if I am not functioning properly I am of no use to my babies. I know I'm going to have to deal with him but it won't be now.

Theresa comes in and we discuss business. I don't expect her to take care of us. I gave her two months rent and I would pay for an exterminator to come out. I'd also stock up the refrigerator and her food stamps would simply be hers. She seemed quite happy and I told her that I would get my own place on the third month. She told me not to be in any rush and I could stay as long as I wanted. The gesture was nice but I wasn't much for roommate living. Most importantly, it was beneficial for me to stay with her. I'm paying full rent and stocking the fridge.

I'm not sure if she had a utility bill. I wouldn't be surprised if it was included in the rent. Theresa said her rent was $550 a month, but I could've sworn she told me that she had low-income housing. I vaguely recall her saying she paid barely nothing in rent. This would be neither here, nor there. I was taught to pay my way through life and I appreciated her allowing me to stay with her, for whatever reason, with all the baggage that comes along with me.

Theresa knew I had a stash but not how much. Unfortunately, she was privy to that conversation with Grandma. I needed to get rested and healed so I can move out. I don't really know her that well. Earl taught me a lot about the streets and the nature of people. Theresa couldn't fully be trusted because I didn't know her. She did come at a time when I needed assistance to help me on my way— an angel. I don't believe she was placed in my life without reason and/or purpose. In time all will be revealed...

CHAPTER 31

AS FLEXIBLE AS A PAIR OF FLIP FLOPS

A couple of months had passed, I'd had my six-week checkup and Lelee had her follow-up infant wellness appointment. I was in a good place. Theresa and I were still living together and I was enjoying the peacefulness with my babies. Well, not complete peace. Earl had been out for months and hadn't seen the kids or I. I'd talked to him sparingly through messages sent via Grandma. He has told Grandma that he accepts that we won't be together but he wanted to see his kids. I didn't trust that one bit. I believed it was simply a ploy. Time had not been kind to our separation and I basked in his absence.

One source of joy became Jerome. I looked forward to our talks, laughs, and quality time spent. My interest only grew over time. He was different. His heart, soul, and spirit were genuinely sweet. You could feel the sincerity of his being. I wouldn't leave the house much and we talked mostly by phone. Occasionally, he would bring Walter from Pompano to see Theresa because he didn't have a car. We would sit and talk when he brought Walter down. There was some apprehension and nervousness with him being around my kids. Therefore, he never laid eyes on them. He was a friend and I wasn't going to bring casual acquaintances around my kids.

It was the best of times while it was also the worst, too. I had settled into being the best mother I could and was away from the craziness of that marriage. I also had a friend in Jerome. Soul II Soul was playing on the radio and I felt they were serenading and speaking to me. They tell me to keep moving and don't stop like the hands of time. Tick Tock! I have a better living than I had with Earl. I just have to keep moving. Conversely, I was living right under the nose of my abuser, in the same city. The abuser who threatened to harm me for doing just as I had done—left him and filed for divorce.

I'm not sure if I was no longer afraid or I was more afraid of the negative influence his lifestyle would bring upon the kids. Nonetheless, it was my responsibility to protect them at all times and at all costs. The only time I ever felt scared was when I left the apartment for grocery runs. I knew beyond a shadow of a doubt, Earl had put the word out on the street. All it would take is for someone to see me in the Northeast Section of town and he would flood the area. I often went out with a hat and shades to conceal my identity.

As much effort was taken to conceal my identity, my car was a dead giveaway. My gold Mercedes Benz stuck out like a sore thumb in this area. I would park the car down the street behind an abandoned house. Whenever I would walk to my car, I was filled with fear of Earl watching or someone had broken into it. I kept no valuables in my car. I made a point to always check the backseat floorboards before entering the vehicle. Earl had a spare key to my car. I had to be smarter than him at all times. It was imperative that I outsmarted him because my life depended on it.

I started to call Grandma less because he was wearing her down. He had found her weakness, which was the kids, and pounced on it. I'd be the first to admit that Earl loved his kids but I had to learn to love me first. Self-love would allow me to make better choices and be a better mother. Once I file for divorce, the visitation would be worked out. Until then, they are with me. I don't trust Earl. He would take the kids and disappear just to bring me ultimate hurt and pain.

It was time for me to check in with Grandma since it had been a few days. I dial her up and wait to hear Earl's newest ploy. The phone rings and Grandma answers, "Hello." "Hey ma!" "Hey baby! I was worried about you. Earl came by here the other day, and said that if he doesn't see his kids I better pull out my black dress," Grandma worriedly states. "Ma, I have heard that a thousand times. What else is new?" "Rona, listen to me! It doesn't matter what your relationship is with him because those are his kids too." I respond, "Ma, I know. But I don't trust him. He won't give my kids back. He is just trying to get to me."

Grandma agrees, "I don't doubt that." I adamantly state, "We will let the court figure out visitations. If he can't bear to be apart from his kids then he should stop killing people and committing crimes. I don't want my kids around that. Ma, there's a lot you don't know. But, trust me, he's trying to use you and the kids—or anyone else for that matter—to get to me. But I'm not afraid, no longer a fool, and I am not going back." "Don't be no fool! I'm praying for you. Rona, be careful! I've been feeling 'funny.' Read the 91st Psalm!" Grandma tells me with serious concern. "Ma, I won't be a fool and I will continue to read that Psalm." Grandma closes by saying, "Check in with me more and take care of my 'flowers.' I love you, Rona." "I will and I love you, too, Ma."

My Grandma is too old for this type of worrying and aggravation. I need to get this divorce finalized sooner than later. There's no better time than the present. I wait for Theresa to get in from work to get her kids; I gather mine up and go see a divorce attorney who I found in the Yellow Pages. I'd always heard some of the best attorneys here were Jewish. I found one with a name that appeared to be Jewish—Attorney Harvey Friedmanstein. His office wasn't far away from me on Commercial Blvd. by the Executive Airport.

A dream or goal unfulfilled is even worse without effort. The time apart from him hadn't drawn me to him. Instead, it allowed me to clearly see and know this marriage was not for me. It wasn't my idea to get married in the first place. I went along with it because he wanted it. Marriage hadn't been on a high priority list, but the divorce was a different beast altogether. With every ounce of my being I wanted to dissolve this marriage. He can keep all the possessions, and give me sole custody of the kids.

The meeting with my attorney lasted hours. I was informed me that Attorney-Client Privilege protected me and, for once, I opened up the floodgates. I told him everything. I do mean *every-thing*. He was obviously taken aback with all the background information. He took my case and I wrote a check for his fees in full. The first hand of business would be get to him served and place a restraining order on him. If the past months had been calm, we were definitely about to enter the eye of the storm. Once Earl has been served, the stakes would be at an all-time high. Come what may, I just wanted peace of mind for my babies and me. I cared not about the house, furniture, money, cars, etc. All those things had been attained by ill-gotten gains anyway. Just let me go on with my babies because that's all I wanted.

Leaving the attorney's office, I wanted to fill Grandma in but it wasn't wise to go to her house. Looking at my watch and knowing her schedule, I'd go by the church to catch her after choir rehearsal. Like clockwork, less than five minutes of pulling into the church parking lot, she heads outside to talk with her church members. She doesn't even see me and I just watch her for a few minutes holding court as usual. Miss Frazier! I loved my mother and admired her strength. I decide to get out the car and surprise her, "Excuse me, Miss Frazier!" Grandma turns around and answers, "Yes! Oh, hey baby! What are you doing here?" "I missed you! I just wanted you to see the kids and it's just not safe to come by your house." Grandma leans in to kiss me,

"I missed y'all too." "Ma, get in for a minute. I've got something to tell you."

Grandma walks over to my car and immediately acknowledges her "flowers" while getting in. "You know we are on church grounds, so don't start me to cussing. What is it?" Grandma advises. "I just wanted you to know I just left the attorney office and I filed for divorce. He's also going to get me a restraining order. So don't be surprised if Earl starts acting up even more." I could see the approval on Grandma's face as she began to speak, "If this is what you want, you know Grandma supports you. I'm proud of you. You're a grown woman. Correct your childish mistakes by conducting your business from now on as a woman." "He should have a temporary order in place and until a hearing is scheduled, the kids will stay with me. Until I have that, I am not allowing him to see the kids. After that, we will plan something. Once I have the restraining order, I will return home and look for a place." "Rona, you know you are always more than welcome. I'm proud of you, you hear? Get my 'flowers' out this car and call me later. I need to get home by sundown." I hug and give her a kiss and do as she instructed.

I felt good! I never want to disappoint Grandma. I want to keep her proud! She wants more for me and I can't blame her for that. With the papers being filed, I'd find a place, get the kids in a Montessori School, and return back to school to finish. Nothing is impossible if you take it step-by-step. There were no hard feelings. The hatred and anger had subsided over the past few months. I just wanted him to go his way and I would go mine. It was as simple as that. Peace out!

The next few days would be spent with my babies. I enjoyed being a full-time mommy. This was our bonding time. As I looked upon my two loves, I began to have even less compassion for my biological mother's absence. I was incapable of deserting or leaving these two. They were the reason for my drive and motivation!

What her absence taught me was to stay present at all cost. Only death would keep me from them. *Only* death and even still I would worry about them. That is called being a M-O-T-H-E-R! How could I be any less than a good mother after being blessed with Grandma as my first teacher and role model? I lived my life for these two and nothing and no one, but death, would prevent me from being present in their lives.

CHAPTER 32

AS FLEXIBLE AS A PAIR OF FLIP FLOPS

A couple of weeks later I finally got the call and the filings had been completed and the divorce and protective order was in place. The protective order was added security when he decided to violate the conditions, which I knew he would. My attorney informed that my divorce could be finalized within 45 days if everything went smoothly. In less than two months I could be out of this marriage, I crossed my fingers hoping and praying it would go smoothly. I headed over to Grandma's house to spend time with her. With having the restraining order in place, I could call the police and have him arrested. I was not out to get Earl but protect me and mine.

At Grandma's we sit and talk. I begin to tell her about Jerome and she seemed elated. However, that wasn't saying much because it wasn't hard to top Earl. Jerome had two legal jobs, several cars, and a heart of gold. If there had been a downside with him, I hadn't discovered it yet. He was courting me like a gentleman should. Our time was limited, due to my having small kids, and he always seemed to understand that I couldn't get out of the house. We were able to have one quick date because Theresa offered to watch the kids. I accepted her offer and he picked me up. He took me to the beach and we had ice cream while walking down the beach. I enjoyed it and thought he was genuinely a good guy. He knew my fragility and handled my heart with care. When life's shoes became too uncomfortable and hurtful, he offered to carry me for some relief. Any other approach wouldn't have worked. At the first sign of my past, I would have kicked the shoes off and took off running.

Grandma's house phone begins to ring and I run into the house to answer it. "Rona speaking!" "Bitch, I want my kids! I want to see them now! Bring my fucking kids, bitch! You already know what time it is! You're out of your league, li'l white girl. Oh, but you will see!" I respond to Earl's aggression fearlessly, "Stop calling here upsetting Grandma with your nonsense! Didn't you receive your papers? Have your lawyer contact my lawyer!" "Have you lost your rabbit ass mind?" I am so unbothered by him and sarcastically responds, "No, I actually found it. Didn't you get the papers?" I know that Earl is enraged and I am finding much pleasure in it. He starts yelling, "That shit don't mean nothing. I want to see my son and daughter. I haven't even laid eyes on her. I want to see my kids, bitch!" I am not concerned by his anger, "I have no problem with you seeing the kids but there is an order in place. You can't violate the restraining order."

Earl begins to laugh. I know that laughter usually follows with rage and anger. He states by doing just that, "Do you *really* think I give a fuck about that either? Listen, bitch, stop playing and bring me my kids." He starts laughing again and continues, "I am going to show you something later but bring my kids to my mama's house." I say, "I will pull up outside and your mom or your sister Tasha can get the kids. But not you! I don't want to see you! I don't want *any* problems out of you! I'm serious!" Earl demands, "You don't give me orders! You and nobody else! You are my wife and I don't care what the judge, God, or you say! Just bring me my kids before I get mad. Come on now!" He hangs up the phone.

I go outside and resume talking with Grandma. I tell her that it was Earl on the phone and he wanted to see the kids. I'm not altogether comfortable with him having the kids, but I'm in possession of paperwork stating I have temporary primary custody. Grandma feels as though he has a right to see the kids, especially since he hadn't seen Lelee. Lelee was now three months old. I could drop them off for a few hours or to spend the night. Robbie was three years old but Lelee was still a baby. They would all be strangers to them in a strange house. I relented.

I would feed and clean Lelee up then I'd drop them off. Maybe Lelee would sleep most of the visit. I don't think I could bear to go through the night without her. I'll let Earl know that I will drop them off for a few hours. During that time, I'd surprise Jerome and go see him. It would be a rarity for me to get out without kids. Maybe we could go walk on the beach again. Whenever I thought of him, it would bring a smile to my face. Over the months, I had grown fond of my new friend.

Earl doesn't give me credit. He thinks that I have no business savvy. My attorney had informed me that if I allowed him to my home or family it would invalidate the order. My coming to his mother's house while he visited the kids would void the order. I needed to come up with a way to get him the kids without seeing him. I had to think. Think, Rona! Ok, I got it! There's a convenience store around the corner from his mom's house. I'll call him and keep him on the phone while I dropped the kids off.

Grandma helped me pack up the kids. I asked Robbie if he wanted to see his daddy and he smiled. Maybe he had missed him. We will see how this goes. Grandma tells me to be careful and check in after the kids were dropped off. I told her I would oblige. Miss Cat's house was less than ten minutes away from Grandma's. I cut through Lauderdale Manors to hit 19th and pulled into the convenience store. Someone was using the pay phone and I waited nervously for the guy to finish. I'm flipping the quarter to calm my frazzled nerves and I close my eyes to begin to pray aloud, "Dear God, Please watch over me and make sure no harm comes to me. Throw a fence around my babies as they go to their father's. Lord, don't allow us to be separated by any means. Order my steps, Lord. In your name I pray. Amen."

I open my eyes to the phone booth no longer in use. I get out of the car and I have an inexplicable calmness over me. Picking up the receiver, dropping the quarter in the coin slot, and I dial Miss Cat's number while I watch my loves securely in their car seats. Earl answers, "Hello." "Earl, listen. I don't want to argue or fight with you." "Then bring me my damn kids, bitch!" I try to defuse his anger, "Calm down and hold on. I am going to bring them over there for a few hours. Then have Miss Cat drop them off to Grandma's." "They are my kids and I'll bring them back when I am ready. You will face me and bring my kids! You hear me, bitch?" I answer, "Yes, hold on! Don't hang up! Hold on for a moment. I have to check on the kids."

I run to the car and jump in heading down 19th to the next block to Miss Cat's street. I pull down the street and get the kids out and leave them at her front door. Lelee is in her car seat and Robbie standing at the front door. I run back to the car in no time, and blow the horn like a mad woman. Earl came to the door and I floored it down the street. Thank you Jesus! I get onto Powerline Road and head north to Pompano to see Jerome. I cannot stop giggling hilariously like a pre-teen schoolgirl. The entire ride to Pompano was filled with uncontrollable outbursts of laughter. I could only imagine his face. I know he didn't think I had it in me. Never underestimate your opponent—that's a cardinal rule!

Jerome lived in Collier City. His background was similar to mine; we both came from a two-parent home with structure. They live off 10th, down the street from the park like me. He was well known in Pompano. His popularity was based on his basketball skills at Coral Springs High. They weren't known to be at good at basketball, football, or track due to the school having few blacks. He reinvigorated the basketball program and was known because of this. Most people in Pompano attended the predominantly all-black Blanche Ely High and they were powerhouses in all sports. They even had an awesome marching that could rock any crowd.

Jerome, with help from other decent teammates, had put Coral Springs High on the map in basketball. They were a force to be reckoned with. Jerome was five years older than I. When he was a senior, I was still in Rickards Middle School. Scholarships had been pouring in for him but he decided to forego college ball and take over his father's lawn business. For all intensive purposes, Jerome was the typical jock—much athletic ability and very little effort made academically. He said he had tired of school after twelve years.

I couldn't understand his decision to not go to college but he hadn't done quite badly for himself without the college degree. For many in my neighborhood, college was a ticket out of the ghetto and poverty. Yes, he had a nice truck and an older-restored classic car but he had two full-time jobs. My feeling was college would allow me to work one job and have the financial means to meet my bills. Who am I to judge? He didn't go to college and has two jobs. I didn't go to college and I've got two kids.

I park the car outside of their gate, which surrounds the nicest yard in the neighborhood. Jerome had the nicest house on the street and in most of Collier City. They lived right next to an elementary school and the teaching staff would compliment them on their beautiful home and flower-laden yard. Jerome's truck was in the driveway and it appears he is home. I ring the doorbell and await an answer. Shortly after, Jerome's sister, Jerniece, opened the door. "Hello, is Jerome home?" "Hi. What's your name and I'll tell him you're here," says Jerniece. "Rona." She suddenly looks surprised and smiled, "Oh! You're Rona! Come in and I will get him. It's nice to meet you. I'm Jerniece, his sister." "It's nice to meet you too," I say. "So you're who he is on the phone with all day? What is there that much to talk about?" she teases while laughing. She continues, "Have a seat and I'll go get him. He might be sleep."

I'm sitting in his living room and they have a nice home. Very nice! It is well furnished and nothing is out of place. This house is so nice that you don't want to touch anything. Wow! Family pictures in expensive frames. Jerome lived at home with his family. They had a rather large home and added on, as the children became adults. He and Jerniece had suite-like rooms in the home, like their own apartments connected to the home. Jerniece reappears and says, "He is putting on clothes. He was napping. He'll be right out. Can I get you anything to drink?" "No, thank you." I just sat there and took in my surroundings. I tell Jerniece, "Your home is beautiful!" "Thank you. I have a call to make. He'll be out shortly, I guess. He is so slow." Jerniece exits the room to her bedroom.

CHAPTER 33

AS FLEXIBLE AS A PAIR OF FLIP FLOPS

Jerome enters the living room with a big smile. "Hey, Rona," he speaks as he walks over and gives me a hug. "Welcome to Pompano," as he laughs hysterically. "Hi, Jerome, you have a nice home." "Daddy and I just give them the money and Niecie and Mama fix the house up. I'll tell them you like it." "Did I disturb you? I wanted to surprise you." "It's ok. I love these kinds of surprises. You should surprise me more often. You must've got a babysitter for the kids." I reply, "Yeah. Let's go get some ice cream. Then we can walk and talk on the pier." "I hadn't planned on leaving the house. This is my only day off, but for you I will," Jerome obliges.

He leans in and kisses me, then he begins to French kiss me. We passionately kiss for a couple minutes and while embracing me I can feel his "nature rise." He was aroused. If there were any questions regarding his attraction for me, it had been put to rest. He takes my hand and places it on his "manhood" while he is kissing me. Oh my goodness! He had a telegram pole in those boxers. I pulled away, I felt it was too much and too fast—literally and figuratively. After all, I had not been intimate in about eight months. The last time had been before Earl went to jail and I was like five months pregnant.

There was no denying that I'd become attached to Jerome but fulfilling his sexual desires was very awkward. I'd not been with another man since I'd been with Earl for the last four years. I had my check-up but declined contraceptives since I had every intention of divorcing Earl and sex with him was completely out of the question. He would never touch me again after I found out about him and Amy. Lord knows I don't need another child. We are so new and still getting to know each other.

I tell Jerome to get dressed and let's go. Jerome cooperates and we headed east on Atlantic Blvd to the beach for ice cream. We laugh, talk, and flirt with each other over ice cream. We feed each other the ice cream and kiss constantly like middle school kids. Hand-in-hand we walk down the beach. I take in the beauty of the beach at sundown. The sounds of the waves crashing on the shore are in beat with Jerome's heart. We embrace and my face rest against his chest with his heart on rhythm with the waves crashing. The cadence is shared by the beats of his heart and the waves coming forcibly into shore.

Once again, Jerome is aroused. As we kiss and caress each other under the moonlight, a wave catches us and we are both soaked. There was no longer a need to avoid the waves after being soaked. Jerome took off his shirt and placed it on the beach sand as a makeshift blanket. He picked me up and laid me on the ground. He immediately begins to kiss me forcibly while undoing my pants and underwear. I nervously try to stop him as I look around to make sure we are still alone in this secluded area of the beach. There is no one there but us. Jerome says, "Relax! I'm not going to hurt you. I promise I won't bite. Well, maybe a little but I just want to make you feel good." "Wait! Someone may see us," I warn. "There is no one but us. That's why I brought you here. I've waited long enough. What are you afraid of?" I unsurely state, "I don't know."

Just then he enters me with a piecing thrust. I moan with ecstasy and a hint of pain due to his length and girth. He places his arm behind my leg and pulls it forward while thrusting deeper. I could no longer resist. I could do nothing but receive his gift. He breathed heavily and kissed me all over. This was very different. It felt different. In some way, I enjoyed it. Sex was not something I enjoyed. However, I could get used to this. Spreading my legs as wide as I could to ease the force of his penetrating thrusts, he begins to moan and jerk uncontrollably. He no longer moves. He lies on top of me breathing heavy.

He whispers into my ear, "That was good, honey!" I say nothing. In my mind, I am smiling. I am glad he liked it. I guess we both knew eventually we were going to be intimate because too much time had been invested. I pull my clothes up once he finally rolled off of me and he had finally stopped kissing me for dear life. I'd often not felt comfortable discussing or even engaging in sex. It was something I had looked at like a chore, kind of like doing dishes— a necessary evil. Jerome says, "I'm so glad that I gave Walter a ride that night. I owe him a beer."

Jerome starts laughing and continues, "You're a good girl. I really like you." "Why?" I ask. "Why? Because I'm not gay. Come on, you're beautiful. You're smart as hell. Your husband was a fool to let you go." "Let me?" I ask. "Yes, because if he treated you like the woman you are then you all would still be together. Well, his loss is my gain. I got you now! I just want to make you happy and see that beautiful smile on your pretty face all the time," he promises. I seek clarity by asking, "You want me? You know all about my situation and you still want me?" "Yes!" and Jerome kisses me and stands me up to hug me. He says, "You deserve to be happy and that's my job. You make me happy and I want to do the same for you." I state, "I wish it was that easy. I need to handle my situation with him. It might get ugly and I don't want to involve you." Jerome comforts me by saying, "I am already involved."

We walk back to his truck holding hands and we continue to talk. There was no denying that I liked him. He was the polar opposite of Earl. I'd never even heard, seen, or had any hint of an angry, mad, or an evil side. His spirit was light-hearted and his smile could light up the darkest room. I hadn't felt this way since Drew. Both came from stable homes with a positive role model as a father in the home. They were both taught and reared by men. With Earl, I'd forced myself to accept him but there was a constant struggle. It was if I'd been forcing a square (me) into his circle.

Jerome takes me to the showers on the pier to rinse off the sand from our feet and shoes. He lifted me up and caringly rinsed off my legs and carried me to the bench. He gently sat me down and placed my shoes upon my feet. I love a chivalrous man. It's not about the house, car, or jewelry that really matters. Earl provided me all those things but I never felt safe and secure. Jerome had only spent meagerly upon me and I was truly secure with my placement in his life. It was still quite new and the marital issues were pressing, but he was a much-needed blessed distraction.

Oddly enough, I'd been away from the kids and I didn't have the normal separation anxiety. In spite of the fact that I'd expected a battle with Earl to retrieve the kids. None of that mattered right now. I was enjoying these stolen moments of joy. They had been few and far in return, except the time spent with my babies. I did need to call Grandma. Once we got back to Jerome's house, I'd call and check in with her. Ideally, she'd tell me that she had the kids but that would be far too simple. We are talking about Earl here. Complexity is the name of his petty games. Jerome turns up the music and raises my arm in the air triumphantly; I am drawn back in this very moment.

We head west from the beach back to Collier City while listening to Quincy Jones' "Secret Garden." How apropos! Jerome had stumbled upon my "secret garden" in all of its ugly but naked truth. How reassuring it is to have someone who is willing to help you unpack all the baggage. This has been long overdue and very blissful. I didn't know what the future held for us, so I savored the present moments. Regardless of my battles, God had sent me an angel. He knew my heart was heavy and my spirit was broken. Jerome was willing to help me heal.

Coming through Collier City now listening to Al Green's "For The Good Times" and it was if Jerome was a local celebrity. I noticed he greeted all with a smile and easy conversation. He knew how to interact with everyone. He was the only son and the cherished "Golden Child," too. People naturally liked him due to his easygoing personality. He was not one to make you feel unwelcomed or not acknowledged. He was a good guy and he was my guy. I deserved someone like him. It only made me want to distance myself from Earl even more. I wanted out and the divorce would be a blessing.

We head into Jerome's house, and he shows me to the phone. He says while I call my Grandma, he's going to run down the street to talk with his friends. I sit at the kitchen table and dial Grandma. I know she's been worried. I was so caught up that several hours had passed since I'd been in Pompano. The phone is ringing and Grandma answers, "Hello." "Hello, Ma! What are you doing?" I ask while listening to her background for the sounds of the kids. "Are you ok? Where are you? Why didn't you call me earlier, gal?" "I'm sorry, Grandma. I dropped the kids off to Earl and came to Pompano to see my friend. I'm ok." "Thank God! Well be safe and I hadn't heard from Earl. I guess he's not bringing the kids back tonight." I am alarmed by this and ask, "He didn't call not one time?" "No, and I have been in the house waiting for him to call." "It's ok. I'll call him when I leave here. But I am okay and there's no need to worry." Grandma says, "Be safe and call me and let me know if you get the kids." I reply, "Ok, Grandma. I love you!" Grandma ends the call by saying, "I love you, too, Rona." She then hangs up the phone.

CHAPTER 34

AS FLEXIBLE AS A PAIR OF FLIP FLOPS

Jerome comes back into the house and we go into his room to watch TV. We sit down on his floor just lounging while watching a karate movie. Karate movies were shown every Sunday on TV. We both enjoyed the karate movies with the horribly delayed voiceovers. They were hilarious. The delay appeared to get worse as the movie went on. Jerniece called out to Jerome to "come here." Jerome gets up to see what his sister wanted while I continued to watch TV. Jerome had only been gone a few minutes before I heard Jerniece nervously stated, "Wait a minute, wait a minute! Rome! Rome!" I'm hearing her shrill but I am watching the movie still.

Approximately six assassins are surrounding Bruce Lee. He only has nunchucks to defend himself. I'm thinking to myself, he's in big trouble. Then my attention is pulled away from the TV after hearing the bedroom door get kicked in off the hinge. I was sitting on the floor facing the TV directly north of me; I look over my right shoulder to the east to a sight that stops my heart from beating. Earl is standing in Jerome's bedroom door with an Uzi. That was one of the last memories I have.

Everything went black and dark. It was peaceful, silent, and serene. Wherever I was, wasn't so bad. I felt no pain and that was a good thing. It wasn't burning hot, so I must not be in hell. I've been told that heaven is blindingly white and there was no light, only darkness. I had no idea where I was but Earl was no longer with me and that was quite all right with me. The silence was broken by the sound of Jerome's voice. I couldn't see anything still but I could hear. The annoying thumps increased in intensity until the pain of the blows brought me to.

I open my eyes to stinging which made it hard to see. There was no need for vision anyway because I was being forcibly led somewhere. I wipe my face to remove the perspiration stinging my eyes and I see a hand filled with blood. I was not perspiring but bleeding! Before I could completely get my footing, I am back in the dark black place. It is no longer silent and I hear yelling back and forth. "Stop hitting her like that. You're going to kill her!" I heard Jerome say. An unidentifiable male voice demands, "Shut the fuck up!" Earl speaks, "This is my wife. She's mine. I do what the fuck I want to her." I could hear Jerniece crying and mumbling something inaudible, possibly a prayer. The unknown male makes another demand, "Lay your ass down, nigga. You try to save her and you die! Real talk!"

Suddenly a crushing blow to my nose caused my eyes to tear and burn. I hurt so badly. The pain is shattering. The concrete on the front porch ripped at my skin, as I was being drug and beaten like an animal. I somehow manage to get off my knees onto my feet and I try to talk to Earl to stop the beating. "Please stop! Please I am so sorry! Please stop!" "Didn't I tell you I was going to do a 'quarter' if you tried me?"

I finally realize he had been beating me with the butt of the gun in and out of consciousness. He mercilessly beats me with the butt of the second gun. He stops beating me to drag me down the street to his awaiting getaway car. The asphalt shredded every inch of my skin it came in contact with.

"You hear me? You're going to die tonight," Earl rages. Hearing those words made everything super real. That had been my greatest fear to be killed by his hands. Maybe I should've known he was up to something because he hadn't called Grandma once looking for me. I'd come to Pompano laughing because I'd won the battle and now I was crying out in pain in a war for my life.

"Stop, please! Don't' hit me anymore. I'll come back. I am sorry, just don't hit me in the head anymore," I cry out to him. He raises his gun and strikes me right in my left eye and I immediately feel a gush of blood from the new cut. The blow awakened me and I began to fight for my life. We were at the trunk of the car and he was attempting to throw me in. I fought and tussled him as if my life depended on me staying out of that trunk. We all know what the message being sent is when one is placed in the trunk—discarding trash and death. I had a newborn daughter barely three months, who would never know me, and a three year old, who may or may not remember me. Oh, hell no!

The debilitating pain in my head due to the blows were no longer felt, all I could feel was anxiety of being laid to rest in the coffin-like trunk. I had no intention of going out without a fight. I'd tried talking to him and the cold, piercing death glare only looked through me without a word said. If his eyes were windows to his soul then he is a product of hell. The only description that would aptly describe it was a death stare. Earl was unable to place me in the trunk of the car and I was literally beating his ass. It was pure determination and adrenaline that brought out that fight in me.

Without rhyme or immediate reason, my feet leave the ground and head first I am body slammed into the trunk. Before I could rise up to get out of the trunk, I see Earl and Tony Rue standing there before the trunk is slammed closed. Tony Rue was the other voice I heard but couldn't immediately identify. Tony Rue was one of Earl's foot soldiers. He was all brute and brawn with no brains. He was no leader and very much a natural born follower. Tony Rue was short, about 5'7", but stocky like a bulldog weighing over

250lbs. He was fresh out of prison for barely two weeks and was still carrying his penitentiary weight.

The car starts after hearing the doors slam. I couldn't see anything, so I had to rely on my sense of hearing. I locate the trunk lock and madly try to get it to unlock with no luck. The "MacGyver Shows" are so misleading. MacGyver I was not and I realized that I needed to pray and ask for forgiveness of my sins so that I may be saved!

As soon as I finish praying, I begin to hear a barrage of gunfire. It was incoming and quite close. I could hear the different sounds of the exchanging gunfire. One gun was a semi-automatic, one was a shotgun blast, and the other was a revolver that fired like "pow, pow, pow." It was safe to say that we were in a gun battle with someone. The bullets were coming in contact with the metal frame. One of the bullets pierced the trunk and I was able to see some light, an outlet to view what's happening. Once the incoming fire had ceased, I dared to look out the hole and saw Jerome's truck traveling at a high rate of speed. He doesn't know that I am in the trunk and his firing could kill me. I could get caught in the crossfire.

Jerome was no longer firing but Earl and Tony Rue were still firing their guns. Suddenly, I was jolted to the other side of the trunk and I could no longer see Jerome's headlights through the hole. The hole became black and there were no more headlights to be seen. I wonder if Jerome is okay. Did he get shot? Crash? My mind is only left to wonder. I begin to cry while I pray for him. This was my greatest fear and Jerome has been thrust in the middle of this mess. I pray he is fine.

The car eventually stops and the trunk opens. I can see a multicolored sign for a water cooler company. I wasn't sure if I needed to start swinging again or try talking him out of this again. He snatches me out manhandling style. He opens the backdoor and kicks me into the backseat. He gets in too. I immediately begin to plead my case, "Honey, please stop! I love you! We have kids! Please don't do this!" He only stares ahead with a blank look while holding the gun on me. "I didn't do anything! Let's just go home. I love you!" I continue. Earl still remains silent as Tony Rue drove the car. I continue, "Honey! Honey! Honey, do you hear me? Let's just go home!"

Earl begins to beat me upside the head with the gun again. I couldn't take much more of the draining blows. Did he hear the insincerity of my words? Raining down skull crushing blows rendered me defenseless. I placed my hands and arms up in a defensive manner to attempt to soften the knockout-rendering blows. The impact of the butt of the gun nearly cracked my skull wide open. The pain was simply intolerable! He finally began to speak as he violently choked me; "You're going to try me with another nigga? Didn't I tell you I'd kill you? You're dying tonight!" "No, I am not! I am not going to die!" I began to fight for my life. I insisted, "I'm not going to die!"

We fight in the backseat while the car has gotten off I-95 and headed down Oakland Park Blvd. Oswald Park is where we ended up. During the struggle, I'd managed to keep Earl off me and kicked him furiously like a kick boxer. His head had even hit the window a few times. I had no intentions of leaving my children motherless.

The car is stopped at the north end of the park past the baseball field. Earl opens the door and grabs me by the legs and snatches me out the car like a bag of trash. My body slams into the concrete and he jumps on top of me pinning my arms with his knees. He unleashes countless blows to my face and head—all uninterrupted and unobstructed. The pain lessens and the blows become barely felt thumps. It's as if I've become numb to the blows.

Drifting in and out of consciousness, I awaken to him beating me and cursing me. He said countless times that death was at my door. I was once again in a familiar place—helpless but hopeful.

No matter the circumstances, I cannot and will not be dying to-night! I have a daughter who would never know me. I would just have to hang on and not give in or up. I hear Earl say, "Pass me your gun." I can't see but I can hear him. He is no longer hitting me. I hear a gun discharge in close proximity. My ears are ringing and I am stunned. I sense that a shotgun blast had been fired at close range. It was so close that my ears are ringing. I open my eyes and I am *not* dead. Earl is holding a sawed-off shotgun.

Tony Rue says, "Chill out. Here comes 'nine.' Them 'crackas' are coming in over there." He points at the south entrance of the park. Earl refuses to give him the gun. "I'm killing this bitch! She just won't die!" Earl says in frustration and rage. They tussle for the gun and Earl raises his leg enough for me to free an arm. His attention is now diverted; I free my other arm and push him off me. I take off running across the field like an Olympic Sprinter towards the Park Ranger's headlights. The lights appear to be the length of a football field away. With the strength remaining, I run blind toward the light and suddenly I lose my footing.

Earl had kicked my feet from under me from behind. I was about a half-length of a football field from the strobe light. He placed his hands over my mouth and got on top of me. I tried to bite his finger off. He punched me a few times and began choking me again. I could barely breathe again and I kneed him in his groin to get him off of me. He screamed in pain and choked me harder before releasing his grip.

I got him off me and was able to get on my feet. I was now able to see that the strobe light had passed us by. I am back on the ground due to an unsuspecting right hook. I drift off into unconsciousness...

CHAPTER 35

AS EMPOWERING AS 4-INCH HEELS

The headlights from the car is now lighting our area up. Earl grabs me up and we head toward the car. I can barely walk and he is beating me for not being able to stand up. Let's see here, let me beat you in the head for hours on end and let's see how gracefully he would walk (serious sarcasm). It would be my pleasure to have the roles reversed, but that would not be my reality right now. We finally arrive back at the car and he tells Tony Rue to turn off the car. He tells Tony Rue to give him a minute and he will be right back. We begin to walk south out the park through a trail to an abandoned house.

I'm not in the position, at this point, to defend myself. I was not in fight mode. I allowed Earl to struggle with my dead weight while I conserved my remaining energy for the next battle. The most eerie part is that Earl had this death glare and was often quiet. The coldness of his eyes scared me. There was very little thought on my part, other than I had no intentions of dying tonight. He took me into the abandoned house and told me to remove my clothes.

He no longer held the gun but placed it in the broken windowsill. I figured he wasn't trying to kill me right now since he placed the weapon down. After all that I endured from him, the sexual assault would be the icing on the cake. He instructed me to lie down on a urine-smelling mattress with exposed springs piercing my back. I dared not resist him and cause him to rage again. I was only there physically. Mentally, I was somewhere else as he forced me to perform fellatio on him. This would be the first time he ever made such a request; he usually got that from the other women and not me.

The thought did occur to literally bite it off; I would be a Lorena Bobbitt 2.0. The problem would be getting past Tony Rue. Tony Rue was standing watch and my darting out of the abandoned house would place me mano-a-mano with him. I decided to not try to escape that route. I obliged and my inexperience would be the reasons for my intentional biting. He pulled away several times and I would relent and make sure he came in contact with my teeth over and over.

My lips were more than twice their normal size. My lips were busted in several places, not to mention my jaw would hurt when I attempted to open it wide. He struck me in the head several times and pushed me back on the filthy mattress. He'd had enough of me shearing him, and it was most certainly done intentionally. He entered me and began to hump me like the animal he is—with his tiny little sausage. I just lie there and silently cry just waiting for it to end. As dire as the situation appeared, I knew this would be the last time he abused me in any way and I wasn't going to die tonight!

Trying to keep my wits and stay alert, I have serious concerns that I may have a concussion or skull fracture from the blows. Sleep would be the death of me, especially if I am hemorrhaging internally. "Think, Rona, and focus!" I say to myself repeatedly. Earl had emotionally disconnected from me. It was obvious by him ordering me to suck his dick—it would be more like a Vienna sausage or a baby frank. He'd intended to "straighten this package" and he had accepted the quarter he proudly stated he would do for me. Having no idea how I would get out of this, but I believed with all heart that I would get out of this severely beaten but alive.

He finished his business and tells me to pull up my clothes and come on. As expected, Tony Rue was standing at the entrance of the park with his gun. We all get into the car and Earl tells him to drive to his mama's house. My heart suddenly drops because I don't want my kids to see me like this. Although I want to see them, but not having to see me all bloodied, battered, and beaten half to death. Their innocent eyes should never have to bear witness to this.

Earl begins to talk, "We're going to mama's house and you need to shower and go to bed." I am thinking to myself that I can't go to sleep. I'll just lie there and wait for him to fall asleep and run out. He asks, "You hear me?" "I don't want to go to your mama's house. The kids are there and I don't want them to see me like this," I plead. "Why not? Their mother is a whore and you don't want them to see your ugly ass?" I begin to cry, "I'm not a whore! I need to go to the hospital. You can just drop me off and I won't talk." "That's exactly what you are! A whore, whore! I know you are not going to talk because you ain't going." I demand, "Why? I need a doctor!" "No, you need to stop being a whore, whore. And I'm going to beat it out of you or kill you in the process."

We arrive at Miss Cat's house and we get out the car. Earl grabs me by my hair and pulls it like a leash. He knocks on the front door and I can see Tony Rue's headlights leaving, providing no extra light but the porch light. Miss Cat answers the door and opens it to let us in. I immediate broke out in tears as I saw her standing in the doorway holding my baby girl. She had her over her shoulder burping her. I suspect it is about midnight because that is usually the time she wakes up to be fed. Miss Cat looks at me and makes eye contact. Could it be possible that she will end this nightmare by coming to my aid? After all, she is in the nursing field and she must know that I need immediate medical attention. She coldly says, "I don't have nothing to do with it. Keep me out of it." She turns and walks to her bedroom while gently patting Lelee's back.

I struggle to see her face. I need to make sure she is okay. As Miss Cat turns left to go to her room, I can see her lying there with her eyes closed sleep. Seeing her allows me to find the much-needed strength to keep fighting and thinking quickly on my feet. Robbie was probably in her bed asleep, although I didn't see him. Robbie was Earl's namesake and he truly was a proud father. He'd bring no harm to him. I knew that much to be true.

Miss Cat, the mother-in-law from Hades, had even surprised me when I expected so very little from her. Maybe she was worse than thought. I'd actually thought she would provide me some assistance or relief. As I looked in her eyes as we entered her home, I saw anything *but* concern. She may have even gathered some personal enjoyment from seeing me beaten so brutally. I am sure she felt that I had it coming to me. This last act would cement our lack of having a relationship from this day forward. How could one woman allow this to be condoned by refusing to assist the beaten woman whose child she held? I wouldn't wish this on my worst enemy—even her and her son. She would never get the satisfaction of seeing me like this again.

Earl takes me into a bedroom and orders me to take a shower. I go into the bathroom and close the door. There's no lock on the door. I turn the knobs to turn on the shower with no intention of washing away evidence. Standing there, I saw a woman in the mirror that caught my eye. She looked next to death. The thick black hair was matted with blood and patches of hair missing pulled from the root. Both of her eyes were nearly closed with a bleeding and crooked nose. Her lips were bleeding and swollen. Knots were all over her forehead. Bless her soul!

I wondered where did this woman come from? I turn around to an open bathroom window and there's no one behind me. I turn around and realize that she is I! I'm unrecognizable to even myself. What has he done to me? I'm so shocked by how savagely I'd been beaten that I couldn't bring myself to tears. I was literally shocked and flabbergasted as I stared at this unfamiliar and un-identifiable me. I decide to make a run for it and I decide to climb out the open window.

Carefully removing the screen and dropping it outside, the window is fully open. I stand on the toilet tissue holder to propel me headfirst out of the window. I am able to get out as far as my waist before Earl appears and begins to beat me back in the win-dow. Each blow to my head and face was worse than other. I don't know how many of those blows to my head and face I could bear.

The thought of running out the door crossed me mind, but I wasn't sure which direction he'd enter the house—front or back. After the last attack, I was stunned and needed to recover my grounding. I doubted I would be swift enough to outlast and out-run him. And the very last thing I needed was another beating to the head. Before I could even finish processing the thought of escaping, the bathroom door flung open. "Didn't I tell you take to take a shower, you dirty little whore?" Earl angrily asked. "I don't want to shower. I need to go to the hospital," I demanded. "Take off your clothes, whore!" He then snatches my shirt off while hit-ting my battered head once more. "Get in the shower and let's go to bed!" Earl demanded and stared at me with every intention of forc-ing me to abide his orders. I begin to take off my pants and under-wear. He stands watch as I pull the shower curtain back and step in. Once he sees that I am in the shower, he closes the bathroom window and locks it. He turns and leaves out of the bathroom.

I stand to the back of the shower and the showerhead barely reaches me. I am now reminded of all my battle scars when the water makes contact with my skin. I can feel the scrapes, scratches, and cuts from the attack. I don't shower. I stand there writhing in pain. Earl comes back in and snatches the shower curtain back, "Get under the water!" he orders while pushing me forward to the running showerhead. The pain has intensified because I can now feel each and every laceration. As the water runs through my hair, I look down and see reddish-pink water running down the drain. There also was a considerable amount of hair that had fallen out, too.

Earl hands me a towel and turns off the water. I wrap myself up in the towel and my hair is still drenched and dripping. My head hurts so bad I dare not apply any pressure, even wrapping a towel upon my head. Earl turns the bathroom light out and pushes me into bed. He leaves the bedroom light on and tells me to "get against the wall and all the way to the wall." He gets right behind me in an effort to block my potential escape. He then locks the gate by placing his arm around my waist and under me to prevent much movement. He falls asleep quickly and I fight sleep for my life.

CHAPTER 36

AS EMPOWERING AS 4-INCH HEELS

Whenever I would catch myself dozing off, I'd refocus on something to stay awake. I fought sleep like this for hours until Miss Cat came banging on the door. She was frantically yelling, "Robert Earl! Robert Earl! Open the door! Open the door, gal! Hurry! Robert Earl!" Earl jumps out of bed to unlock the door and Miss Cat bolts in, "It's police outside all around the house. They're everywhere, all behind the house too! Should I let them in?" Earl says, "Yeah, but give me one minute first, then you can let them in. Let me hide these guns first and talk to my wife." Now I am his wife, what happened to "dirty little whore?" Ok, since we are changing faces, I'll put my mask on too.

Earl closes the door and begins to stash his guns and then sits on the bed next to me. "You know I didn't do this right?" he asks. I am thinking to myself that this must be a joke, and a bad one at that. You are exactly who did this to me. Is he insane? He continues, "I'm on bond and a new charge would revoke my bond. Tell them that you and one of my girlfriends had a fight. Ok?" His tone had instantly changed from abusively demanding to soothing. He was a chameleon. He switches it on and off. I wasn't buying it. I said nothing. I just sat there.

Police burst through the door with guns drawn and immediately pounces on Earl. They snatch him off the bed and body slams him onto the floor. He didn't resist as I thought he would. It would be in vain anyway. He was outmatched and outgunned. He simply yelled out to me, "Honey, Honey, tell 'em!" I did not speak a word. The officers snatch him up and take him out of the room in handcuffs. A nice looking younger detective approaches me. He is dark and handsome and very well dressed. The nice looking detective informs the remaining officers he would like to speak with me in private. Miss Cat refuses to leave the room. After he informs her he would have her arrested for obstruction of justice, she relented. She stated before leaving the room, "Rona, you need to tell them the truth so they can get out of my dam house! My son has been home all night. He ain't done anything!" I was not surprised or shocked by her statement. She had shown me her permanent hand when she refused to assist or even offer any medical care.

Miss Cat leaves the room rolling her eyes at us both. I am not taken aback by her defending her precious son with no regard for me. He could've killed me. He damn near did! The handsome detective begins, "I'm Detective Lacey with the Pompano Police Department. I need for you to tell me who did this to you so you can get immediate medical treatment." I hold my head down to gather my thoughts. I ask, "Can I ask you a question?" Det. Lacey answers, "You can ask me anything you like." "If I told you who did this, will you keep them long enough for me to get out of town?" I ask. I needed confirmation that I would have enough time to get out of town. It wasn't uncommon in domestic issues like this that the aggressor simply is taken downtown to "cool off" and released home angrier than when he left. Det. Lacey assures me, "If you tell me who did this, you won't have to worry about him for a very long time." I look at him in his eyes and I believe him and feel he is trustworthy. I walk out of the bedroom into the living room where Earl is being detained and Det. Lacey follows.

The time has come for me to "straighten this package." I walk in there and I sound like a broken record as I repeat over and over while pointing at Earl, "He did it! He did it! He did it!" The officers immediately take him into custody while he's yelling out to me the entire time. I was deaf to his pleas for help, as he had been deaf to mine. Miss Cat runs and kicks me in retaliation for naming her abusive son. I now have two-for-one and both are arrested. I give them Grandma's information so she can get my kids. I am trying to hold it together but I am finding it hard to stand up without assistance. I was badly injured and I knew it.

Det. Lacey grabbed me by the arm to lead me outside to the waiting ambulance. I can hear Earl yelling out to me. He was where he belonged—arrested! I looked at him as we past the police car and I stop to address him. He whimpers, "Honey, what are you doing? Honey, why am I being arrested? I didn't do anything. Honey, what's going on?" I look him straight in his evil eyes completely disgusted and unaffected by his pleas. I speak to him with conviction, "I am straightening my package!" I walk to the ambulance and fall out while receiving care.

I awaken to smelling salts being placed under my bloody nose. Finally, I see bright lights. Could this be heaven? My eyes are barely able to make out the faces and figures due to being swollen shut. I think he'd beaten out my contacts because my vision was the furthest thing from being clear. I could hear medical talk and blaring sirens so I must be at the hospital or en route.

I begin to realize that I made it and I did not die at Earl's hands. I begin to cry and give thanks to God. I cry out, "Oh, God! Thank you, God! My God, thank you!" This was it! I made it out alive. I was beaten, battered, and bruised but I am here getting medical attention; Earl has been arrested. I just knew in my soul this would be the last time he'd ever lay hands upon me. I just knew if I got through this alive it would *never* happen again! I never lost hope in that, no matter how dire the situation. He wasn't going to get away with this. In addition to all the other charges that are forthcoming, he has completely violated the restraining order. I can't erase the memories in my head of him coming into Jerome's house and those haunting memories of him with guns blazing to kill me. All these acts were done while he was on bail. I am sure that bond will be revoked.

The injuries that I'd sustained required a hospital stay. I had surgical staples in my head, six stitches over my eye, and fractured eye socket and jawbone but I was alive. My injuries were mainly in my face and intentional. If he didn't kill me, he'd leave me to be damaged goods. He wanted to destroy my face. The amount of swelling I had gives me the impression that he may have accomplished his goal. I found it difficult to even look at myself in the mirror. It was too depressing of a reflection. My hospital stay was quite blurry to recall due to the medication given. My retina had been reattached by laser surgery and a splint had been placed on my nose and chin with countless bandages covering my head.

It seemed as if I was there for a day or so, but it had been a couple weeks. I did have a cloudy recollection of periods being questioned by Det. Lacey. He was often there keeping me abreast and taking statements. Finally I was released after being away from my babies for eternity, or so it seemed. Det. Lacey did me the honors of driving me home to Grandma's after I was discharged. After my eye surgery, I'd been given those dark shades for which glaucoma patients wear post-surgery. Even the dim light of the lamp next to the hospital bed would be too bright for my sensitive eyes. The bright Florida sun was unbearable and simply brutal. The tinted windows of his unmarked car provided little aid. My eyes tear and run incessantly. Det. Lacey hands me his handkerchief from his nice suit.

I simply cup my hands around the shades to further block the light and this provides me some relief. "Thank you for the handkerchief. I need to tell you something," I inform him. "What is it?" Det. Lacey asks. I continue, "Earl committed a murder. He murdered Orion. He came and got me after it happened. I want to testify against him." Det. Lacey wasn't surprised by this information, "Yeah, we've been in contact with the State Attorney's Office regarding his bond. They asked if you'd now be willing to talk to them about that." I agreed, "Yes, I'll talk to them. I told Earl if he let me go and leave me alone that I wouldn't talk. I meant it. He tried to kill me. Why am I protecting someone who tried to kill me? I sure will talk to them and I will tell them everything." All bets were off when he tried to kill me, I would no longer be loyal and uncooperative with the State.

Det. Lacey has always had a direct, real way of conveying his point based on what he has seen first-hand in the streets. He counsels me, "Listen, I've seen good girls, pretty girls like you get messed up with 'cats' like this and they go right back. Rona, if you go back, *he will kill you*! You really need to leave him." I hear him and say, "I already did! I filed for divorce! I had no intention of ever going back. That is why he did this. You don't have that to worry about. I am never going back. Look at me! Look at what he did to me." He turns his head to look and says, "That's why I say, don't go back. It will only get worse. You're a smart girl. You're beautiful! You don't have to deal with that type of creep." He called me "beautiful" and I thought of Jerome. He always said I was. I reply in disbelief, "Beautiful? I look like a beat up mummy. He did that on purpose, he always tries to damage my face so no one else will want me.

The stories shared with me made me understand that I was not the only one that has gone through this. He assures me, "Trust me, it is bad but I've seen far worse. Many girls didn't make it out like you. They usually end up in a homicide folder. You did well because you are alive. I know you fought for your life because it's obvious he has been in a fight with someone. He has some nice reminders of you." We both share a laugh and he continues, "You will heal and still be beautiful. I care little about your look, but your *outlook*. You need to understand that you can't change your mind with the sweet jailhouse talk. He will try! I've met with him and he told me he just needs to speak to you and the charges will be dropped." I am sure he said exactly that because he'd get my cooperation through beating me to death or just simply death. I assure him, "There's no chance of that. I'm prosecuting and not changing my mind. There's no turning back. I wasn't raised like this. My kids deserve better. I want nothing else to do with him or his mama."

We are a short distance from Grandma's house. I left her in one piece and I am coming back all battered but I have peace. But, thank God I am here! I want to see my babies and hug Grandma. I'm coming home with no fear of Earl and his antics. I have not known peace and didn't have peace of mind. All I wanted was peace and the past years have been tumultuous. I needed rest for my weary soul. The mere sight of the house number 841 was stronger than any analgesic I could be given to diminish the pain. *I am home!*

CHAPTER 37

AS EMPOWERING AS 4-INCH HEELS

I t was good to be home. Thank you Jesus! God had kept my babies in His perfect care. Lelee had started on formula now since I'd been in the hospital and unable to breastfeed her. She appeared to have gotten bigger and Robbie was still my very smart lad. I couldn't even fathom not being with them everyday. Grandma had done as she always did, step in and take care of her family. I had no worries while the kids were in her care. She had raised two generations and was now caring for the third.

Grandma couldn't believe the events. She said her left eye had been jumping after I had left to take the kids to Earl that day. She didn't know who or what it was, but it was a sign of trouble to come. So she kept praying. Grandma was a prayer warrior! She started her day on her knees and usually ended the day the same way—and countless prayers throughout the day. She kept us covered in prayer. I don't doubt that it was Grandma's main line to Jesus as the reason I am here.

She said after we talked that evening, she had a funny feeling. She said she went into the bathroom and prayed for everyone in the family. Her request for a protective fence to be thrown around us was her consistent prayer. It is truly by the grace of God that I am here! The doctors had informed me that my injuries were so severe that had I just gone to sleep, I could've developed a blood clot and died or from internal bleeding. My staying awake saved my life. To this very day, I don't know where I found the strength and fortitude to fight for my life. There is no doubt that Earl had intended on killing me.

Over the next few months, Grandma helped me recover. She was a real help with the kids while I healed. She made sure I ate three home-cooked meals a day minimum because I had lost a considerable amount of weight. She also kept the curious and nosy persons away so that I could recover in peace. Once the news hit the streets, the gossiping vultures were in full force. I just didn't discuss it with anyone outside of the family. The State Attorney's Office had advised me to not discuss the case.

I spent so much time talking to prosecutors, investigators, detectives, attorneys, and even co-defendants that I really had tired of discussing it. I mainly talked to Grandma to keep her abreast of what was going on. Earl had been charged with home invasion, attempted murder, and armed kidnapping with rape. His bond on the murder charge had been revoked and I had provided a deposition as a witness for the State. Earl's Defense attorneys were asking for a speedy trial on the murder charge, in hopes that State wouldn't be prepared. Darnell had already pled guilty but refused to testify against Earl.

I'd even had a meeting with Darnell and told him that we were out looking for him that night. Earl wanted both of them dead so they wouldn't talk. I know that Darnell believed me but he was too concerned with harm to his elderly mom. Resultantly, he was going to eat the time alone. Having Darnell would be a plus, but the State had a star witness in me. I'd seen the crime scene and had been told by Earl's account. I was going to take the stand against him in the murder trial and mine.

Jerome had been calling for some time and had come to the hospital several times but I was out of it. I wasn't mad at him or anything but I really didn't know what to say other than giving *sincere* thanks. I did want to personally thank him for prosecuting and getting the police involved in the first place. I had made some progress in my healing in the several months after the incident. My initial avoidance was due to me not wanting him to see me all bruised and beaten, but Grandma told me he had come to the hospital several times and seen me. I couldn't keep him away. He kept calling and would drop by unannounced. I would make a beeline to my room and hide.

Grandma didn't fully understand why I'd been avoiding Jerome. I hadn't been fully forthcoming. My period never returned after the incident. I was hoping that it was due to stress, but I'd begun to feel nauseous after Labor Day and had decided to go to the doctor. I was pregnant and nearly five months. I was pregnant from Jerome. Earl had raped me but I had cut him with my teeth so he couldn't have a "happy ending." Jerome had ejaculated in me that night on the beach approximately five months ago.

Another baby was the *very* last thing I needed. An abortion at this stage of my pregnancy would not be an option. I'd gone to see about adoption but struggled with that since my biological mother abandoned me. That was the problem and I doubted that I'd be able to give up a baby that I've carried for nine months. The mere thought of giving the baby up was too close for any type of comfort. I was unsure that I could live with that. I'd only known Jerome for nearly the same months I was pregnant, or so it felt. My fear was that he would think that I trapped him. Lord knows this was not the case! The trial was a few months away and I would be good and pregnant. This would be the first time that I face Earl and very pregnant.

I came clean to Grandma and told her that I was pregnant from Jerome. She liked Jerome and thought he was good for the kids and me. I shared with her my concerns about Jerome's reaction to the news. She asked what I planned to do and I said that I'd just keep avoiding him. He didn't deserve all this craziness. He was trying to be nice and ended up staring down a sawed-off shotgun in *his* home. To add insult to injury, he had also impregnated a married woman.

I had no master plan other than staying away from Jerome. It wasn't as if I didn't want to be bothered by him but I believed that I was protecting him from my crazy world. Even I didn't want to be bothered with *my* craziness. He was now a part of this craziness and the ante had been upped now with a child. I had difficulty wrapping my mind around being a mother to his child. This was all too much too fast.

Jerome had sensed the distance and called daily speaking with Grandma. I'd talked to him sparingly with him always questioning my distance. He was trying to respect my personal space, especially after my near death experience. However, he could sense that things had changed with him and I. I didn't share my true feelings or pregnancy because I assumed his reaction would be anything but jumping up and down for joy. He had a pass from me. Maybe it was best if he just lived his life without me. This may be completely illogical thinking but it was my mindset at the time.

Grandma's position was that I should tell him. It was fear of rejection mainly. Rejection is one of my greatest fears. I guess it has to do with unresolved feelings and emotions stemming from my biological mother abandoning me. She was at the root of my fear of rejection. The idyllic image I had of him would be no more if he rejected his child and me. I'd rather retain his image and not have to be hurt from him turning his back on us. We'd talked enough for me to know that he hadn't wanted any more kids at this time. I guess the universe decided otherwise.

Sitting in the front yard and catching the cool Florida breeze with Grandma, while Robbie played in the yard, was a daily ritual. Lelee was asleep in my arms and I rocked her gently while the cool breeze blew. Miss Nezzie, our next-door neighbor, sat on her porch and we all talked while enjoying the sunset in the horizon.

We had a birds-eye view of the activity in and around Sunland. The park was a popular hub in Lauderdale and we lived right next to all the action. You could see each and every car that entered the park.

The loud banging systems clashed with the wars of subwoofers, tweeters, and hard-pounding bass. LL Cool J could be heard in one car and another would be jamming Jam Pony's Slick Vic was bumping that "Body Mechanic." Jam Pony's tapes were made by the local DJs, who were known to set off any party. The guys with the expensive systems often played Jam Pony religiously. Jam Pony touched something in you that you couldn't help but move to the bass beat. As it is often said, "Jam Pony was often imitated but never duplicated." Their mix tapes sold well and flooded the streets. It wouldn't be unusual to have four out of five cars passing by jamming them "Pony Boys" out their speakers. Bass music was the preferred music and that's what Florida was known for—bass!

The genre of music had changed and I could hear some slow old school music. Hmmm, and they are jamming too. It was a break from the norm and I could hear Al Green's soulful voice. A burgundy Chevy truck pulled up at a high rate of speed with the music blaring. It was Jerome! Oh Lord, my initial reaction was to run in the house. I was holding Lelee so that wouldn't be an option. I hadn't seen him since the incident. It had been many months and I wasn't ready to see him yet.

My heart was literally racing at a million miles per second. It must've knocked Lelee awake because she began to cry with her eyes wide open. I was rocking her to calm her down and Grandma reached for me, "I'll take her. Jerome is here and you need to talk. If you don't tell him, then I will. Enough of this mess." I am in shock, "Now?" Grandma answers, "Yes, Rona. I had him come down here because you had something to tell him. Now give me the baby and y'all talk." I guess I don't have much of a choice in the matter, now do I? My hand had been forced.

She takes Lelee in to the house after greeting Jerome with a hug and kiss. They both had a mutual like for the other. She called for Robbie to come in but I told her he could stay. I was watching him and I might just need him to be used as an escape, if things became too heated. Jerome picked up Robbie and swung him around. He threw the ball with him and just played around with him for a while. I watched carefully because this was the first time he had been in contact with him. Robbie enjoyed his playmate and appeared to enjoy Jerome.

The playtime ended when Robbie said he had to use the bathroom. He ran into the house and playtime was over. Jerome looked good, as usual. He had always been a clean-cut guy with a perfect smile. As he walked towards me, the smile from playing with Robbie became a confused look. He took the empty seat next to me. His face showed me complete confusion regarding what I had to tell him and I was just as confused as to how I had even arrived at this point. We both were confused.

CHAPTER 38

AS EMPOWERING AS 4-INCH HEELS

The silence is finally broken by Jerome speaking, "Hey Rona! You look good!" "Thank you! So do you!" I respond. "What's going on? Grandma said you wanted to talk to me," he states. "Yeah, but I didn't want to now, " I say. "What is it? And why not now?" I begin to cry and the words escape me but the tears hold me hostage. Jerome comforts me, "Rona, don't cry!" He begins to hug me and continues, "I'm here. I've been wanting to just hold you." "I'm sorry! I'm so sorry for everything. I never meant for all this to happen," I inform him. Jerome's tone is soothing to my spirit and he says, "It's ok! We're fine! It's not your fault! But I'm here for you! I'm not going anywhere. Ok?" "But, but...I'm pregnant!" I blurt out.

Jerome begins to smile and asks, "You are?" "Yes, I was scared to tell you. That's why I had been avoiding you. I know you didn't want any kids right now," I explain. "So that's why you've been pushing me away? I thought you changed your mind about us. I didn't know what was going on. I missed talking with my friend." I confess, "I missed you so much, too. This has not been easy without you. I had no one to talk to other than Grandma."

The smile on his face has grown even bigger as he asks, "So we're having a baby? When is the due date?" "I am five months and due in December." Jerome is completely surprised, "You're five months? You're not even big." "I know. I carry small." Jerome searches for answers, "This is September and the baby will be here in a couple months?" I answer him, "Yes." He continues, "Alright! Then we are having a baby in December." He reaches for my hand and our fingers interlock as he says, "I will be a good father and we're having a baby!" His laughter was contagious and we both laughed and smile.

This went better than I had expected. It was if a ton of bricks had been lifted off me. Yes, we're having a baby. He truly seemed happy and I was thankful to have my friend back. We sat in the yard and talked for hours recounting our experience, our feelings, and our future with our baby. I had made it through the storm and Jerome was my rainbow. He made me happy because his heart and soul was pure. Our union had come at a good time. The trial was approaching and I could use his support. Reuniting with Jerome allowed me to have some semblance of peace and carefree living. Life was good! I'd healed from the physical injures. My babies were growing like weeds. Robbie was my little man and Lelee was getting out of the way for the new baby. She was crawling and already getting into mischief. My meetings with the State Attorney informed me that Earl was heading to prison for a considerable amount of time. I was rebuilding my life and correcting previous mistakes. I was even proud of myself for creating a better environment for my babies.

Several months later, it was time to go to trial and testify against him on the charges of second-degree murder. This would be the first time I'd seen him since he had attempted to kill me and this would be a test. I wasn't afraid but timid. Once you've stared and looked at death in the face, fear is no longer anything to fear! It was more like apprehension. I didn't know how I would handle seeing him. There wasn't much care given for him seeing me quite pregnant now. I'd grown and was less than two months from delivery.

Not many outside of the family even knew I was pregnant. I didn't venture out much and stayed home mostly.

Honestly speaking, I was somewhat embarrassed about the court appearance revealing my pregnancy. My pregnancy would lead to much speculation that I was carrying Earl's third child. The thought had crossed my mind a time or two but I knew it wasn't his. When Earl raped me, he hadn't reached completion. He couldn't due to the bite marks from the fellatio. It was too painful for him and he eventually gave up. Conversely, it wasn't forced with Jerome and he ejaculated inside me. I knew this was Jerome's child. There could be a small chance but I highly doubt it.

Earl had alleged to his Defense team that I was unfaithful and "loose with my caboose." And here I am preparing for court with another man's baby while married to an abusive man. There is no doubt that this is not a good look. I couldn't change made up minds, nor did I care to try. After the hell I'd gone through, I cared not about opinions of others. Try walking a mile in my shoes before they judge. If I had chosen to be as Earl accused me, he couldn't say anything about it. I'd simply be playing catch up to all the dirt he has done. I was not into payback but bounce back. I was done with Earl and I was ready to close that chapter.

I had mixed emotions about testifying. I'd been placed in a position where my testimony could potentially send the father of my two kids to prison for up to life. I was going to face my abuser and show him that he didn't shut me up. I was in essence snitching which was frowned upon in my community. Above all else, I was gong to "straighten this package." My testimony would be the beginning of the end.

Earl had attempted to call from jail. We would just hang up or tell the operator that we don't accept collect calls. There was only one reason he had been calling and that was for my silence. I'd been silent too long. When I offered my silence in exchange for my freedom, the counter offer was an attempt on my life. Now I have my freedom and will no longer be silenced. I wanted no part in a murder trial but there was no way in hell I was going to continue to protect him when he tried to eradicate me. What part of the game is that? One I want no part of.

I prayed to God to give me the strength to walk into the courtroom and simply tell the truth. I needed God to be with me as he brought me in from the wilderness. This was the last chapter. Once I get these testimonies behind me, it will be over. Luckily, I had a great support system and a zealous prosecuting attorney. To God is the glory! What seemed so hopeless and terminal has become hopeful and limitless. My perspective had changed and everyday was now a gift.

Arriving to the courthouse, I head to the office of the State Attorney to have my parking validated. I meet with the lead prosecutor Barry Schwartz. "Hello there. Are you ready for your big day?" he asks. "Hi and as ready as I will ever be. I'm ready to get this all over," I answer. He understood, "I bet. How's the pregnancy going? Do you need anything to make you more confortable?" "I'm fine. All is fine. I have a couple months to go, " I answered. "We better head to Courtroom 'A' to get this show on the road," he states. Off we go to slay the dragon.

We take the elevator to the courtroom and upon exiting the elevator we walk right to Miss Cat seated outside of court glaring at us. Awkward! I am not surprised to see her here. I am sure she's a witness for the Defense. Her eyes tell the story. Yes, I am pregnant and I'm sure she's trying to ascertain information to take back to Earl. She has the nerve to speak to me, "Hey Rona, you're pregnant? How far along are you?" Geez, she doesn't waste any time questioning me and I've no desire to even speak to her. "Yes, I'm pregnant and in my third trimester," I answer back. She wastes no time in asking, "Whose the daddy? Robert Earl?" With complete disdain I answer, "It sure isn't." "Whose is it?" "You don't know him but he's the one your son decided to burst into his house with guns!" I fire back. "So y'all had been messing around for awhile? Earl said you were cheating on him." I hold nothing back, "I'm not like your evil son. I met him after I left your son. As far as cheating, I should've cheated on him. He didn't deserve my fidelity." I am over her and her inquisition.

It gets quite loud and the bailiff asks us to keep it down. We both had our reasons for disliking the other and that wasn't going to ever change. How can I even respect her as a woman when she has never shown me any type of respect or acceptance? The dislike was mutual. I wasn't raised to disrespect my elders but she was dancing on my very last nerve.

Before I enter the courtroom to testify, I bow my head and pray. I am asking for the strength to tell what I know without fear. If he were convicted of both crimes, then I wouldn't have to worry about him for a very long time. Earl threatened me with death constantly as my only way out and here I am alive and out! Now he will know what it feels like to fight for his life.

CHAPTER 39

AS EMPOWERING AS 4-INCH HEELS

My name was called to take the stand. I walked in with my head held high and looked straight ahead. The stride in my brand new shoes is one of boldness and bravery. In my peripheral view, I could see a packed courtroom on both sides. There is complete silence, other than the sounds of papers being shuffled by the Attorneys. I step into the witness box and am sworn in. Earl is almost seated directly in front of me. I look away and give no eye contact.

The questions begin and I calmly answer them. During my line of questioning, I'd sometime look at Earl directly. I told the jury what I saw when we returned to the scene of the crime. I was sending a nonverbal message to him. He no longer held any control or power over me. Looking him in the eyes showed him I was not afraid! I was in total and complete control. This queen would not be sacrificed for a faux king. Checkmate!

I really wanted to come across as credible. It was important that I did well on the stand. The case was hanging on my testimony, but also my present and future peace. There was no mention of the pending charges for which I was the victim. It could only be introduced if I was asked by the Defense. If the Defense opened the door then the State could enter. The Prosecutor rested and I prepared for the barrage of questions that the State had prepared me for with the Defense. To my complete surprise, the Defense rested with no questions. What? I don't understand, but this will only speed up my return to my babies.

The attorney called me later at home and said I was phenomenal in court. I was better than he expected I would be. He said the jurors hung onto my every word. I simply told the truth, no more or no less. I was a tad bit nervous, but I had to show him that I am stronger because of him. No longer his victim, I'm a survivor! He couldn't break me! He didn't kill me because he was not the one to decide my fate.

The radio is playing Miki Howard's "Love Under New Management" in the background. I hung up the phone and began to sing the words while thinking that I am in love with Jerome. I am in "love under new management." I felt nothing seeing Earl, other than a reminder of the hell he put me through. Jerome makes me happy and it feels good to be treated like a woman. We were tested quite early and as much as I tried to push him away he stayed! How could I not love him for that, if for nothing else?

The next few days I waited on word of the verdict. His guilty conviction would automatically be prison time. Every time the phone rang I thought it was *the* call, but it was not. I decided to occupy my mind to take the focus off the verdict. I had started to prepare to move in January after I had the baby in December. I was starting from scratch, so I had to furnish the entire place. I wasn't working but had a business going on that provided me a nice income. This also relieved me from having to exhaust my savings.

The cd offers that would be in many of the magazines I read, was my product and I sold them wholesale to music stores. I could order ten compact discs for just the shipping, which was less than two dollars, and sell them for five dollars per cd. I basically turned Grandma's address in to an apartment complex. My business was booming. I have received as many as 24 boxes of compact discs at one time. I was making approximately a thousand dollars a week by waiting on the mail and having the freedom to be with my babies. I was stockpiling all the things I would need to furnish my place after I had the baby.

The phone rings and I am informed the verdict comes back as guilty of second-degree murder. Yes! The lead prosecutor tells me that he doesn't think he could've secured a conviction without my testimony. The jury found me to be credible and Earl taking the stand did not help his case. His testimony was quite disingenuous and somewhat pompous. This does not surprise me. Earl doesn't fear anyone and truly thinks he is smarter than most.

I am told that we are halfway there and they are going to move on with the next case—my case—quite quickly. We will start preparing in the next weeks. The next trial will be different. I won't be testifying to what I was told and saw but what I experienced first hand. I will be reliving this experience again. I am ready! I am going to face him and tell the truth.

Jerome was a blessing to have as a sounding board and much needed distraction. The time spent with him was always light and fun. He made me smile and I love that about him. He reminded me that I was strong enough to do what I had to do. Jerome felt that if a man treats a woman like I've been treated, then he must be dealt with accordingly. I was thankful he would be my side to see this through.

My doctor's visit consisted of choosing a date to deliver my baby. I was due December 21st, and Dr. Walker was trying to get the deliveries out of the way so there wouldn't be any Christmas surprise deliveries. Jerome and I chose the 19th of December, and with weeks remaining I needed to prepare for the arrival of the baby.

I was kind of superstitious. I really didn't do much shopping for the baby until my last month. I'd heard the heart-breaking stories of babies lost and the mother is left with mounds of baby items. It is still possible to have a child stillborn but the mortality rate at full-term is significantly lower. My spending caught Jerome off guard. I spent about a thousand dollars and asked nothing of him. I needed only his muscles and not his handouts. At this point, lifting anything and raising my arms above my head were not advisable.

I'd been taught that my babies were my responsibility. I'd also been shown this. Whatever the father chose to do, he simply did. But what was not going to happen, my being dependent upon his financial support. Jerome was probably taken aback that I had access to cash like that while being unemployed. I was unemployed but innovative. The cd hustle kept me quite comfortable financially. My money was my money and his was his. We didn't discuss money and I am sure he questioned to himself about my finances.

After buying out Zayre's in Lauderdale Lakes, we head home to place the things up and get my bag packed for my delivery. This pregnancy happened so quickly that it flew by. Thankfully, I wasn't as sick as I was with Lelee. It wasn't a bad pregnancy but kind of smooth when the nausea ceased. I carried this baby neatly with my hair growing much. I was ready to have this little person and get this chapter behind me. I was looking forward to life with my three and me.

The morning of the 19th arrived and I had to be at Hollywood Memorial Hospital at 5:00a.m. Jerome had come and got me to have our baby. He had to work that day and spent the day on the phone with me through delivery. My bags were packed and I was ready to deliver. I was checked into a birthing room to deliver. The birthing room was nicer than some luxury hotels. It was very modern and didn't have a hospital feel to the room but a welcoming feel.

Jerome stayed as long as he could before he had to get to work. He kissed and hugged me before leaving with a big smile upon his face. I was just relaxing in bed watching the "Price is Right" and talking on the phone. My labor was induced and things changed abruptly. I could no longer talk on the phone due to the discomfort of the contractions. I tried the techniques learned from reading about childbirth and Lamaze to lessen the pain.

Once again, nothing was given for pain. My Bahamian doctor and I were going to have it out. I was in so much pain and my requests for pain meds were denied. The doctor orders, "Just hang in there. It will be over in about thirty minutes." "I am in so much pain. I don't know if I can make it for thirty minutes more," I told him. "You want a healthy baby, right? It's just a little pain for a healthy baby. The pain meds will lower the baby's heart rate," he advises. I was not hearing any of this. I am in so much pain that I want immediate relief. I demand, "I know my Patient Bill of Rights. I want a damn C-Section *now!*" "A C-Section is not an option. I will be back in thirty minutes and we will be having a baby," the doctor said as he walked out of the room.

Great, the clock is on the wall facing me and the half hour seems like an eternity. Why would you tell a woman in labor "thirty minutes" and not return in the assigned time? It had been thirty-five minutes and I started buzzing the nurse. Nearly an hour later, the doctor arrives with the Labor and Delivery Team. I give the doctor a tongue lashing for his poor time management. I am prepped and ready to finally deliver. I am told to begin pushing when I feel the next contraction.

Here we go, the contraction is here and less than a minute apart. I push for dear life. I wasn't about to have a repeat of the fiasco with Lelee's forced delivery. I can feel the baby coming down my birth canal and I am told to "stop pushing." The baby's umbilical cord is wrapped around its neck. Great, here we go again. If he'd given me a C-Section, we wouldn't be in this situation. The doctor starts pushing the baby back in to untwist him. The pain is on another level. Ugh! I push the baby out while the doctor pushes him back in.

The umbilical cord is removed from the baby's neck and I can continue to push, but I'd never stopped! The pressure of the baby is becoming more and more. It's almost over. I feel myself being ripped and I mean literally ripped! The size of the baby's head had torn me! I screamed out in pain and it's over. The doctor happily says, "Congratulations, you are the mother of an 8lb. 1oz. baby boy."

CHAPTER 40

LIFE IS A JOURNEY, WEAR COMFORTABLE SHOES

After the baby was cleaned up, he was handed to me. I couldn't believe this beautiful baby is mine. He had a head full of hair; he was light-complexion with slanted eyes. He was gorgeous! If I hadn't been there to see his delivery first hand, I wouldn't believe he was mine. I didn't think he looked like Jerome or I. He was just a beautiful baby with Chinese eyes. Now I am panicking! What if Jerome questions him? I was too tired to process everything and soon fell asleep after they took him for his initial tests.

Shortly after waking up in my room, I opened my eyes to flowers and a card. The roses were beautiful and blue with a card. I reached out for the card to read and Jerome came walking through the door. He had an unlit cigar hanging from his mouth and was wearing the biggest smile I've ever seen. He gave me a hug and kiss. He was glowing as if he just delivered a baby. The decision had been made to keep the baby and seeing Jerome's face was validation. Jerome said to me, "That's a beautiful boy we have." "He is! I saw and couldn't believe he was mine. He's beautiful," I said. The door reopens and more visitors shuffle in. Jerome's mother, Miss Mable, speaks as she walks in, "How are you doing, Rona?" "I am fine but I am still kind of tired," I respond. Miss Mable continues,

"He's a big boy! He looks just like his daddy, especially with those Chinese eyes." Jerome's Uncle Fred says to him, "You made that one, boy! That's a Randall!" Jerniece agrees, "I can't wait until I can hold him."

All of their beaming faces showed clearly the love and joy they had due to the new edition to their family. Miss Mable stating that he looked like Jerome put my mind and nerves at ease. If anyone would know his physical similarities, it would be her. It was also a good feeling to have a pleasant relationship with the family. They never mistreated or disrespected me, even after the horrible incident at their home. They were good people. Miss Mable was a class act, unlike Miss Cat. She was honest, kind, and genuinely a good woman. I see where Jerome got his beautiful spirit. His father, Buck, was even a more beautiful soul with a hearty laugh to match. Jerome got his ways from both of them. Buck loved me and I loved him. He was a good man and they had an undeniable father-son bond.

Jerniece was a good girl too. She was in her late 20's and still lived at home. She had maintained her banking position since high school. Her free time was spent with her mother, Miss Mable. They were literally inseparable. Jerniece had bought Rome literally a wardrobe for a month. I promised them once I had my six-week checkup that I'd bring him to visit. It was obvious they loved him on sight and I would make sure that he knew and grew with his family.

Discharge day finally came and the nurse had come to get the final papers signed. The paperwork included an application of birth. I chose to name him after his father, Jerome. Luckily, I looked over the application of birth because Earl was listed as the father. I demanded that it is changed immediately. The nurse advises me that I am married and my husband had to be placed on the document. I refused information on the father to prevent his name from being listed. As soon as my divorce is final, I will correct this. Jerome is present to bring us home. As we head home, I begin to think to myself that I now am a mother of three. Progress and an upgrade have been made because this is the first time the father of my children was present and not incarcerated.

Grandma's house would be my home and then I would move into my own apartment next month. It felt good to be home and live with my three blessings and new man. I've got a new life now that I have made it through the storm. I'm still here! Thank God! Now I need to focus on my babies, these three required me to be my very best. Beginning with reuniting my family by introducing Robbie and Lelee to their new little brother Rome. To some degree, Robbie had more experience with a growing family because he was the oldest.

On the other hand, Lelee was not immediately welcoming. Robbie instantly embraced his little brother. Lelee immediately decided that he wasn't wanted nor welcomed. Her mission was to take him out. They were nine months apart and she had to get out of the way for a new baby. She was talking, teething, and walking at six months. She was like a midget assassin who couldn't be trusted alone around the baby. I would place him in his bassinette to sleep and a bottle and pacifier prepared in case he awakened. Lelee would grab the edge of the bassinette and lean backward causing it to tilt over. Rome went rolling under the bed and she'd take his pacifier and bottle.

This war of attrition went on for the first few days. She was a silent assassin and had to be watched closely when around Rome. She was a cute, little walking doll with a pit bull streak in her. It was evident that big things come in small packages. She was a foot tall and ran around like she was a giant. As the kids became older, you could see their personalities forming. Rome was just a newborn baby but it was apparent that Lelee was a warrior. Robbie was a calm spirit. He didn't get into mischief like Lelee. He would sit still and quietly play with his toys. He was an obedient and loving child. He lovingly watched over his younger siblings. There was a difference in personalities between them but they all shared the same physical traits—both were bow-legged.

Robbie was more bow-legged than Lelee. He walked like an orangutan, monkey, or ape. I'd consulted with his doctor who referred me to an orthopedic surgeon for a consultation. The medical term is Rickets, which is a vitamin "D" deficiency. The doctor appeared to be quite concerned with it, but I'd known guys who were bow-legged and quite gifted in athletics. Those guy stood out and the guys in my 'hood loved the bow-legged girls, too.

I'd only had Rome a couple days ago and I had an appointment to take Robbie to see about his legs. I get the kids ready to go, against Grandma's wishes. She didn't think Rome or I should be out unless it was absolute necessary. It had taken a couple months to get this initial appointment and I didn't want to have to wait another several months. I am heading to my car when I heard the phone ring. I stop to pick it up before leaving. "Rona speaking!" "You are going to go to sleep one night and the last face you are going to see waking up will be mine and then you will die!" The caller hangs up.

I continue on with the kids. Earl has obviously found out that I had Rome and it's *not* his. I was not even fazed by the call and carried on to Robbie's appointment. Earl was no longer a concern because he was headed to prison. It was over! He could send verbal threats but the physical abuse was over.

The doctor's office was packed to capacity. Luckily, there was a waiting room filled with toys to occupy the kids. I enjoyed the light casual adult conversations with the other parents. In speaking with them, I came to know that my kids were fast, well developed, and smart for their ages—mainly Lelee. At barely ten months, she was walking, talking, and off the bottle. She was even potty-trained! The other parents thought she was older, due to her well-developed ways, but a preemie because she was little. Robbie was smart and knew his colors and numbers. He was very well mannered with constantly saying "please" and "thank you." The time spent with them had been wisely used. I was proud of them!

We are finally seen by the doctor after waiting for hours. The kids had become restless after playing for hours with their toys. The doctor looked at Robbie's legs and stride as he walked across the room. It took hours of waiting to have a ten-minute visit with the doctor. He recommended that his legs are broken and reset. This would require that he relearn to walk. He would be in leg casts to heal. There was no way I would subject my happy, healthy son to that. The day was nearly wasted with this visit.

Robbie would grow out of most of it and wouldn't have to regress to not being able to walk. I had to nearly run to keep up with him as we walked to the car. I didn't want him to lose his ability to walk or run, even temporarily. Robbie was very quick, happy, and playful. There's nothing wrong with being bow-legged. The decision had been made and we all headed home to rest. I was happy! I was hopeful! I was going to make it for my three depending on me. That idle threat from Earl was not going to prevent me from facing him again in court for my case.

The upcoming trial and my testimony would cause me to recount the entire episode. I was going to have my day in court. I had to "straighten a package." I was no longer consumed by fear! I wasn't completely afraid of him. To some degree, I carried fear with me of him but I was no longer consumed completely. Much of that fear had been replaced with a courageous anger. After all the shit he put me through, he has the audacity to try and take my life. The girl he did that to no longer exist and a brave, courageous woman was here to stay.

CHAPTER 41

LIFE IS A JOURNEY, WEAR COMFORTABLE SHOES

The kids are now home, fed, and in bed. Finally, I am able to relax a little. I normally sleep with them to stay on their schedule but I am unable to slow my racing mind for sleep to find me. I am sitting in the den lost in thought and Grandma notices and takes a seat next to me. "Rona, what's on your mind? What's going on in that head of yours?" "A lot, Grandma! Everything, Ma, everything!" Grandma always made me feel better. "Talk to Grandma. What is it, baby?" I confide in her, "I just have a lot on me. Earl called and threatened to kill me, the doctors want to break Robbie's legs and reset them, and the big trial is upcoming. I also will be scheduled to move during that time." It has just been a long day and I just need to relax it off.

Grandma is interrupted from responding by the ringing phone. She answers the phone and tells me it is for me. "Rona speaking." "Hi, Rona! This is Barry Schwartz from the State Attorney's Office. How are you?" I answer, "Hi Barry. I am fine. I was going to call you." Barry sounds surprised, "Oh, have you heard already?" I am puzzled, "Heard what?" "Robert Jackson tried to escape and attacked a guard with another inmate. He was able to get to the second floor but didn't have the credentials to get out." I am in disbelief, "Oh my God!" "He didn't make it out the jail and we now have him on lockdown. I just wanted to keep you informed. Don't worry, he's not going anywhere, " he assures me. I can only pray this to be true.

I felt as if I'd been sucker punched once I hung up the phone. Breathing didn't come easily. I'd informed him that Earl called and threatened me earlier this morning. He must've hung up the phone on me and attempted the escape with intentions of bringing harm to me. Oh my God! When will it end? This had become jarring! Maybe I would not be completely free. The "what ifs" kept crowding my thoughts. What if he had gotten out and caught me off guard? What if he ever got out, would I truly be safe?

I needed to seek out counseling. There has been enough that has occurred to me to easily escape into some type of harmful behavior or lifestyle. I did not and I could not go that route! As a matter-of-fact, I didn't drink or smoke. I'd just been keeping everything bottled in and this final threat by Earl opened the floodgates. My sweeping everything under the rug did not resolve anything. There were things within me that needed to be addressed. I couldn't deny that I needed some help.

The progress I'd made had become stifled. I began to feel anxiety about the trial, paranoia of Earl escaping, and feeling overwhelmed by the insurmountable odds stacked against me. My appetite had escaped me and I'd lost a fair share of weight. The baby weight was gone and then some. Upon my six-week checkup, I had been diagnosed with stress-induced anorexia and depression. I was prescribed an appetite stimulant and an anti-depressant.

As part of my therapy, I had to go to meetings for Eating Disorders Anonymous. I never felt that I should have been there. My loss of appetite was not intentional but subconsciously. The majority of the people here consciously stuck their fingers down their throats. I listened as they shared stories of binging and purging. It was incomprehensible to me. What was I expected to share? "Hi,

I'm Rona! My ex-husband tried to kill me and my appetite lessened with stress," I thought aloud. I realized that a traumatic event occurred to me and I need to learn how to handle the stressors.

I got both prescriptions filled and I began to read the product insert of both. The major indication for both was that both causes drowsiness and alcohol intensifies it. I was cool with that because I didn't drink. Once I started eating with more regularity, I am sure I would feel better. I was tired physically and needed to heal completely. My body was in literal shock. My body hadn't fully healed from the brutal beating and the two births eleven months apart. My body, spirit, and mind needed to heal completely.

The anti-depressant was a different story altogether. The medicine could cause insomnia, loss of appetite, and nervousness. No, thank you! I was great at that without any assistance from the anti-depressant. I didn't take the anti-depressants and opted instead for the Victims of Domestic Violence counseling provided through the courts. I needed to cope and do so better than I had been doing. The drugs may assist some but I chose to allow faith to be my drug of choice. To be hopeful, in a hopeless situation can be a powerful drug!

My kids needed me and I had to work through these issues. The counseling was good for me and I identified a lot of warning signs in my marriage, and even when we were dating. I know now that all the time he was promising me he'd do " a quarter" if I didn't abide him was programming. He was programming himself to do just that if I left him. I had dismissed them, as only idle threats made out of anger, but this would not be normal behavior. Control is a large part of it and he'd beaten down my ego and my self-esteem was in down under in Australia. The less I felt for myself made him feel more empowered and in control. The counseling allowed me to get it all out and take it all in. It also prepared me for my testimony.

Several months into the counseling, I felt good and was getting stronger each and every day. I got my mojo back. I was ready to go

forward. I found an apartment and furnished it completely starting anew. The trial was weeks away and I was mentally prepared to
go to battle. My babies and I now have our own place. It is a very
nice place with all new furnishings for our new life. Life was good
and things were looking up. I found a place in Lauderhill and in
the same complex as my cousin Shirley, who was the daughter of
Aunt Pearl.

Two weeks had quickly passed and the trial had begun. The
weeks leading up to this day are somewhat of a blur. The move had
me so occupied and I had no time to even think about the trial.
I talked to God the entire drive to the courthouse. My prayer was
that I did not believe God had brought me here to this point to
ever leave me now. I was praying for strength to face all and tell
my story. The drive was a haze and I entered the courthouse as
"David" to face "Goliath."

I go through security to reach the elevators to go to the courtroom. I get off on the 7th floor and am met by Attorney Barry
Schwartz. He assures me that everything will be fine and I will do
well. I have this numbness, calmness, and detachment at this present moment. I hadn't cried one time. It's as if I am subconsciously
on autopilot. This would be the final chapter. I would have my day
in court for what he tried to do—take my life. There was no sense
in delaying the inevitable; he would be accountable for his actions.

Miss Cat and some female, whom I assume is one of Earl's jailhouse jump-offs, and *Amy* are the first faces I see as I enter the
courtroom. They all glare at me as I head to the State's table to
talk briefly with the Attorneys. She could give me hateful looks all
she wants but I am going to do something she should've done for
her son—teach him right from wrong with ramifications for mal
behavior. It was strange because I wasn't nervous or afraid, simply
there in the moment.

I can hear a door open and chains being shuffled. "Goliath"
has entered the arena/coliseum. My heart begins to beat a little
faster and I feel the need to make eye contact. I want to see him

and I want him to see me. I'm not afraid anymore and I've healed and here to face him. I turn around without any hesitation to see him smiling at me with his gold teeth. He's just trying to intimidate me and psyche me out. Better luck with that in a next lifetime because those old ploys no longer work with the new me.

The Bailiff instructs the courtroom will be in session in a couple of minutes. I take my seat on the first row opposite of Earl's family. I could've had my family and friends all here but for some reason I felt I needed to cross the finish line alone. I'd been the only one who got me into this jam. Other than God, I was good being here alone. With God on my side, my clique was deep enough. I was mentally prepared for battle. I hadn't known how I would act when this day came. Some times God gives His toughest battle to his strongest soldiers.

Earl sat there staring at me and I only felt hatred and not fear. He disgusted me. The blinders were off; he'd beaten them off. I saw him for what he really was—not worthy of having me. At times, I'd stare and snarl at him while shaking my head "no." I was letting him know that I am no longer a victim but a survivor and fighter. Bring it! Today is not a good day! The judge takes the bench and opening statements are made. The State simply opened with asking the jury to take into the credibility of the victims.

I turned around to keep an eye on Miss Cat and notice her, the "jailhouse jump off" and Amy were no longer there. They had been escorted out of the courtroom because they were witnesses. Now that is interesting! How can the "jailhouse jump off" be a witness? I don't even know her. I no longer concerned myself with the women in his life. What was Amy going to testify to? The fact she fucked my husband and it was somehow my fault. I was just glad that I was no longer a part of the circus. Let me tighten my straps on my shoes...

CHAPTER 42

LIFE IS A JOURNEY, WEAR COMFORTABLE SHOES

The State opened with calling me to the witness stand as the first witness. I walked to the box and was sworn in. I take my seat and notice a jury of men and women seated to the left of me. They will decide his fate today but I've got the truth on my side. Luckily, I had no fear of speaking in front of a crowded room. Much thanks to my church, I was used to speaking in front of a large crowd. I'd always been told that I was very articulate and today would be show and prove.

I was very confident that I was smarter than Earl, his mother, and random women. They ran off emotions and no logic or rationale. I am not saying that I am not emotional but I am a very analytical sort. My positions are based on learned evidence rather than solely opinions and feelings. They weren't very articulate and I'm sure they'd be caught up in their lies. I took a deep breath and acknowledged the jury with greetings. The Attorney began his line of questions on my childhood aspirations, schooling, athletics, and now as a grown mother of three.

The questions are answered as descriptive and concise as possible. I knew what he was doing. He was trying to get the jury to know me—humanize me. The Attorney had informed me, "To not hold back, if I needed to cry then cry." I had no intentions of crying but recounting the story opened up the tear duct floodgates. When asked about my children, I began to cry. Damn! They found the key to unlock the floodgates. Earl had seen me cry enough already. He viewed my tears as a sign of weakness and he would pounce on that. He had seen me cry tears of sadness over the years far too much. The Attorney asks, "How many kids do you have? And please state the ages?" Through my sobbing I state, "I have three kids—two with the defendant. The ages of my children are four years old, a fourteen month old and a three month old. " "I can clearly see that you love your kids. Is that the reason for the tears?" I reply, "No." "Then, why the tears?" the Attorney asks. "I love my babies with all my being. My tears are because my children could have been motherless. I could've been killed. It simply brings me to tears to think that they would not have known me. It just makes me very sad because they don't deserve any of this," I answer.

I look directly at Earl. I may be crying but it's a sign of me releasing but still strong! He will hear me today! Like it or not, I am here and he will pay for what he has done to me and mine. "Goliath" is no match for a strong, educated, scorned woman! My glare pierces his armor and he looks down. I continue to look at him still. He will face me today! He had the opportunity to walk away and I would keep quiet. No, that wasn't a viable option for him. Now there will be no more compromising and only a demand for justice. The attorney asks, "Are you still married to the defendant?" "Unfortunately. We are now legally separated but due to his trials we were unable to get a date to finalize the orders. I believe it's just a delay tactic," I boldly state. The Defense Attorney jumps up and loudly states, "Objection, your honor! My client's only case and charges would be this only one. We haven't introduced any other statements regarding anything else." The judge ruled, "Sustained. Strike the court cases from the record." I am laughing on the inside and it may have been removed from the record but the jurors still heard it.

Earl will be revealed for what he is today! He's a convicted felon who has been thumbing his nose at the law from day one. He has finally met his match. He's no worthy opponent; he's unworthy— period. He is sitting there looking like a lost little boy. Finally the layers have been pulled off. You are just a scared little boy that inflicts his pain unto others. "Are you here today out of the hurt from the divorce to get some revenge?" the attorney asks. I answer with conviction, "Most definitely not! I am here today because the defendant tried to kill me. That's the *only* reason. I'm not hurt by the impending divorce. Why would I want to remain married to the man who tried to kill me? That simply defies logic."

It is what it is! The marriage was over before it began. He'd been involved with others since he met me. He has no concept of a faithful marriage. Bitter from the demise of the marriage? Not so much! I needed to take all the necessary steps to rid myself of him. I felt I was stifled in my current relationship because of having Earl be the "pink elephant in the room." Jerome couldn't even sign the birth certificate because I was legally married to him still. I had to refuse information on the father and have it updated once the divorce is finalized.

Jerome had been super supportive and been a father figure to my other two. My mind was too cluttered to even build on us. I just existed. It was just smooth sailing but I was still kind of distant emotionally. I would even say that I was emotionally reserved. I needed to get the trial done and build more on Jerome and I. Jerome deserved the best of me because he had given me the best of him. He and Jerniece were even testifying in court on my behalf. Jerome stated he would be going to court on Earl because that could've been one of his sisters placed in a trunk to be killed. Jerome was adamant that he wasn't a man for what he did to me. The attorney asks, "Did you believe that your husband would kill you that night?" I bravely answer, "I do believe that was his intent. He had told me countless times he was going to kill me and I was going to die tonight." I watch the jury as they receive my testimony and I could see sympathetic eyes.

Earl did kill me that night, in a figurative sense. I'd been termed smart with the books, but I had no street sense or common sense. The somewhat sheltered, naïve young girl was gone—dead. When you look death in the face, your outlook changes. Much like a phoenix, the death of the naïve girl rebirthed into a much wiser, strong woman. All the while, he is trying to kill me but he is giving me life. In a sense, this was my rite of passage. I am alive! I am here! I thank God for grace!

My testimony lasted over a couple of days. By the end of tiring day one, I needed to go home to my kids to recharge. They were the source of my strength. It was them who I lived for. I had to be strong for them. They allowed me to grow up and be the best version of me for their benefit. Childish things and games were done. I had three depending on me! I couldn't, nor wouldn't, let them down!

The Defense was now up to cross-examine me, "Is it true that you had an abortion during the marriage and had not informed my client?" "Yes, but I did not want to bring another child into an abusive marriage," I counter his attack. "You had a right to inform the father of the child and you did not or did you? Was my client the father of the child?" "I felt it was my decision alone. I was nearly raising one child alone already. He was most certainly the father. He threw away my birth control pills and forced himself on me sexually right after the abortion; it was done to replace the one I 'killed' in his words." The attorney continues, "Do you feel that my client would harm his kids? Has he ever harmed his kids?" I fire back, "No, only the mother of his kids."

The light bulb has been turned on and I get it. They are trying to paint me as the bad guy. The attorneys prepared me for this.

I've just got to stay calm and tell the truth—no more or no less. They are playing dirty bringing up the abortion. No one knew about that but he, Libby and I. The mere fact they are bringing this up is a sign of desperation! It is going to be all right because God is with me! The Defense attorney starts in again, "Is it true you left my client at the Dade County Youth Fair?" "Yes, I sure did! We got into a fight and I left. He hit me that night, too!" "Isn't it true that you've assaulted several of my client's girlfriends and *your sister*?" I almost chuckle, as I answer, "No, that's not true! I've been assaulted by several of them and had to defend myself while pregnant with *his* children." The Defense Attorney goes for the jugular, "Haven't you pulled a gun on my client and pulled the trigger but it jammed?" "Yes, in defense from a brutal beating by your client," I answer.

They are going in but I stay calm and throw in occasional jabs. Although the judge had stricken some things from the record, the jury heard it. It was not erased from their memory. The gloves had come off and I guess this is why Defense attorneys are paid the big bucks. He is trying to paint me less than what I am. I can't show any negative reactions. Earl is enjoying this and I know these are his questions being asked by his attorney. I see him constantly writing down things and much whispering. I notice that they do not ask one question about why we are here—the night of April 1st. The armed kidnapping, home invasion, attempted murder, and convicted felon with possession of a firearm charges were never mentioned by the Defense. "Is it true that you left your kids on the street and sped off on the first of April?" the questions continue. "No, I left them at his mother's front door." The attorney closes, "The Defense rests…"

CHAPTER 43

LIFE IS A JOURNEY, WEAR COMFORTABLE SHOES

The trial was wrapping up. Jerome, Jerniece, and some of their neighbors—who I didn't even know—had given their testimony. Jerome and I no longer talked in depth about that night. We just grazed over those talks. We both were trying to move past this. I was on standby, in case I was needed back in court. The state attorney kept me up-to-date with the court proceedings. I was told that Miss Cat took the stand and painted her darling son as a choirboy. There was also a parade of women who testified that he was very gracious with his generosity and never hit them.

I really wasn't needed to put the nail in the coffin because the Defense was doing a great job at it. The state attorney stated the jury had connected with me and literally frowned upon the parade of women talking openly about being involved with a married man. The kicker was when Earl took the stand. I was told he came across again as cocky and disliked. He openly testified that he "beats his wife's ass because she is hard-headed."

He even validated my feelings of being not a person but property. He said that I was his "property." I'd begun to feel that way. He showered me with gifts and cash to control me. When he became angry with me, he'd throw it up in my face. Because he did every-thing for me, he felt I was his. He had purchased me and owned me. Well, you live and learn! When you learn better, you do better!

I'd decided to not be present for closing arguments or the ver-dict. There was going to be a guilty verdict because that was the only verdict to be made. Besides, I'd seen more than enough of Earl. Once the verdict was made, he would then be sentenced. At this time, it will be all over! The divorce would be granted any day now that the trial would be ending. The Lord has mercy! This has been a long road but I am here.

My cooking skills had improved and I decided to cook a nice dinner for Jerome to just show him that I appreciated him. I'd spend the day preparing him a nice meal after leaving court. I invited him over and put on some Anita Baker to get the mood right. I was not about to allow the trial or upcoming verdict to con-sume my thoughts or life. I'd changed and worn out many shoes on this journey. I had even lost my sole, at times, but still walked on with the remnants of the shoes—in spite of the callouses. That was all behind me and I was moving forward. I'd been through hell and it was time to experience heaven. I refused to believe that my future would be worse than my past. Conclusively, I believed that the rest of my life has to be a cakewalk since I had such hard-ships in the beginning.

The phone rings and I go to answer it, "Rona speaking." "Hi, this is Attorney Barry Schwartz." I nervously acknowledge him. He continues, "The verdict came back rather quickly and he was found guilty on all counts. You were excellent! I will be in touch soon for the sentencing. Then, I will need you to go have a great life!"

I wasn't surprised! I had the truth on my side. I would gather no satisfaction by hearing the guilty verdict. It simply would be a formality. I was there and experienced his wrath first-hand. I knew he was guilty! And there were no "ifs, ands, or buts" about it.

Hanging up the phone, we had even more to celebrate and be thankful for. I began to smile and look up giving thanks to the heavens above. I go to my stereo and crank it up. I was in my zone, finishing the dinner while the kids played outside. I now look into their smiling faces and I am happy. I never had aspirations to be a mother, but now that I am, I couldn't imagine life without them. I get them all washed up before dinner is served.

Jerome arrives after the kids are bathed and dressed in their pajamas. He gives me a kiss and begins to play with the kids. I can tell they have genuine love for him. He's a good man and I am curious to see where this will go. I love his sweet spirit and he has been so supportive and patient with me. I truly thank God for sending him my way.

I fix their plates while they horseplay in the living room. Rome is asleep and the noise doesn't awake him. We all sit at the table and say grace before we dine. This is now my family. What God has brought together let no man, woman, cat, or dog come between. Jerome likes the dinner and finishes his plate. He usually eats many small meals throughout the day, but he finished his entire plate in one sitting. I am now convinced that he enjoyed the meal.

The kids finish their meal and we all dine on a strawberry cheesecake for dessert. I give them small slices because I don't want them to get a sugar rush right before bedtime. They consumed their dessert in no time flat, and they are shuffled into the bathroom to brush their teeth. We get them nestled in bed to watch television in their beds. I now have time to talk to Jerome. Well, not exactly, Rome has awakened and needed his diaper changed. He begins to whimper as a warning before he engages in an eardrum-curdling cry. Jerome had been waiting on him to wake up and takes over. He changes the diaper, gave him his bottle, and put him back to sleep. What a good father!

While Jerome is on daddy duty, this will give me time to shower while they bond. As the water runs all over me, I gather my thoughts so I can talk with Jerome. I have to do this! There's no way I can let my past hurt my future, and most importantly, or my present. The therapy really helped me make strides. I can't assign negative thoughts upon Jerome when he has only been positive. I felt good and I was much stronger than I'd been in the past. It's true, what doesn't kill does make you stronger.

I've always loved water. I swam often and associated water with cleansing. As the steaming hot water streamed onto my skin, I was washing away any self-doubt, unhappiness, anger, rage, insecurities, hatred, and any thing else that would not build me up. I just stood there and allowed those negative layers to be washed away. "I will not, won't stop climbing that mountain until I reach the top," I repeat over and over.

Time escaped me and I'd been in the shower so long that all the hot water had been used. The water was now ice cold, which means it is time to get out but I hadn't even lathered up yet. Great, now I have to wash up in cold water. I guess Jerome had put Rome to bed because I could hear music playing low. Jerome loved his "oldie but goldie" music. Diana Ross' "Ain't No Mountain High Enough" was playing. He turned me on to this type of music and whenever I hear it, I think of him. The bathroom mirror is steamed up and I wipe off the dew while singing with Diana.

My face appears and I smile at her. Now this face I am familiar with. I love her! I fought to be her! I am she! The music changes and "Zoom" is playing by the Commodores. As I look into my eyes, I see peace and joy! My spirit is no longer broken. For so long, I couldn't face myself and I am truly blessed to be in a better place—"Zoom, Zoom."

I'm finally ready to have a talk with Jerome after brushing my teeth and applying my face cream. He is in the living room enjoying his favorite brew. I sit next to him and he grabs my hand. He looks me in my eyes and says for the first time, "I love you, Rona!" I respond, "I love you, Jerome!" Life is good and these are the moments that make life worth living. I seize the opportunity share with him, "Jerome, I just want to say thank you again for daring to care and love me. Thank you for being so patient and supportive in my darkest hour. You became a guiding light for me. You even came to court for me. Thank you for *everything*. I mean it!" Jerome smiles and holds me close as he says, "You're welcome. You're a good girl, Rona! You deserve a good man—me! You don't deserve to be beaten on. We're together and we're family, right?" I kiss him and agree, "That's absolutely right!" We spent the night talking and listening to music. It had gotten late and Jerome was about to head home. We embraced and kissed through our adieus.

The next few weeks were uneventful, in comparison to the past chaotic weeks. I'd received the call from my attorney and the divorce had been finalized. I was free! I rushed to the courthouse to meet my attorney to receive the finalized orders. Before I could take in the divorce, the sentence hearing had come. This would be the last round. As soon as the hearing started, it was over. He received thirty years!

Walking out of the courthouse was such a good feeling. It was euphoric! The sky was bluer. The birds were chirping beautifully with a cool breeze was on my back. Most importantly, a smile upon my face! I did it! I survived it! It is over! My stride was even different in my shoes. I no longer had any pain and discomfort. It was if the dead weight had been lifted and my load and stride was lighter. The sun shined brightly and my soul was carefree and light. I slayed "Goliath." That chapter is now closed and I look forward to a new chapter living happy and having peace of mind.

Many celebrate the Fourth of July as Independence Day, but not I. March 5th, today, is my Emancipation Day going forward. It is a day I will look upon with much hope, respect, and divine inspiration. I've gained my independence and I will never lose it again. I am skipping to the car and scuffing my brand new shoes in the process; I care not about the shoes because I chose to stand up for myself. I was no longer falling prey to love. Arriving at my car and before I place the key into the ignition, I take a moment to take it all in. I breathe deeply, inhaling the joyful newness of my life and exhaling the pain of the past.

I unlock the car and sit in the driver's seat. I look into the rear-view mirror and see the tears of joy running down my face. It is well with my soul, for these are triumphant tears. I give thanks to God for bringing me through! I look into my eyes and say, "I will not, won't stop climbing that mountain until I reach the top!" I kick off my brand new shoes and turn the key to start the ignition...

EPILOGUE

"Hurts Like Brand New Shoes" is a metaphor for life's bumps, obstacles, trials and adversity. The walk of life can be painful and hurtful. Often times, the walk can be uncomfortable and not by our own choosing, but we tolerate it and make due. The pain associated with living may be unavoidable but the direction in which we take is solely ours alone. We come to know that in the hurt is where we find tolerance and comfort. You've broken through and broken in life's "shoes."

It is my hopes that through this journey of personal insights, you will trust your own process. Know that there is beauty in the struggle and you can endure the hurt. What was meant to break you, in turn, built you up. This novel is from many different "shoes." May you endure the pain while walking—fearlessly and bravely— even if life can often "hurt like brand new shoes."

ABOUT THE AUTHOR

Cyntrenna Palmer was born and raised in Fort Lauderdale, Florida. Her love of writing and literature led her to receive a degree in English from the University of South Carolina. "Hurts Like Brand New Shoes" is her debut novel. She resides in the Upstate of South Carolina with her husband and multitude of shoes.